A PRIZED PUPIL!

Also by Leslie Scrase:

Days in the Sun (children's stories, with Jean Head)
In Travellings Often
Booklet on Anglican/Methodist Conversations
Some Sussex and Surrey Scrases
Diamond Parents
Coping With Death
The Sunlight Glances Through (poetry)
Some Ancestors of Humanism
An Evacuee
Conversations (on Matthew's Gospel)
  between an Atheist and a Christian

A Prized Pupil!

... of a boys' boarding school in the 1940s

Sequel to AN EVACUEE

Leslie Scrase

UNITED WRITERS
Cornwall

UNITED WRITERS PUBLICATIONS LTD
Ailsa, Castle Gate, Penzance, Cornwall.

British Library Cataloguing in Publication Data:
A catalogue record for this book is
available from the British Library.

ISBN 1 85200 096 1

Printed in Great Britain by
United Writers Publications Ltd
Cornwall.

Dedication

I thought that I would dedicate this book to all the boys I remembered from my own boarding school days. But the list grew and grew.

Then I thought I would dedicate it to all those whose friendship I particularly valued and value from schooldays: people like the Lotts of North Devon and David Selleck in Canada. But that list was still far too long and it was impossible to determine who should be included and who left out.

Eventually I decided to dedicate the book to three people who have died and who therefore cannot object.

The first is Jackson Page who I respected and loved as a man, as a friend and as a teacher. He was the only secondary school teacher I ever had who made me want to study and want to learn. There are generations of boys from that school who would acknowledge an immense and lasting debt of gratitude to him.

Guy Wright's early death robbed the world of a fine man. For me, he was the man who opened up the world of music. He allowed some of us the freedom of his room and of his music collection. He enriched, broadened and deepened both my knowledge of music and my appreciation of it. I know that many others share that debt.

Last but certainly not least is John Shapcott. Anyone who knew John will understand this dedication. In these days when homosexuality has become a respectable and accepted part of social life, it is difficult to speak of that other friendship between men which has nothing to do with sexuality at all.

Men in the forces (when they were single sex), men from single sex boarding schools and sports teams will all know what

I mean. There can be a friendship between men which binds them with steel in a relationship which can often last for life. It needs no expression in words. It can survive long periods of separation, long periods in which there is no contact at all. It is so powerful that it deserves the name of love in spite of the misunderstanding to which that word can lead.

More than most of the men I have known, John had the ability to inspire that kind of companionable and deep friendship, that kind of love. But he not only inspired it. He gave it in full measure.

I wish I were a better writer, for these three men deserve a better dedication than anything I can manage. This book then is to the memory of:

Jackson Page;   Guy Wright;   John Shapcott;

with love and with lasting gratitude.

Leslie Scrase

Disclaimer

It would be foolish to deny that there are autobiographical elements in this book.

Inevitably this means that some of my friends may suspect that they also appear. If that is the case, I hope that they are pleased with the things they find.

If at any point they are not pleased, let them remember that this is purely a work of fiction and none of the characters bears any resemblance to any person living or dead.

And to those of my family who are looking for autobiography may I stress that this is a work of fiction. Not everything in these pages happened to me as a boy at school. In one particular respect I can only add: more's the pity.

A Prized Pupil! is a second novel telling the story of the life of Roger Wallace. The first was also published by United Writers Publications under the title *An Evacuee*. I owe my publishers a real debt of gratitude.

'For though now old
Beyond the common life of man, I still
Remember them who loved me in my youth.'

Wordsworth's shepherd Michael

Contents

1

A Bucking New Snip

It was the 12th of September 1942. Roger had already been a wartime evacuee for three years. Now he was going to boarding school. He waited impatiently outside the Quayside Hotel in Beddingford, hopping up and down in ill-restrained excitement.

An Austin 10 drew up outside a tiny cottage on the High St. Miss Holly came out in her dull Sunday clothes and dark blue Sunday hat. She climbed in the car beside her nephew and the two of them drove down to the river. They pulled up at the hotel and got out of the car, amused at Roger's delight that they had arrived at last.

"Hello dear," said Miss Holly. "This is my nephew who's gwain to take ee to school. Take us in to your Mother dear and you can all get started."

Introductions were made and Roger and the man half lifted, half dragged Roger's metal clothes-trunk out to the car. They heaved it up onto the car's open boot and roped it up. Miss Holly kissed Roger good-bye and walked off to look after her nephew's hardware shop. Roger and his mother got into the back of the car and they drove away in silence.

They drove west out of Beddingford alongside the river and then began to climb Five Mile Hill. In spite of the load the black Austin 10 pulled steadily up the hill and as they climbed so Roger's excitement grew. But there was a fair bit of apprehension too. What would boarding school really be like? Would it be, as he expected, like *Tom Brown's Schooldays* or *Stalkie and Co.*? He could hardly contain himself.

"Do stop fidgeting dear. You're making me all hot and bothered jiggling about like that."

His mother was feeling anxious too. They had had so many problems with this boy since he was evacuated. She was sure that all he really needed was to come home but her husband wouldn't hear of it. And he was probably right, the bombing was pretty bad. She did so hope that boarding school would give her son the stability he needed.

The road finally levelled out shortly before Stubble Cross. From there onwards they had about four miles to go, uphill and down through open country with high hedges. They passed a number of farms and a tiny village. They drove past a nondescript set of grey buildings, another farm perhaps, and then came to a cross roads. There were no road signs. These had been removed so that invading Germans would have no help in finding their way around.

The driver turned right and came to the beginning of a real village. As they entered the village there were two shops side by side: a cobbler and a bakery.

"I think I'd better check where the school is," he said. He dithered for a moment or two and then chose to make enquiries in the bakery. A woman was serving bread straight from the ovens. The smell was wonderful.

"Perspins College? You've come right past it my dear. Go back to they cross roads and turn left. 'Tis the first set of buildings on the left."

They returned to the grey buildings they had thought were a farm. There was no obvious entrance. They stopped by a rough courtyard. Boys directed them through a short, dark passageway to the Headmaster's study. They knocked and the Head came out of another door at the side of the passage. He led them straight through into his house where a small group of new boys and their parents struggled to make polite conversation. The Head introduced Mrs Wallace, Mr Holly and Roger, rubbed his hands together and said, "Now the school's complete. You new boys are the last arrivals. Time for a spot of tea. Don't you think so Jennifer?"

It was a very quiet and genteel tea, presided over by the Headmaster's wife, Jennifer. She was tall and slim and very quiet, almost remote. Yet she seemed to carry an aura of calm peacefulness with her, of gentleness too. How on earth had she come to marry the Head? He was such a bull and a real human dynamo.

Tea was an awkward, uncomfortable affair and was followed by equally awkward farewells between parents and children. But the Head seemed more at ease when the parents had gone, leaving their sons and their sons' ration books in his care.

"Come on then boys. I'll show you your dormitory and then you are on your own."

He breezed out of his house and through a series of corridors with the boys struggling to keep up. He took them up a small flight of wooden stairs. A large dormitory faced them but they turned away from it along a short landing to a much smaller dorm. The Head threw open the door and said, "Here we are: New Boys Dorm: Dorm 16. You are the first boys to enjoy such a thing. You're new. I'm new. And a dorm full of new boys is also new. You and I will grow into the school and its customs without interference from older boys. We shall help one another. Now, choose your beds and get your trunks."

An older boy was standing quietly behind him in the doorway.

"Oh. This is your dorm prefect. He'll show you round and generally look after you."

With that he was gone. The older boy said, "My name's Thomas. I'll get to know yours bit by bit. Let's go and get your trunks."

Their trunks were an untidy group at the end of a corridor but Roger's wasn't there. Thomas helped the boys to the bottom of the stairs and then showed them how to take them head over heels up the stairs. Then he turned to Roger.

"What's your name?"

"Roger Wallace sir."

"You don't call me 'sir'. I'm only a dorm prefect. Now, show me where you arrived at the school."

"I'm . . . I'm afraid I'm a bit confused sir . . . sorry . . . Thomas. We seem to have been whizzed through so many corridors. But it was by a sort of courtyard by the road."

"Good. That's not far away." He led Roger through to the courtyard and there was Roger's trunk standing on end by the roadside. Mr Holly had obviously just tipped it off the car and left it. "This one yours?" asked Thomas.

"Yes."

"Well you grab that end and I'll carry backwards."

By the time they got to the bottom of the stairs Roger felt that his arms were going to drop off. Thomas noticed and heaved the trunk up the stairs himself. Then the two of them carried it into the dorm. There was only one bed left right by the door. A buzz of conversation stopped as they entered the dorm.

"Get yourselves unpacked. You put your things in these buffaloes," he said. "I'll be back in a while to show you where to store your trunks."

With that, he left the dorm and conversation began again. Some of the boys were farmers' sons and knew one another – in fact half of them were related to one another: first, second or third cousins once or twice removed. Roger never did get the hang of their family relationships. The rest came from away, mostly from the London area. Roger looked around.

He wasn't a farmer's son so he didn't belong to that group. But it was three years almost exactly since he had been evacuated. He didn't really feel that he belonged to the London group either – besides his home wasn't quite in London. As he began to empty his trunk he wondered just where he really did belong. He supposed that he belonged right where he was for the time being.

He looked around the room. It was long and low and on the dark side, with a worn, uneven wooden floor. Six iron bedsteads were ranged along his side of the room and seven on the other. The 'buffaloes' were old wooden chests of drawers. There was one between each bed.

Each drawer was reserved for its precise allocation of clothes – the same for each boy. Including the clothes the boys were wearing there were three of everything except handkerchiefs and each item was marked with a Cash's name tape sewn on. The idea was that one set of clothes was worn, one was being laundered and repaired, and one was in the buffalo. Clothes were changed on Sundays.

It was pretty much the same with the beds. They provided their own sheets and pillowcases (three of each) and the school supplied one underblanket and three over blankets. The boys made their own beds before breakfast every morning and kept the dorm clean and tidy.

As they unpacked they chatted and Roger soon found himself

included. Tension and anxiety washed away and he began to feel at ease. They all seemed to be boys he could get on with. He felt that he was going to be OK.

Thomas returned. Only one boy was still unpacking, Roger's next door neighbour. He seemed a bit dreamy and was putting his things away one by one instead of hauling out great heaps and stuffing them in the drawers as the other boys had done.

"What's your name lad."

"Peter Jonas sir."

"Well Jonas, you'll have to learn to buck up a bit. Our lives here are governed by the school bell and all our odd jobs have to be done on time. Here, let me help you. Oh, and I've already told Wallace that you don't call me 'sir'. You only call the masters 'sir'. Understood? . . . There that's complete. Now, bring your trunks and follow me."

They dragged or carried their trunks to the stairs and clunked their way down and through more corridors out to the edge of a huge sports' field with two rugby pitches end to end. They dragged their trunks to a tower.

"That's the water tower," said Thomas. "It supplies all the water for the school. And our trunks are stored here at the bottom. He opened a door into the tower. It was already piled high with trunks but somehow there seemed to be room for theirs.

Thomas led them back to the centre of the school to a grey, asphalt quadrangle enclosed within grey buildings and, as the boys were to discover, almost always roofed over with a grey, drizzling sky.

"I'm going to leave you here. Stay in the quad until the bell goes and then line up in twos against that wall. You'll be allocated to your houses. The school has three: Alpha, Beta, and Gamma named after letters of the Greek alphabet. Alpha is red. Beta is green and Gamma is blue. Your school badges will be in your house colours. Oh, and you'll all be in Class 2 which meets in the Assembly Hall up those stairs." He pointed across the quad.

"Why class 2?" Jonas asked.

"Class 1 is a sort of preliminary class for under-age boys. Class 2 is where the proper school begins."

With that he left them on their own, but they were not to be left alone for long.

2

Bath Tickets

"Come on you new snips. Line up over here."

They looked at one another. Thomas had said to line up after the bell. They hadn't heard any bell. But one or two of them set off straight away so the rest followed. A tall boy lined them up properly. Other boys stood with him, one of them with an exercise book in his hand.

"Name?"

The tall boy addressed the first boy in the line. He felt intimidated and his reply came out almost as a whisper.

"Speak up. Give us your name again."

"John Parsons."

"John Parsons eh. Well Parsnips, say 'sir' when you speak to me. Now. Try again and get it right this time."

"John Parsons sir."

"That's better. Next."

At the end of the line Roger whispered to his neighbour, "Thomas said we should only say 'sir' to masters."

"I know," came the reply, "but we'd better do as they say."

Meanwhile each of the boys was giving his name to 'sir'.

"Bradders, inspect the new snips will you."

Another boy stepped forward, stocky and cheeky. He was no taller than they were. What was going on? He began with poor John Parsons.

"Let's see your ears. Hm. Hands? Not bad. Shoes? Just look at those shoes. Come straight off the farm have you? Those won't do. I'll inspect those again before breakfast tomorrow. Next."

He moved on down the line. Something was seriously wrong with every boy.

"What's your name again?"

"Philip Jonas sir."

"Well Philip Jonas I've just seen your ears. Good God man, real flappers. And look at the muck in them."

Jonas went crimson. How was he to know that his ears were perfectly clean?

"That's half the line," said the tall boy. "Those who have been inspected go straight to the staffroom for your bath tickets. Through that corridor over there," he pointed, "and up the stairs to the first floor. The door is facing you. Off you go. At the double."

The boys ran off and the inspection continued. Roger was condemned for dirty finger-nails and then the second batch were sent to the staffroom for their bath tickets. They headed for the corridor and up the stairs past Philip Jonas. He was sitting disconsolate on the stairs. Roger stopped.

"What's up with you?"

Jonas looked up. He had been so full of his own misery that he hadn't noticed the boys thundering past.

"Have they sent the rest of you to get your bath tickets?"

"Yes."

"Well don't go. There isn't any such thing as bath tickets. It's just a joke they play on new boys. And don't go back in line either. Those other boys are no older than we are. I'm going to hide in the lavs until the bell goes."

The two of them went down the stairs and arrived at the bottom just as four of their tormentors came looking for them.

"What are you new snips doing here? Get back to the quad into your line."

"You can't tell us to get into line," answered Roger. "You're nothing more than we are."

"Hark at him. Cocky for a new snip. Scrag him," and the four boys grabbed Roger and dragged him back across the quad while Jonas made his escape. Although Roger continued to struggle they held him firm at the end of a somewhat depleted line.

"Right," the tall boy was saying, "we need new boys for the choir. Parsnips what songs do you know?"

"None really. I knows a few hymns I suppose." And then his face lit up. "And I know 'Rule Britannia'," he said.

"Go on then. Let's hear it."

Shyly Parsons began to sing but as he grew in confidence he sang with more gusto. Sadly, he didn't know that he was tone deaf. His singing sounded awful but his tormentors were delighted. As he drew to a close the tall boy said, "Not bad. Not bad at all. You could be just what we are looking for. Sing it again."

Parsons let rip and this time the boys found it hard to stifle their giggles but Parsons didn't notice. He was giving the song his all.

"Yes. That's pretty good. Let's have it just one more time."

He sang and the boys fell about laughing. He stuttered to a halt. What was wrong? They hooted at him. He went white with anger and embarrassment. What was it? Why were they all laughing?

But they never told him. With a bit of luck they could keep this one going for days. They went on down the line making each boy sing in turn. Finally they came to Roger.

"Right Wallace. Let's hear you sing."

Roger actually had a pretty good singing voice. He'd often sung solo at his last school. But he remained silent.

"Come on boy. Sing."

"No. You can't make me sing."

The tall boy was amazed. "What did you say?"

"You sent me for a bath ticket. Well I didn't go because there's no such thing. So there. Now you tell me to sing. Well I won't sing. You're nothing more than a bully. You can't make me sing."

"Can't I just. You see if I can't. We'll soon deal with you." He punched Roger in the stomach.

That set Roger off, struggling as hard as he could to get free from the four boys who had hold of him. Some of the other new boys realised that they had been conned and took Roger's side. Soon there was a proper mêlée with Roger and some of the others flattened on the ground. Suddenly there was a shout that sounded like K.V.

Like lightning the old hands disappeared leaving the new boys alone and Roger picking himself up off the ground. None of the new boys knew that K.V., the Latin 'cave', was a warning cry telling them that a member of staff was coming.

"What are you doing down there boy?"

Roger looked up at a tall, slim, fair-haired young man.

Something told him to be careful.

"I fell over," he said.

You're a new boy aren't you. What's your name?"

"Roger Wallace."

"Well don't just sit there on the ground. Get up and say 'sir' when you speak to me."

All these flippin' boys demanded to be called 'sir'. Roger was fed up with the lot of them but he played safe.

"Roger Wallace sir."

"Go and get cleaned up and report to me at the staffroom." The young man strode away.

Roger went and cleaned himself up as best he could. He was angry.

"They're all the same. That boy can't tell me to go to the staffroom. Who does he think he is. 'Sir'! If he wasn't so tall I'd tell him where to put his 'sir'. He won't kid me into going to the staffroom."

The bell rang and boys began hurrying to the quad from all directions. They lined up in three different rows denoting the houses to which they had belonged. The new boys had lined up against the wall and were now given their houses and told to join their lines.

Roger was in Beta house which wore green badges. There was a good deal of pushing and shoving as the boys joined their lines and tried to establish their seniority.

"I arrived at school at 3 o'clock. You didn't get here until 4 so I'm senior to you."

"How old are you?"

"That's got nothing to do with it. It's when you arrive that counts."

Roger couldn't be bothered with all that. He stood at the back of the line.

The school marched up a set of worn, stone stairs and turned left into a large hall – alpha first, then beta and gamma. They all crammed into old wooden, double desks and sat down – all except for a few of the oldest boys who stood in the aisles at the back. The desks were stained with generations of boys' ink, carved with their initials, notched and rutted from generations of pocket knives. They had a well used quality that made boys feel at home. But for Roger the comfort was not to last very long.

The tall, fair-haired young man who had spoken to him in the quad came in and stood on the platform. He was a teacher! But he looked so young. Roger's heart sank. How was he supposed to know? If the teacher had been wearing that gown he would have known. He should have worn it. It wasn't fair.

They sang a hymn with fair volume. The teacher read from the Bible and said a prayer and then he made a few announcements.

"The new boy Roger Wallace stand up please."

Roger stood.

"Report to the staffroom immediately after assembly and wait for me there."

"You're for it," whispered Bradders. "That's Smarty and he can't half make you smart."

That was a lot of comfort. Roger went to the staffroom and waited outside. It wasn't long before Mr Smart arrived. He looked smart too with his fair hair all slicked down with Brylcream. His suit looked new with sharp creases in the trousers. Even his gown looked new.

"Come in boy."

There was no one else in the staffroom.

"Why didn't you come when I told you to?"

Roger started to explain about the bath tickets and how he wasn't going to be fooled twice, although he wondered if he ought to tell Mr Smart that he thought he was a schoolboy. Luckily he never got the chance. Mr Smart interrupted him.

"No excuses. You thought that because you are a new boy I wouldn't know who you are. You thought you'd get away with it."

"No sir," Roger protested, although he admitted to himself that Smarty was perhaps partly right. He had hoped to get away with it.

"Don't 'no sir' me. I know what you boys are like. You had been fighting down there in the quad hadn't you?"

He didn't even wait for Roger's mumbled "yes sir". He just went on, "Well you're going to have to learn fast that I won't tolerate misbehaviour or insolence, and I certainly won't tolerate disobedience."

"But sir . . ."

"SILENCE. Bend over that chair."

Roger was stunned. It was so unfair. He looked daggers at the teacher and then he turned and bent over the chair. Mr Smart took a gym shoe and whacked Roger hard, four times.

"Now go straight to your dormitory and get to bed. You have missed your cocoa."

Without a word Roger stood up and walked out. "So this is what boarding school is going to be like," he thought. He walked across the grey quad, closed in by its surrounding walls, high buildings and the darkness. It was grim, just like a prison.

3

The Sheet

It was after lights out two nights later.

"Wallace are you awake?" It was Jonas whispering.

"Yes."

"I need to go to the lav to do a leg." (The new boys were already using the school slang.)

"Well go then."

"I'm scared of the dark and we're not allowed to put any lights on."

It was true. At 'lights out' they took down all the war-time blackouts from the windows so that they could let some fresh air into the dormitories. But after that no lights could be used because they might attract German bombers.

"I'll go with you to the lav," Roger said.

They got out of bed and crept out into the corridor. Then they saw a torchlight flash in the next dorm.

"Look out. It's Smarty," whispered Roger and they both hurried back to their beds.

On silent gym shoes Mr Smart swept along the corridor and into their dormitory. His torch flashed from bed to bed. All quiet and everyone in their beds. He was surprised.

He could have sworn that he had heard a noise. Perhaps he had better come back and check later. He moved noiselessly away. After a couple of minutes Roger asked, "Do you still want to go?"

There was a long pause. "It's too late. I couldn't wait and old Smarty scares me stiff. I've wet my bed."

"Well don't just lie in it," Roger answered. "Get the wet things off your bed. We shall have to dry them."

He jumped out of bed and helped Jonas take off his bottom sheet and blanket. By now all the boys in the dorm were wide awake.

"Where can we dry them?" asked Jonas.

"We'll hang them across the stairs. They'll be dry by morning. Then you can put them back on your bed and no one will know."

So they took the sheet and the blanket and draped them across the stairs. Soon everything was quiet again and the boys began to drop off to sleep. Suddenly there was a muffled oath from outside. "What the . . ." and then the sound of swift footsteps to the dormitory door and the flash of a torch. It was Mr Smart.

"Who hung those bedclothes across the stairs?"

Silence.

"I'm waiting."

"I did sir," answered Roger.

"You've wet your bed have you?" said Mr Smart with disgust.

"No sir but . . ."

"Don't lie to me. I've just walked into them. The bedclothes are not just wet. They smell."

There were muffled giggles all round the dorm.

"Silence!" roared Mr Smart.

"Sir, I know sir but . . ."

"Don't 'but' me boy. Get your dressing down on and go up to the staffroom."

Roger put on his dressing gown and his slippers and made his way to the staffroom.

A few minutes later Mr Smart arrived and called him inside.

He looked at the boy with obvious distaste and said, "We understand that some boys can't help bed wetting. When they do, they go to Matron and see the doctor and receive help so that they get over it." (He wrote a short note). "You will go to Matron in the morning and take this note with you."

"But sir . . ." began Roger.

"Don't interrupt me. I have told you that we don't blame boys who can't help wetting their beds, although boys of your age ought to have got over that kind of thing long ago", he added. "What I will not tolerate is lying."

Roger tried once more, "But sir . . ."

"Be silent. If you haven't got the guts to admit the truth that you are a dirty boy, we'll just have to put some backbone into you. I want you to understand quite clearly that I am not punishing you for your filthy habits. I am punishing you for your gutless lying. Now take off your dressing gown and bend over that chair."

He took his gym shoe and gave Roger four furious whacks on the backside. "Now get back to your dorm and report to Matron in the morning."

Roger was angry and bitter as he went back to bed but when he got back to the dorm Thomas was there. As a prefect he came to bed much later than they did. The other boys were telling him about Smarty walking into the wet bedclothes.

Thomas looked at Roger and said, "I'm glad he did. If he hadn't, I probably would have done and then you'd have been in trouble young Wallace."

They all giggled at that and Roger began to feel better. But he already hated Mr Smart. "Served the rotten swine right," he thought.

In the morning he went to see Matron. She was a kind and motherly little grey-haired woman and he found that he was able to tell her what had really happened. She did her best not to laugh and asked, "So which boy was it who wet his bed?"

Roger hesitated.

"You don't need to worry. He won't get into trouble and if you don't tell me I only need to read his Cash's name tape on the sheet."

So Roger told her.

"Very well Wallace. We'll put some clean things on Philip Jonas' bed. I don't expect he'll wet it again. But you tell him, if he does have trouble I want him to come and see me. Now run along and don't get into any more trouble with Mr Smart."

"Thank you Matron." Funnily enough Roger was so grateful that he almost felt like crying. But then he thought of old Smarty walking into those bed-clothes and laughed instead.

Jonas was waiting for him so he told him what Matron had said and how nice she was.

"I'm sorry you got scatted. I was too scared to own up. It should have been me he hit with the slipper," Jonas said.

"I don't think Smarty would have whacked you. He's got it in for me. I don't know why."

"Does he scat very hard?"

24

"Hard enough."

Roger knew nothing of some staff conversations that were taking place. The first was when Mr Smart reported to the Head about his night duty rounds. He told him about Roger and added, "In Beddingford there is a solicitor called Hilton who is a friend of mine. Wallace lived in his house for a time as an evacuee. He had all sorts of trouble with him. He told me that the boy is deceitful and will tell any lie to escape punishment. I have already had to beat the boy twice. We are going to have to watch him very carefully and keep him firmly under control."

The Head listened and thanked Mr Smart for his report but he wasn't altogether convinced. He preferred to go by his own judgement and his own assessment of the boy had been much more favourable. Oh, he had no doubt that Wallace would often be in trouble. After all, he was a cheeky, lively lad but he had clear, honest eyes. He seemed a straightforward enough boy. Time would tell.

As Mr Smart was walking away from the Head's study he met Matron. "Did that boy Wallace come to see you this morning about his bed wetting?"

"Yes he did, but he wasn't actually the bed-wetter. That was actually another of the boys. He was just trying to help the boy dry his bedclothes."

"Then why didn't he say so?"

"Perhaps he was trying to protect his friend," said Matron quietly.

"Hm." He went on his way. Matron was too soft with these boys, he thought, but a tiny question mark about his own reaction to the incident lodged in his mind.

And now it was Matron's turn to speak to the Head. She painted a much more favourable picture of Roger and spoke of his loyalty to his friend.

The Head was pleased on two counts. He was pleased that it was not Wallace who had wet his bed. He knew that he was expected to be sympathetic to boys who did, but the fact was that he despised them. Something wrong with their moral fibre, he thought.

But he was also pleased that Roger had protected his friend. "You feel that Mr Smart never gave him a chance do you?"

"I didn't say that sir. I wasn't there and I don't know the details

25

b

of what happened so I'm not about to criticise Mr Smart. But he did get one fact wrong that needs to be put right. I have already told him and now I'm reporting to you that Wallace was not the bed-wetter." She understood the pre-historic attitudes of these men. If they thought Roger was a bed-wetter they would have a down on him that might never be erased.

"Then who was? Who was the boy who didn't have the guts to own up?" As the Head demanded to know he exuded an almost brutal masculinity.

She smiled grimly to herself. She had been right about his prejudices. She looked him in the eye and lied.

"Wallace wouldn't tell me who the boy was and I haven't checked yet with the maid who replaced the dirty sheet and blanket."

She was just as determined to protect Philip Jonas as she was to secure fair treatment for Roger Wallace. By the time she saw the Headmaster again he would have other things on his mind.

4

Bath Night

The following morning the first bell rang at 7.15 and Thomas had them all out of bed and into the washroom. They stood at wash-basins and washed in cold water. There wasn't any hot. Thomas stood and watched. He sent a couple of them back to wash their necks properly.

When they were washed and dressed and had made their beds, he checked them over and sent them to the shoe cleaning room. Each of them had a small locker with brushes and shoe polish. They cleaned their shoes and milled around aimlessly until the second bell at ten to eight. They lined up in their houses, were inspected for cleanliness, tidy hair and clean shoes, and then they marched into the dining hall.

Eight to ten of them sat at scrubbed wooden tables. Huge saucepans were brought in, steaming hot, and each boy was given a dollop of stodgy porridge. There were jugs of milk on the table to thin the porridge a little, and they were allowed a teaspoon of sugar. Then came a thick slice of toast and a tiny pat of butter to scrape over it, and marmalade. It was to be the same every day except Sunday when they each had a boiled egg which could be anything from rock hard to watery runny.

After breakfast some cleaned the dorms, others cleaned the classrooms, and others the locker rooms and other spare rooms of the school. And some simply walked the quad, the corridors and play areas hunting for litter. At ten to nine the bell rang again and they lined up in their houses in the quad. The master on duty had already inspected the school to see that they had done their cleaning and tidying. Now he inspected them once more before marching them up into the hall for assembly. Once in the hall they stood and waited.

The Headmaster led the staff onto the platform and announced a hymn. One of the senior boys read from the Bible, the Head prayed using a book. Roger noticed that. Most of the prayers he had ever heard in church or in school had been without a book, often long, meandering affairs that wandered twice round the world and back again. These were brief. They didn't make a lot of sense but they were brief. Roger preferred them. Then he remembered that in old Hilton's church the prayers had come from a book. He wondered what sort of church the Head belonged to.

After the prayers the Head made some announcements and then sent most of the boys off to their classrooms. The new boys stayed put. The assembly hall *was* their classroom. Their days followed one of two patterns. Each lesson lasted forty minutes. On Monday, Wednesday and Friday they worked until 12.10 and were then free to lunch-time at 1 o'clock. Then they worked from 2 to 4 and were free until tea at 5. They went back to the assembly hall at 6.30 for homework, or prep. They had three subjects a night to work at, half an hour a subject. Then came cocoa and bed at 9 with lights out and blackouts down at 9.15. Older boys did more homework and went to bed later.

Tuesdays, Thursdays and Saturdays were similar. But in the mornings they had classes right through to lunch time at 1. They had no classes in the afternoons. On Tuesdays every boy belonged to a scout troop or to the 'pioneers' who did practical work around the school, gardening or repairing things and very soon learning the way to skive off.

Thursday afternoons were for sport. Every boy played rugby in winter and cricket in summer plus cross country running. Saturday afternoons were also for sport. It was a small school so every boy was either playing for the school or supporting the school. No one was excused.

And then came Sunday. A change of clothes; best suits, and off to church or chapel in the morning.

After lunch every boy wrote a letter to his parents and then went for a walk. It was about the only time in the week when boys got out of the school grounds. They were back in school for tea and all of them went to chapel in the evening.

It was a routine into which they settled very quickly.

The only slight variation came on bath nights. The school only possessed ten baths so baths for the boys had to be arranged to a very tight time-table. Roger's bath night was on Fridays and it meant that he missed half an hour of prep.

Roger welcomed the break from prep. Almost from the very beginning he had made up his mind that if prep was supposed to last half an hour a subject, he would spend half an hour and no more. Quite often it was impossible to finish the work set in the time. Too bad. If he hadn't finished he didn't finish. He didn't see why he should use up his precious spare time doing prep the way many of the boys did.

Half an hour off prep for his bath was a bonus. The main block of baths had seven bathrooms side by side. The block was called simply 'the baths' but that was not where Roger went. He had to go to 'the tilehouse'. It was a large low-ceilinged room with a floor of concrete slabs and tiled walls.

Along the first wall from the door there was a row of hooks on which the boys could hang their towels. Along the next wall there were about thirty wash-basins. Against the third wall, end to end, there were two baths and a third bath stood in the middle of the fourth wall.

After rugby or other sport the boys entered the tilehouse wrapped only in their towels. They washed down at the wash-basins and then jumped in and out of the first bath, in and out of the second bath and in and out of the third bath, rinsing themselves off in each bath. By the time two rugby teams had been in and out of the baths the colour of the water was pretty rich.

This was where Roger and two other boys came for their bath at 6.30 each Friday. George Watson should have been the second boy but he had done a swap with Parsons. The third was the tall boy who had sent all the new boys for their bath tickets. He was the same age as the others but looked three years older. His name was Henry Wilkins and he had been at Perspins for a whole year. Like all Perspins boys, he was intensely conscious of his seniority over these new snips. Roger disliked him, not just because of that bit of teasing. He just didn't like the boy.

The first couple of bath nights passed without incident but on the third Friday, Henry Wilkins arrived late. The other two boys were already lying lazily in the end to end baths.

The vacant bath was in the most draughty spot of a very draughty room. Wilkins stripped off and said to Parsons, "Out you get Parsons. That's my bath."

Parsons was an inoffensive chap and already suffering for it. He began to get out of his bath.

"You stay where you are," shouted Roger.

Parsons hesitated.

"OUT. This minute."

"Don't you dare."

"Don't interfere Wallace. It's nothing to do with you. As senior boy here, I choose which bath I shall have. You new snips go where you're told."

"Who says?"

"I do."

"Stuff that."

Parsons had taken no part in this conversation. He simply slid quietly back into the warm water and soaked himself. But by now Wilkins had had enough of talk. He grabbed the bar of soap from the empty bath and hurled it at Roger.

As quick as a flash Roger threw the bar from his bath back. Then he threw the bar Wilkins had thrown at him and while Wilkins was trying to pick up one of those slippery bars to respond, Roger leapt out of his bath and over to the wash-basins.

One after another in lightning succession the wash-basin soaps flew across the room at Wilkins. He backed away towards the door. Most of the bars missed him but one caught him on the head and another in the stomach. With a yell he opened the door and escaped into the quad – stark naked.

He pulled up very suddenly when he found Mr Smart and Miss Elliott the housekeeper chatting together in the quad.

"What the devil's going on? Get back into your bath at once," ordered Mr Smart and he followed Wilkins into the tilehouse.

Roger was standing there with a bar of soap poised for action. It was lucky he didn't actually throw it.

"You Wallace. I might have guessed. Wherever there's trouble this term I find you at the bottom of it. Well: what have you got to say for yourself?"

"Nothing sir."

"It WAS you who drove Wilkins into the Quad?"

"Yes sir."

"Clear up this mess. Get yourself dressed and report to the staffroom."

"Yes sir." Roger began picking up the bars of soap and putting them back where they belonged.

"That'll teach you to pinch my bath," said Wilkins.

"Oh no it won't," Roger replied. "It's first come, first served."

Parsons had finished his bath by now. "There's no need for you two to squabble," he said. "I don't mind having the draughty bath in future."

Wilkins didn't have the sense to drop the subject. He rounded on Parsons and said, "You'll have the bath I tell you and so will Wallace."

"Oh shut your gob," said Roger but both he and Wilkins were very surprised when Parsons said:

"Yes. Shut up Wilkins. If you hadn't come in here causing trouble tonight, Wallace wouldn't be in trouble now. It's all your fault and you didn't have the guts to admit it."

Before either of them could add to that, Parsons had grabbed his towel and gone. Roger also took his towel and went to get dressed before going to the staffroom. Henry Wilkins decided that he hadn't got enough time for a bath so he washed quickly at one of the basins.

When Roger was standing in front of Mr Smart he fully expected another scatting with the gym shoe but Smarty said, "I'm going to put in a report about you to the Head. We'll see whether his punishments are any more effective than mine. Now get yourself to the assembly hall for your hour's prep.

"Yes sir."

He made his way to the assembly hall but couldn't concentrate on his work. He felt homesick – but where was his home? He didn't have a home of his own any more. For one reason or another he had had to leave every evacuation home he had been happy in except Miss Holly's. And now old Smarty had got it in for him. It looked as though boarding school would be a disaster. He wished he was back with his mum and dad. Or with Miss Holly or Barbara – he knew they liked him.

When nothing happened that week-end Roger began to hope that he had heard the last of the bathroom episode. But of course he was wrong.

Lunch was the biggest meal of the day. The Headmaster and his wife, the housekeeper and some of the other staff all sat at the top table. All meals began and ended with 'grace' in Latin. After lunch that next Monday morning the Head made his usual announcements ending with, "Bishop, Jones, Elliott, Mallins, Stebbs and Wallace all report to my study immediately."

Roger's heart sank. He made his way through a series of passages to the small room beside the Headmaster's house – his study. The other boys arrived, lined up and talked in hushed tones.

The Head arrived like a whirlwind with his gown swirling out behind him. He called Bishop inside.

The passage where they waited smelt heavily of old leather and polish. Roger quite liked the smell. It made him think of the smell of his dad when he cuddled into him. That was a pipe tobacco sort of smell always associated with warmth and security. Why such different smells were associated in his mind he never knew but it was as well that he liked *this* smell. He was going to spend an awful lot of time waiting in that passage before his school-days were over. Bishop came out and sent Jones in. Roger thought to himself, "Who'd have a name like Wallace. They always do things in alphabetical order so I'm always one of the last. It isn't fair." When his turn came Roger went into the Head's study and stood behind a large armchair. The Head was seated at his desk beside a window and facing the door. The smell of old leather and furniture polish pervaded this room too.

"I have a report here from Mr Smart about an incident on your bath night."

"Yes sir."

The Head didn't tell Roger that Mr Smart felt that he was a trouble-maker and a bad influence on other new boys.

"Would you like to tell me what happened?"

"I had an argument with one of the other boys sir, and I chased him out into the quad without any clothes on. Mr Smart and Miss Elliott were in the quad sir and Mr Smart said that he was going to make a report to you sir."

"Why isn't the other boy here too?"

Roger didn't know how to answer that. Eventually he mumbled, "Please sir, I don't know sir; perhaps because he was the one what got chased sir."

"English boy, speak English. 'He was the one who was chased'. And don't mumble boy. Speak up, speak out, speak clearly. Do you understand boy?"

"Yes sir."

"You seem to have been in trouble ever since you arrived."

"Yes sir."

"I think perhaps we had better move you from the new boys' dorm to a dorm where senior boys can keep an eye on you. You will move your things to dorm twenty-three. There is one other new boy there Lendicott. He may be glad of your company. After tea today report to Cardew the dorm prefect and move your things to the new dorm immediately."

"Yes sir."

"Now Wallace, we can't go on having bad reports about you. I'm going to punish you today and I hope that it will be for the last time."

He crossed the study to an alcove in the corner and took a cane from it. He flexed the cane and said, "Remove the cushion from that armchair in front of you and place it on the floor. Then bend over the back of the chair and grasp one of the rungs."

Roger did as he was told.

"No boy, not like that. Grasp the third rung from the back of the chair. It arches your bottom more sharply so that you feel the power of the cane better."

Roger took hold of the third rung and felt the touch of the cane as the Head took aim. One, two, three strokes followed. Roger gasped with each one and grabbed the rung more tightly.

"Stand up boy."

Roger stood and tried to hide his discomfort.

"After a caning, retrieve the cushion and replace it on the chair. Then stand and say 'thank you, sir'. Finally, wait to be dismissed."

"Yes sir." He picked up the cushion and put it back on the chair. "Thank you, sir."

"Very well. Dismiss and remember to report to Cardew after tea."

"Yes sir." Roger walked carefully out of the study. He tried to look as though he had not been hurt. Then he went right across to the other side of the school and out into the cricket field where he could be alone. Not until he was safely there did he let the tears

33

of pain and anger go.

Not only had Smarty got it in for him. He had put the Head against him too. It was a pity that Roger couldn't see the effect he had had on the Headmaster.

"Gutsy boy. Seemed straight as a die. Loyal too. Wasn't prepared to get the other boy into trouble. Probably end up as head boy one day."

5

An Artist and a Poet

Out on the cricket pitch, Roger walked to try to ease his feelings. Round and round the boundary of the field he went. At least there was one good thing. Old Smarty wasn't the housemaster in charge of dorm 23. Dickson was the housemaster there and he was a decent old cove who never knew what was going on. And Joe Lendicott was in the dorm too. He was pleased about that. Joe sat beside him in class and the two of them got on well with one another. So Roger began to be more cheerful and as he cheered up he started to sing, "Hang out your troubles on the Siegfried line . . ."

"Heard you Wallace. Said you wouldn't sing for us didn't you but I've heard you."

The voice came from the other side of the hedge but Roger knew who it was. It was bloody Wilkins. "Oh shut your mouth," shouted Roger but he felt sick. "I'll get even with him one day," he said to himself. "I swear on the bloody Bible I will." He was blissfully unaware of the incongruity of the combination of swearing and Bible. Swearing was something he had never done. His family didn't. But he found he was beginning to like words like 'bloody' and 'bugger'. They were so expressive.

After tea Roger reported to Cardew in the prefect's room. Several of the boys in dorm 16 helped him to move his stuff to dorm 23. It was another fairly small dorm but a much lighter room with a high ceiling and plenty of windows. The other new boys were quite envious.

Prep. followed and then cocoa and bed. Cardew had moved

things around so that Roger and Joe were next to one another and that was smashing. But after lights-out when everyone was quiet, Roger's spirits took a dive again. He lay in bed wondering if coming to boarding school had been such a good idea after all. He felt homesick again.

Cardew came to bed after the lights were out. He saw that Roger was still awake and he came and sat on his bed.

"Where do you come from Wallace?"

"Beddingford. At least, I came here from Beddingford but that's not my real home. I was evacuated there. I come from near London."

"Where exactly?"

"Just outside Croydon."

"What, near the aerodrome."

"Yes, that's right."

Cardew began to talk about it as if he had known it well. In fact, he had only been there once when his dad wanted to see it. That was when it was still important, before the war. But the way Cardew spoke you'd have thought he knew the whole area. Roger listened and felt proud of his home – his real home. What a smashing chap Cardew was. Perhaps boarding school would be all right after all. He felt happier already and it wasn't long after Cardew had left his bed before he was asleep.

Most of the new boys had the odd bout of home-sickness. But they were kept so busy and there was so much that was new in their lives that it only was the odd bout. They were quickly making new friendships. And in the case of the more local lads, family relationships helped them settle. But for one or two of the more sensitive lads, boarding school was utter misery and torment. If boys didn't fit the school mould they were given hell. Parsons was one of the boys whose life was made a misery and Philip Jonas was another.

The fact that he had wet his bed had leaked out and older boys tormented him about it. If he had been any good at sport it would soon have been forgotten, but he wasn't. He wasn't interested in sport – not in any sport. Once, playing rugby, he had found himself with the ball in his hands and set off for the line full tilt. Everyone in his team started yelling. How nice to have encouragement at last. He ran his hardest, crossed the line and downed the ball. Perhaps sport wasn't so bad after all. He had a real sense of achievement.

But then it all fell apart when he discovered that he had run the wrong way and planted the ball over his own line.

He started to find ways of getting out of games afternoons. Then he would just wander off on his own. He liked rooting around for bugs or beetles, or just sitting on an old tree stump gazing into space. Other boys were never sure whether he was thinking or whether there was just a blank. He reminded them of that scribble in the bogs: 'Sometimes I sits and thinks and sometimes I just sits.'

But there was more to Jonas than they realised. Fortunately one or two of the staff began to recognise it fairly quickly. Sometimes it was to his benefit and sometimes not. He certainly pleased the other boys one maths period.

Mr Barlow held up his homework exercise book and said, "Jonas, as far as I can see you haven't done your maths homework."

"No sir. I looked at it but I couldn't understand it and it didn't interest me."

The others waited for Mr Barlow to explode. They hardly dared breathe. Mr Barlow looked at Jonas with astonishment and then he realised that the boy wasn't being impudent or rude. He was just stating what he thought were the simple facts of his life.

"If you don't understand, it is for you to ask me to help you to understand. Lack of understanding is no excuse for failing to do your homework. And whether you are interested or not is beside the point."

How true that was. Mr Barlow wasn't really very interested either. He was only interested in making model trains that ran round his garden, and in the model railway club he ran on hobbies' evenings, but he couldn't tell the boys that. So he said to Jonas, "Maths is one of the most important subjects you will ever study."

"But why sir? What is the point of it all? When will I ever need to know that 'a minus b equals c'?"

From most boys that would have been pure cheek but Jonas was not being cheeky. It was a simple question asked in all sincerity. The rest of the class could hardly believe their ears. Jonas was asking for trouble.

But he wasn't and Mr Barlow recognised that he wasn't. He answered the boy seriously.

"To obtain school certificate or matriculation you have to have maths as one of your subjects. Without it you will be unable to go to university. So you see, you cannot make your way in the world without maths."

"I'm sorry sir, but I don't see it that way. I don't want to go to university. I want to be a poet or an artist and I can't see that maths is any use in those professions."

"You can't make a living as a poet or an artist. Maths is essential if you want to make a living. And incidentally, it will help you to understand the principles of perspective in art."

Jonas chose to ignore that last remark. He replied, "But sir, other great poets and artists have been prepared to starve for their work. I don't see why I should be any luckier than they have been. Perhaps a creative person needs to go through a period of poverty."

Mr Barlow looked at the boy with incredulity. The lad was perfectly serious. He wondered if he had any talent. He must ask his colleagues. Meanwhile it was time to take control of this conversation and bring it to an end.

"If you don't mind my saying so, I consider that to be a lot of tommy rot. Find a way to earn a living and to practise your art as well. If you have real talent your art will come to take over, and when it does you will earn your living from it. In the meantime, I would like you to do me the honour of trying to understand my subject. You will also make a genuine attempt to do your homework – and at very least to present me with something neat and well-produced."

That was a real sting in the tail. Jonas was totally incapable of doing anything neat. He couldn't look neat, with his hair sticking out in all directions no matter how he tried. His clothes were never neat, and he always had at least one shoe-lace undone and one sock down. His written work was always covered in blots and smudges. Neatness and Philip Jonas just didn't go together. But as he listened to Barlow, he determined to try, so he simply answered, "Yes sir."

And that was that. He spent ages trying to be neat and producing homework that was almost non-existent. Barlow always gave him as many marks as he could possibly scrape together because he recognised the boy's effort. He made no attempt to bully Philip into anything more.

The other boys were astonished that Jonas got away with it. There was a brief chance that he would become a kind of hero, but how could a boy who wanted to be a poet be a hero. And they were envious. They could never have held such a conversation with a master. They were envious too when he began to build a decent relationship with the English and Arts master.

There was one occasion when Mr Emerson came into the class and without more ado pointed to a dark corner of the room.

"Bradley. What colours do you see in that corner?"

"Black sir."

"Is that all – just black?"

"Yes sir."

"Wallace. What colours can you see?"

"Well it isn't really black sir."

"Go on."

"I suppose it's sort of grey sir."

"You suppose it's sort of grey," Mr Emerson repeated with heavy sarcasm. "Jonas, let's see if you can help these blind Samsons. What colours do you see?"

"Purples and violet and yellows sir."

Oh thank heaven. There is one boy in this wilderness of savages with an eye for colour.

Roger and Bradley looked at one another. They were blowed if they could see purples and violet and yellows. They wondered who was the daftest, old Emerson or Jonas. Daft or not they liked them both so they didn't join in the mockery and ragging of Jonas that followed at break time – but they made no attempt to interfere with it either.

The ragging was merciless and there seemed no end to it. Jonas was an obstinate and courageous boy. The taunting and bullying made him miserable but he never gave his tormentors the added pleasure of seeing him lose his temper or break down in tears. Nor did he alter his ways or compromise. He liked Mr Emerson and he liked the sarcastic way the master spoke of the boys he taught. He called them 'savages' and 'philistines'. Jonas began to think of them in that way. He was an artist. They were dull, tough, insensitive and sports mad.

More and more Jonas began to feel that there was no good reason for him to stay in such a primitive, uncivilised hole. He would run away.

And that is precisely what he did.

He checked his pocket money and then went round borrowing as much as he possibly could from every boy who had shown him a modicum of friendship. Roger lent him tuppence. He kept a much blotted and smudged sheet of paper listing his debts and then he waited for Sunday to come.

On Sunday afternoon the boys all filed into the assembly hall and wrote their letters home. And then it was time for the Sunday afternoon walk. Jonas set off on his own and headed for the railway station six miles away.

It was not until he arrived there that he discovered that there were no trains on a Sunday at that tiny little halt. Oh well, he would just have to wait that was all. He made himself as comfortable as he could in the waiting room and fell asleep. When the railwayman found him there the following morning he rang the school.

The Head drove out and fetched him. He was very decent.

"Running away boy? What on earth for? Can't have that you know. We are all part of a team. Work together, play together. You understand? Bit homesick were you? Need to toughen up boy. Let's have none of this sloppy sentimentality. Got to be a man. Right boy? Understand do you? Good. Let's have no more of it."

A week later Jonas ran away again. This time he headed towards Beddingford because that was the nearest sizeable town, but it was thirteen miles away. He walked uphill and down towards Stubble Cross. He'd only gone a couple of miles when he had to wait while a farmer drove his milking herd across the road towards the milking sheds. The evening milking had to be done in time to tidy up and go to chapel. The farmer looked at the boy – about the same age as his Tom who was also boarding at the school, and also new that term.

"You'm a long ways from school boy."

"Yes," said Philip. There wasn't much else he could say.

" 'Twon't be long afore 'tis tea time. How about stopping by to the farm for a little while and 'aving some tay with us?"

"Oh, yes please," Philip answered. He hadn't realised how hungry he was and he jumped at the offer.

"Come on then boy. You just follow me until I get those cows sorted out."

So Philip followed into the yard. He waited and watched

fascinated. He had never seen cattle so close before.

"You know my Tom I expect? Tom Rowden?"

"Yes, he's in the same class as me." Philip liked Tom. You couldn't not like him. He was so steady and decent and straight – quiet too.

"Come on then boy. Come and meet Tom's mother."

Mr Rowden took Philip to the farm, took off his boots and introduced Philip before going off to wash. It wasn't very long before they were sitting down to a magnificent tea. Mrs Rowden was famous for her table. It might be war-time but the table was laden with treats such as Jonas had never seen in his life – and certainly not in his life at Perspins.

He tucked into bread and jam and Devonshire cream and followed that up with trifle and more cream and then cakes. He ate until he was so full that he couldn't have walked a hundred yards, let alone all the way to Beddingford. And all the time they were asking him questions about himself. They sat him in a comfortable chair by the huge wood fire and in no time he was fast asleep.

"What shall us do with the boy mother," asked Mr Rowden.

"You get yourself ready for chapel. Then you can take him back to school. But don't take un to the Headmaster. I don't suppose they know the boy's missing yet. Take un to Mr Emerson. Us knows he. Us doesn't know the Head properly yet. Mr Emerson will see to the boy."

"Ess," replied her husband. "I reckon that's just what we should do."

"An' I reckon us can invite the boy's mother down yer to stay when 'tis exeat time."

"Gyaw mother, you'm a genius. That's just what us'll do."

Mr Rowden got ready for chapel and then they woke Jonas and told him what they were going to do, but Mrs Rowden was rather careful about the way she put her plans to Jonas.

"Now boy, you've got a week-end exeat coming up zoon. Why don't ee come back yer with our Tom and enjoy a few days here on the farm? Our Tom will be glad to share his room with ee and us can give ee some proper food too, not like that old stuff they gives ee at school. An' p'raps us can manage a rather special surprise for ee too."

"Thank you very much Mrs Rowden. I'd love to come." Jonas

felt that life was looking up. A whole week-end of Mrs Rowden's food. Wow!

"Of course it does mean you'll have to go back to school now, but Mr Rowden says he'll drop ee back to Mr Emerson's house."

The excitement had gone from the boy's face. But yes, he would have to go back to school now people knew he had run away. And if he had to go back, old Emerson was the best person to have to face.

"I'll get my coat on then shall I?"

"That's it boy. Us'll zee ee zoon."

So Mr Rowden took him back to Mr Emerson. It was nearly time for chapel but Mr Emerson decided to keep Jonas with him for a while. He wasn't a religious man and he felt that he could be more use to the boy than any sermon. His wife brought them cups of tea and biscuits and left them to chat.

"Now Philip," said Mr Emerson kindly, "what's this all about? It's the second time you've run away isn't it."

Jonas was astonished. He had been addressed by his first name. NO ONE used first names. He didn't even know that old Emerson knew his first name. He found that he could talk to him.

"I don't feel that I fit in here sir. I'm no good at sport and – well that's all anybody seems to do. Even in our spare time everyone seems to kick a ball around or make socks into a rugger ball and throw them around."

"I'm no good at sport either Philip. But you may have noticed that I support the school teams."

"Yes sir."

"We can't all be good at sport any more than we can all be good at art, but we can learn to appreciate other people's skills and to support them."

"Yes sir."

"I don't suppose anybody in school knows that you are missing. I shan't say anything but if you are called to see a master about your absence, ask him to speak to me."

"Yes sir."

He called his wife. "Let's have a game of cards or two until it is time for Philip to nip back into school."

Life really was looking up. And back in school Jonas found that most of the teasing and bullying died away. Any boy who could run away not just once but twice, deserved a bit of respect.

So apart from Wilkins, they left him in peace. And when the school magazine came out they even read the first poem he wrote for it:

> *'I love cats.*
> *I hate rats.*
> *Cats eat rats.*
> *Three cheers for cats.'*

6

War and Wickedness

Tucked away out in the heart of the country as it was, Perspins seemed to be completely cut off from the war. But for the black-outs and the food rationing you wouldn't know that there was a war on. There was no television of course and most of the boys never even heard a wireless. And because there was no cinema, they never saw the news programmes about the war.

Mr Barlow used to show them old films on the school film projector on Saturday nights but those had nothing to do with the war. And they were always breaking down. Sometimes they never did get to see the end of films.

Yet news did filter through from letters from home and from announcements by the Head. For eighteen months it had nearly all been bad. The only bright spots were the escape from Dunkirk and the Battle of Britain when British fighter pilots had more than held their own against all that the Germans could throw across the Channel.

The rest of the news was all bad. The boys were not told about the U boats sinking vast numbers of ships in the Atlantic. Nor that Germany had invaded Jugoslavia and Greece, driving British forces out of Greece and the Greek islands. The invasion of Russia had seemed like good news because it gave Germany another enemy and removed the danger of invasion but the Germans were sweeping the Russian armies further and further back. They seemed unstoppable.

So did the Japanese. There had been great excitement when they came into the war because they brought the Americans in. But now their armies were advancing like a plague of locusts. The

Dutch, French and British colonies in the Far East all fell to the Japs. To the British it seemed impossible that Singapore, Malaya and Burma should all have been lost, and lost so quickly. Would India be next?

Once again, these things were kept from the boys – though most of them seemed to get to know. The one thing they did all know about was North Africa. That was a field of warfare that caught and held the imagination. Armies swept to and fro across the desert like great tides rushing in and out on the shore. Unheard of places like Sidi Barrani hit the headlines and Tobruk returned to the news again and again as first one side and then the other fought for supremacy there.

The Italians seemed to have no great heart for the war and vast numbers of them were captured by advancing British troops. But Rommel's German panzer divisions were a different prospect. They drove the British and their allies back to the very borders of Egypt and Rommel seemed poised for final victory in North Africa.

But the demands of the Russian campaign meant that men and supplies were being taken from Rommel and his lines of communication were so long that keeping his front line forces supplied was a nightmare. At the same time, the British were pumping men and materials into Egypt. For the first time Rommel found himself opposed by superior forces. But they were still forces that had taken a beating; forces with immense respect for German power; forces whose morale was low. Could a defeated army be turned into one that could achieve victory? Their new general, Montgomery, believed that it could and set about ensuring that it would.

In October 1942, one month after Roger went to Perspins, the battle of El Alamein began. Over the next few weeks it became the first major British land victory of the war and was proclaimed by Churchill as the turning of the tide. In his turn, the Head announced the victory with great pride to the school and reminded the boys of the names of all the old boys serving in the forces.

Roger thought about his brothers. Alfie was flying on bombing raids over Germany, he knew that. And he also knew that his second brother was in Africa. But was he at El Alamein?

Back at home his father was pretty sure that he was. Before

Eric had gone to Africa, he and his father had bought identical maps. When Eric wrote home, he took his air letter and placed his map on top of it. Then he took a pin and pushed it straight through marking the spot where he was. Censorship took no notice of a pin hole. When the letter arrived his father took his map, pushed a pin through Eric's pin-hole and his own map and so discovered where Eric was.

Eric had done his final training in South Africa and arrived in the North just in time for El Alamein. His squadron of Hurricanes flew in constant support of the troops on the ground, giving them air cover and battling for supremacy in the air, a supremacy that was achieved for the first time.

But Perspins was isolated from all that – isolated from everything really and immune to everything except its own life. It was exciting to hear about the victory but it was much more exciting on a Sunday afternoon to smash the cups on the tops of telegraph poles or to go scrumping apples from the farm orchards near the school.

Years later Roger was to write about his memories of Sunday afternoon walks:

After our Sunday dinner time
we wrote a letter home,
and then we all went for a walk,
a sober Sunday roam.

The chapel folk were rather shocked
if we did other things
for playing games was wickedness
on a day for prayers and hymns.

A sober Sunday walk it was,
a sober Sunday roam:
how many telegraph cups we smashed
before we got back home.

We hunted all three village girls –
they were not too hard to find –
and if we grew too fresh with them
they never seemed to mind.

A sober Sunday walk it was,
a sober Sunday roam,
and many apples boys could scrump
before they got back home.

We took our Scout troop's cooking things
on our sober Sunday roam,
dug vegetables and tickled trout
before we got back home.

A sober Sunday walk it was
and a rabbit's on the wire
or a pheasant's caught and cleaned and cooked
on a roaring open fire.

We opened up the squire's dams
on our sober Sunday roam,
rowed on his lake, swam in his pool
before we got back home.

The chapel folk were rather shocked
if we did other things
for playing games was wickedness
on a day for prayers and hymns.

So a sober Sunday walk it was,
a sober Sunday roam.
How saintly Perspins boys became
just before they got back home.'

It must have been quite a relief to local people when the boys
went home for a weekend exeat or for the school holidays.

7

An Exeat

From September to Christmas the boys were allowed home for two week-end exeats. These were not much use to Roger. Croydon was too far to go and at nine pounds return on the train, too expensive, even if his parents would have allowed him home to risk being bombed. But there were plenty of boys in the same boat, so Roger didn't mind.

All the same, when Jonas came back from a week-end with Tom Rowden and kept on and on about all the food they had had, he had to admit that he felt pretty envious. So when Joe Lendicott asked him if he would like to go on the next exeat to his farm Roger jumped at the chance.

Eight weeks into the term, one Saturday after breakfast, Joe's father picked them up. The car was a bit of a bone shaker but they only had ten miles to go – all through narrow country lanes with high hedges.

Roger had never been on a farm before. The car turned off the road and bumped up a rough lane into a wet, muddy yard full of cow muck which a man was beginning to wash away. The cows had already been milked and were back in their field.

As the car drew into the yard two dogs ran out from one of the barns surrounding the yard, barking like mad. Joe's father turned to Roger and said, "Roger boy, don't ee go to stroke the dogs. They idn house dogs to be stroked and petted. They'm working dogs and guard dogs. You put your hand out and they'll go for ee. So just you stand still with your hands by your sides. Let the dogs sniff round and get to know ee. Then they'll leave ee alone."

They got out of the car and Roger stood quite still, trying not to look as frightened as he felt. The dogs stood a yard or two away, snarling. Then they came cautiously up to him and sniffed his ankles. They worked their way round him as he stood rigid with fear. And then they trotted off quietly back to the barn.

"There boy. They know ee now. They won't bother 'bout ee no more just so long as you don't bother with they."

But Roger wasn't listening. He was staring at the man who was hosing the yard down. Suddenly he set off running.

"Sam," he cried. "Oh Sam!" and he ran smack into the man, throwing his arms around him. The man barely had time to drop his hose on the floor.

"Why it's young Roger Wallace ain't it. Cor blimey. Who'd of thought it. Where 'ave you sprung from then."

The Lendicotts looked on in astonishment including Mrs Lendicott and her three younger children who had all come out of the farm to welcome their guest.

Sam looked up, grinning all over his face. "We used to know each other before the war," he said. "I used to work for Roger's dad sometimes. Now boy, let me get on with my work and you go and meet the family."

Joe made the formal introductions to Mrs Lendicott and to his younger brother and sisters Jack, Stella and Phyllis. Then the three boys put wellington boots on and went out to explore the farm. There were cows and sheep, a few pigs in their sties and what seemed like hundreds of hens and the odd cockerel, and a few ducks. There was a tractor (a Massey Ferguson that the boys were very proud of though Roger couldn't see what all the fuss was about) and there were four huge working horses. But the one creature that really shook Roger was a massive shorthorn bull with a vicious looking pair of eyes and a ring through its nose. It was kept all on its own in a very sturdy building at one end of a barn.

"Why has it got that ring through its nose?" asked Roger.

Joe pointed to a long pole with a hook at one end. "You have to be careful with bulls," he said. "They'm treacherous beggars. But their nose is a bit sensitive so us puts that hook through its nose ring and then us can control it, keeping it at a safe distance with the pole."

As Roger looked at the bull he hoped that he would never be

asked to control it. By lunch-time the boys were ravenously hungry. They sat down at the long, scrubbed oak table in the farm kitchen with the rest of the family and Sam. The kitchen was a low, dark room with an uneven floor of slabs. All the cooking was done on a massive kitchen range which kept the kitchen permanently warm and dry – too warm in summer.

Joe's dad was tall, slim and wiry. He had to stoop when he was in the kitchen. He eased himself into his chair at the top of the table and his wife placed a plate with a huge pasty and masses of vegetables in front of him. She did the same for Sam and Joe and then came to Roger.

"I 'opes you likes pasty boy," she said.

"I've never had it before," answered Roger, "but I'm sure I will."

"Niver 'ad pasty. Well bless my soul. The poor boy an't niver 'ad pasty."

Joe's mother was amazed. She watched Roger as he began to eat. There was no question about it Roger certainly liked pasty. She was delighted and served Jack and her small daughters, leaving herself until last.

"So you two knows each other," said Joe's father to Sam.

"Yeah. Very well. I used to live in a . . ." (he paused) "in a small place in the woods and this lad and a friend of his found it. Once we got to know each other they was always poppin' round. Decent pair of lads. I knew both their dads and I used to work for this one's dad sometimes when he was a bit short of labour."

"Remarkable, and both of ee 'ave comed right across country down yer."

"Yeah. 'Ow come you're down 'ere young Roger?"

"I was evacuated down to Beddingford and then the school went home last summer. Dad wouldn't let me go home because of the bombing."

"Dead right he was too. It's bin pretty awful round about there. Juney's pub's gone west and the big shed in her garden."

"What your . . ." Roger nearly put his foot in it. He knew that Sam had lived in a shack in the woods and had transported it to June's garden before he left the area. "I mean, that shed you built in June's garden?"

"That's the one. So your dad was very wise not letting you

home. What's happened to that young rip you used to be mates with, that Jimmy Smith?"

"He went home with the school."

"Missed him I expect. You two was always together wasn't you."

"Yes," said Roger. He hadn't thought about Jimmy for a long time.

"And what was it brought you down here Sam?" asked Mrs Lendicott.

Sam shot Roger a warning glance. He wasn't sure whether the boy knew what had caused him to leave Croydon in such a hurry, but if he did, he didn't want him letting on.

Turning to Mrs Lendicott he said, "I used to live in a small place in the woods. Then the council cut the woods down and built a new housing estate. So I moved into some more woods further out – that's where Roger knew me. I always liked to be in the country away from people.

"But it was obvious that the town would grow again and I'd be on my way once more. Then my friend Constable Willis told me about a mate of his who lived down here – Constable Stanbury."

"Oh yes. Eric Stanbury did work up Lunnon way for a time before he got transferred back yer to his home."

"Well my friend told me if I came down 'ere, constable Stanbury would put me up until I could find a job and a place to live. And as you know, constable Stanbury put me in touch with you."

'And all that is more or less true,' thought Joe's father, 'but it isn't the whole truth. Stanbury told me you had been accused of something you hadn't done and you had such a record for misbehaviour that your police reckoned you would be found "guilty", so they advised you to get away – and actually helped you into the bargain. Well, there's no need for anyone else to know all that.' So all Joe's father actually said was, "And you've fitted in very well since you came. We shall miss you now you're leaving us again."

"Leaving us!" It was quite a chorus from the family.

"Sam has decided that he ought to go and join the army. He's probably right and with his skills he'll probably end up in a commando unit behind enemy lines somewhere. But we shall be sorry to see you go Sam. You're almost one of the family. Sam only told me this morning so I haven't had a chance to tell the rest of you. You'll have to write off and zee if we can get one of they land girls Esther."

Roger felt bleak. No sooner had he found someone from home than he was going to be left all alone again. It would almost have been better if he hadn't seen Sam at all.

By this time they had finished their pasties and Mrs Lendicott was bringing round mugs of tea. Joe said, "Roger doesn't never drink tea mother. He only drinks milk and water."

Roger tried to hush him up because he felt embarrassed but after Joe had spoken he said, "Could I have a glass of water please."

Mrs Lendicott winked at Joe as she gave Roger a glass and said, "You just go and help yourself boy."

So Roger went to the sink. Where were the taps? He looked all over the place. Feeling very stupid he said, "Excuse me but where are the taps?"

"Taps? Bless the boy. Us don't have taps. Taps idn no use without running water and us doesn't 'ave none of that. If you want water you have to pump it from the well in the yard." (She never mentioned the big jug of water standing close by.) With another wink to the family she told Joe: "You'd best go and help your friend."

So the boys went out to the well. Roger put his glass beneath the spout and Joe lifted the pump handle and pushed down hard. Once, twice, nothing: "The spout must be blocked. Just look up and see if you can see anything."

So Roger looked and Joe pumped once more. Whoosh! Roger was soaked. Everyone roared with laughter and he felt a complete fool and looked it too.

"I'm sorry boy," said Joe's mother, still chuckling away. " 'Tis a joke us loves to play when townies come to stay. You go and get they wet cloos off and Joe will lend you some of his – and there'll be a glass of water on the table for ee when you comes down." She rubbed Roger's head. "You'm a proper sport, I'll give ee that."

That afternoon they went out shooting rabbits. Joe took Roger out to the cage that housed two ferrets, white, long and slender with pink eyes. He showed Roger how to handle them and they put them in a sack which Roger carried over his shoulder. After seeing their sharp white teeth, Roger wasn't too happy to be given the sack to carry.

Mr Lendicott, Sam and Joe all had guns and young Jack carried nets. The two dogs followed close on Mr Lendicott's heels. There were rabbit holes in all the hedges but the men had one particular hedge in mind in 'Ten Acre Field'. They put the nets over some of the holes and stood back in the field with their guns. The two dogs settled behind them.

"Now boys," said Mr Lendicott in his gentle, almost lazy voice, "put the ferrets to the holes."

Young Jack took one of the ferrets and Roger did the same. They took them to the hedge and set them down open rabbit holes. Then they ran back to join the men.

For a little while nothing happened and then a rabbit burst from one of the holes. Joe fired and one of the dogs ran forward and brought the rabbit to Mr Lendicott.

"Well done boy," he said quietly, though whether he was talking to Joe or to the dog no one knew.

"I want a turn with the gun," said Jack. Roger had never fired a gun in his life but he thought he'd like a turn too.

"You have the gun all the time when I'm away to school," Joe answered. "Today's my turn."

"That's not fair. I want a go and Roger should have a go too." Jack grinned inside himself. That was clever that was, bringing Roger into it.

"I don't suppose Roger's ever used a gun," Joe answered in a superior way. "P'raps when us 'ave finished I'll give him a go at a target."

"Be quiet you boys. 'Ant ee zeed thick ferret? Ee's comed out too far down. Fetch'n Roger. Us wants 'n back up yer, this end."

So Roger ran and fetched the ferret. Back up the hedge he went and put the ferret to another hole. He was hardly back in his place when three rabbits broke cover. All three guns fired but only two rabbits fell.

"You missed," grumbled Jack to his brother. "You should have let me have a turn. "

"Shut up. I can't concentrate with you nattering away all the time."

After one or two more kills they moved further down the hedge and bagged some more. Some of the rabbits ran out into the netting and were caught. Others broke loose and most of those were shot. By the end of the afternoon they had killed twenty-four rabbits.

The ferrets went back into their sack for Roger to carry again. The rabbits were carried by their hind legs back to the yard. The two men and Joe and Jack too, cleaned and skinned them. Roger watched, fascinated at their skill with their knives. Sam had two of the rabbits to take back to his cottage and Mrs Lendicott took four more. The rest were hung ready for sending to Beddingford where both meat and skins could be sold.

During the day Roger had copied the other boys and peed in the hedge whenever he needed to. But now he asked Joe, "Where's the lav?"

" 'Tis outside, round the side of the house."

So Roger set off. Joe's father said quietly, "You'd best go with the boy. I don't suppose he's zeed one like ours."

So Joe ran after Roger. His dad was right. It was an earth closet such as Roger had never seen before.

"When you've finished you take a shovel of soil from the bucket there and cover your mess with that. Only don't go using all the soil. Dad won't be very pleased if you empty the bucket every time you have a bog."

"What happens when the bog is full?" asked Roger.

"Dad never lets un get full. He keeps an eye to it and empties it when he thinks 'tis full enough."

"But where does he put it all?"

Joe grinned. "Us grows some bootifull vegetables," he said.

"Ugh. What those vegetables we had today?"

"Ees. Lovely wadn' they?"

When Roger finally returned to the yard, knowing what Joe was like, he said to Mr Lendicott, "Do you really empty the toilet on the vegetables to make them grow better?"

Joe's father and Sam both laughed.

"Yes and no," Mr Lendicott answered. "I put it all on a heap and then next year I dig it all into the soil for next year's vegetables but by that time you wouldn't know where it came from."

"It's like 'orse and cow shit," said Sam. "We use that on the fields to make them more fertile. It's just the same as that really."

Roger could see the sense of it, but he still wasn't sure that he liked the idea too much. Sam took his two rabbits and set off for the small cottage where he lived – a cottage which belonged to the farm. The others went and got themselves cleaned up ready for tea. After lunch Roger had felt that he would never be able to eat again but he found that he was hungry again after the afternoon in the fields.

Tea was all ready for them in the dark kitchen with its scrubbed oak table. They ate thick slices of bread covered almost as thickly with Devonshire cream made from their own milk, and with home made jam. By the time Roger had eaten two slabs and drunk a glass of rich, farm milk he felt he had better not eat any more but he did hope that there would be more cream before he went back to school.

After tea the girls went with their mother to see to the hens. Roger went too because it was all so new and fascinating to him. Then, as evening began to draw in, the girls went to bed and Joe's dad lit two oil lamps and set them up.

"Golly," thought Roger, "they haven't even got gas here, let alone electricity."

The boys played Ludo with Mrs Lendicott until supper time. But they also went to bed fairly early.

With the kitchen so warm and lit with an oil lantern, they soon found themselves feeling very sleepy.

Each of them took a candle, climbed the stairs and made their way to a low bedroom underneath the roof. It looked out of the back of the farmhouse and across the fields but in the darkness there was little to be seen. Roger kept Joe and Jack awake for a while, telling them stories of Sam's life when he knew him before the war. There was plenty of giggling in their bedroom before they finally dropped off.

(Sam's hilarious escapades are told in the previously published book: *An Evacuee* published by United Writers Publications Ltd.)

8

The Day of Rest

They were woken early next morning by a man's shouts and by a terrific kerfuffle that seemed to be going on right underneath their window. They ran and looked out. There in the field below them they could see Mr Lendicott dodging round an old bath which was full of water, and a pile of bales of hay. The bull was chasing after him. Hay was flying in all directions.

"Come on," shouted Joe, and the three boys ran downstairs and out through the yard calling to the dogs as they ran. Fairly close to Mr Lendicott and the bull there was a gate into the field. Joe let the dogs in and shut the gate again quickly. He said to Roger and Jack, "Just shout at th'old bull and wave your arms around to distract un – but stay this side of the fence."

So there was Mr Lendicott running for dear life, the bull after him, the dogs barking and going for the bull's ankles, and Roger and Jack dressed only in their pyjamas, jumping up and down waving and shouting.

Halfway between the gate and the running track lay Mr Lendicott's pole with the hook in the end. Joe climbed the gate, timed his run to the pole, threw it back to the gate and ran straight back and climbed over. Then he took the pole and began to whack the bull as hard as he could whenever it came within range. Most of the time it didn't take a scrap of notice but at last Joe caught it right across the nose. It stopped in its tracks and Joe shouted, "Come on Dad. Over the gate."

His father ran for the gate and vaulted over. He called the dogs away and the bull stood eyeing them all. It took a while for Mr

Lendicott to get his breath back but at last he took the pole and hooked it through the bull's nose ring. He opened the gate and led the bull back to its solitary home in the barn. It was like a different animal.

"Well done you boys. That could have been very nasty. Now you'd better get in and get washed and dressed – and don't forget to wash your feet."

In the excitement it never entered their heads to ask why the bull was out in the first place. As they washed and dressed the cows were being driven into the milking sheds. Mrs Lendicott came in from the hens with a large bowl full of eggs. Joe and Roger went out to the milking sheds and found Sam busy milking the cows. Joe took a bucket and stool and joined in the work. Roger watched, fascinated.

"Do you want to have a go?" asked Sam. "Come on. Mabel here is quite docile but keep away from her back legs. If she gets an itch and kicks out you could get a nasty wallop."

So Roger took his place on the stool and Sam showed him how to work the teats to persuade Mabel to give up her milk. He worked at them and watched the milk squirt into the bucket but he wasn't much good and when Sam took his place back he soon had a great deal more from the cow.

"Try to imagine that you're a very hungry calf sucking like mad," he said, "and don't be too gentle."

So Roger tried again and gradually began to get the hang of it, though the cows would always give up more for Sam than they would for him. And he found it much harder work than he would have imagined.

The cows turned their heads and watched from time to time and they shifted their feet uneasily at this stranger, but mostly they just munched away at their feed and let him get on with it.

After the milking, Joe let the cows out into their field and it was breakfast time. There were huge helpings of bacon and eggs and fried bread and all the toast, butter and marmalade they could eat.

By half past ten the family was all dressed in Sunday best. The two little girls looked very pretty in their frocks, ankle socks and shoes and gloves and with ribbons in their hair. But Joe's dad looked all wrong in a suit somehow. Although he was so tall and slim, his hair wasn't used to being slicked down and his neck wasn't comfortable in a collar and tie.

Off they all went to chapel. When they arrived they filed into a pew and Joe's dad left them. At 11.00 precisely, a steward came in from the minister's vestry followed by Joe's dad. Roger was astonished to see him climb into the pulpit to announce the first hymn. He hadn't known he was a preacher.

The service was the usual hymn sandwich: five hymns with readings and prayers and a sermon scattered in between. Roger liked singing so he enjoyed the hymns and during the readings he had a look around him. It was a small, bare chapel with nothing on the walls and with high windows you couldn't look out of. The pulpit was at the centre in the front, several steps up from the floor and in front of it there was a bare table with a runner on it and a vase of flowers.

The time came for the sermon. Joe's dad said, "My text this morning is 'Near 'Nuff'. I expects you've all done jobs on the farm and when you've finished you've said, 'Tidn' perfect but 'tis near 'nuff. And down on the farm it may well be. Wadn' it G.K. Chesterton who said, 'If a job's worth doin', 'tis worth doin' badly'? Well there's some truth in that too. But not a lot. If a job's worth doin', 'tis worth doing as best we can. An' the same's true of life. Near 'nuff idn' nowhere near good enough as a motto for life is it? Us gotta do the best we can all the time. Jesus told us to try to be perfect because his heavenly Father is perfect. Well of course, none of us can be perfect can us. But us can try. I think it was Charles Kingsley who said somethin' like, ' 'Tis better to aim at a thousand and miss, than to aim at a hundred and get it.' That's not his exact words but," (he grinned), " 'tis near 'nuff. So let's all go home today promising Jesus and promising one another that us'll aim as high as we possibly can and live our lives as best we can. Near 'nuff idn' never enough."

Roger had never heard a sermon like it. He actually enjoyed listening to it and he reckoned he'd remember it too.

After chapel they walked quietly back to the farm and sat down to another huge dinner. After they had cleared away, the boys changed their clothes and went for a walk with the rest of the family right round the farm. Sunday wasn't a day for working but it was a day when Joe's father could quietly check his hedges and his fences and have a general look around, making a mental note of anything that needed attention.

Back in the farmhouse, they dressed in their Sunday clothes again and went into the best room. It was the first time Roger had been in there. It was another low, dark room, full of old armchairs and sofas that looked as though they had been in the family for generations. Joe's dad settled beside the huge open wood fire with a book. His wife opened the top of the old harmonium and sat and peddled and played hymns – one after another after another. All the children stood around her singing as best they could.

"You got a vine voice young Roger," said Mrs Lendicott. "I yeard ee in chapel this morning and I thought so then."

"He sings in the school choir," said Joe.

"I 'spects he does," his mother replied, "which is more than you will ever do. You got 'a belly full of music but a bad road out' as they say. But that doesn't matter as long as you enjoys it. The Lord loves a bull's bellow as much as ee loves the skylark I reckon. An' boys love a good tay even when they've had a good dinner, zo I'd best go and get it ready."

A good tea it was, and then it was time for Mr Lendicott to take them back to school so that they could go to evening chapel. Both boys took a tuck bag with them to put in their tuck locker back at school. Every afternoon for days they were able to supplement their meagre school rations with Devonshire cream, butter, jam, eggs and even a couple of slices of rabbit pie.

Roger felt that he had never eaten so well in all his life and he did his level best to say 'thank you' properly to both Joe's parents. It was the first of many visits and his first taste of the wonders of west country farmers' hospitality.

The walk in crocodile to the chapel and the service taken by the circuit superintendent all seemed a pretty miserable come down, even if Roger did feel a little bit proud that he was sitting in the choir. Oh well. It wouldn't be for too long now. It was time to start counting the days to the end of term.

9

Counting the Days

From the very first day of term a few boys had marked off the days to the end of term. Some of them had devised quite stylish charts which were pinned to the inside of their desk lids.

After the second exeat many more joined in. Counting the days to the end of term became a serious business and it was marked by three strange customs.

Three Sundays from the end of term, before the morning chapel parade, every boy in the school had found himself some sort of buttonhole which he wore all day. So, as the boys marched in crocodile to the chapel half a mile away, all those buttonholes signalled the approach of the end of term.

The following Sunday was stranger still, and very obvious on boys in the younger classes who were still wearing short trousers. All the boys wore odd socks and some of them made the most of the opportunity with a rugby sock on one leg with its rings of red and black, and a white ankle sock or a lady's stocking on the other. Because this was an old school tradition they got away with it, although the Head made it quite clear that he disapproved of the more outrageous pairings.

Dress was normal on the final Sunday of term. The procession to chapel began in the quad and moved off through a narrow passage to the outer quad known as the Parade (because it was used by the cadets as a parade ground). At the end of the passage was a heavy door with stout hinges. This was fixed open to allow the boys to file freely past. But on this last Sunday of term that is precisely what they did not do.

Each boy stopped, faced the wall opposite the door, put his hands on the wall and kicked back once, twice, three times (more if he thought the master on duty was not paying attention, but that often led to a clip round the ear). Then he moved on and rejoined the crocodile march to chapel. 'Kick Door Sunday' was always the last Sunday of term.

Throughout those weeks there was mounting tension and excitement rippling away under the surface of school life. Nor was it only under the surface. Like a live volcano, it kept breaking out in a whole variety of ways, most of it at night.

In Roger's dorm word went round that there was to be a dorm feed. All the boys had tuck lockers with private supplies for supplementing their school teas. Now they emptied them. They called on local shops, bare because of rationing, to see if they could find anything, anything at all that could be shared. And in letters home they had begged for supplies:

> *'Dear Father,*
> *how's mother?*
> *Ate my cake and*
> *want another.*
> *Love from Roger.'*

At last the night arrived. Cardew had told them all to go to sleep. He would wake them at midnight. But sleep and excitement are unnatural bedfellows. Few of the boys dropped off easily. If they slept at all it was only just before midnight when they succumbed and they were no sooner asleep than Cardew was shaking them by the shoulder.

"Wake up you lot – and keep quiet. Wallace, you're the youngest. Put your sheet on the top of the bed like a table-cloth."

Roger did as he was told.

"Now lads, bring your stores. And you Joe Lendicott – keep cave. We don't want to get caught."

Soon Roger's bed was piled high with the oddest assortment of food you would wish to see: cooked chicken legs, cakes, biscuits, sweets from their sweet ration, boiled eggs, a couple of tins of condensed milk – all sorts. And the boys tucked in with Joe and Roger taking turns at the door, keeping a wary eye out for any night-roaming member of staff.

At last most of the food was gone and boys began to drift back to bed. Cardew helped Roger collect up the remnants in two piles, one for throwing and one for the boys to share out and use at tea time the following day. Roger took a much-soiled sheet out onto the landing and gave it a shake. Then he put it back on his bed and was asleep in no time. The pent up excitement of the night had gone.

At breakfast the following morning they heard that dorm twenty-eight had been caught by the Head. He had caned every boy. It seemed to add spice to their own success somehow.

A few nights later they were attacked by the boys from the dorm on the floor above theirs. Down they came wielding pillow-cases and knotted towels and the fight was fast and furious. This time they were caught. Even Dicky could hardly fail to hear the rumpus. He stood blinking through his glasses, letting the boys slowly wake up to the fact that he was there.

Little by little the fighting died away until they were all standing rather sheepishly waiting for his condemnation and punishment. When all was silent he said, "Well, well, well. What uncivilised behaviour. End of term must be approaching. If there is any retaliation from the members of dorm 23 for this unwarranted attack by the savages from above, it will be necessary for me to impose the severest punishments. I'll hold those in reserve. For the moment, get to bed all of you and let's have no more of this unseemly hostility."

How lucky they were and how decent they felt he was.

It didn't stop them dealing with the two bucking new snips in proper fashion as the last few nights of term approached. First there was the tossing in the blanket. It wasn't a Perspins tradition but some of them had read about it in *Tom Brown's Schooldays* and it seemed a good idea. Roger having read the book, was expecting it and both he and Joe found that it was pretty good fun. They were tossed higher and higher until they had managed to touch the ceiling ten times.

But on the last night of term, Perspins tradition took over. Joe and Roger were stripped to the waist. First Joe and then Roger had to start from the door and crawl right round the dorm under the beds until they returned to the door. The rest of the boys stood on the beds with pillows and knotted towels and each time the boys showed themselves between the beds or crossing from one side of the dorm to the other, they were lashed. Pillows didn't hurt though they were sometimes knocked off their hands and knees, but the knotted towels left them red and bruised. Both Joe and Roger soon realised that the secret was to get around as quickly as possible, but because it was a small dorm they were sent round twice and took quite a leathering.

Neither of them complained. It was part of their initiation. Afterwards Cardew congratulated them.

"Well done you two. You've finished with the 'bucking new snip' label. When you come back next term you'll be 'new bucks'."

It was a meaningless promotion but the two of them felt quite proud all the same. And then it was time to go home, only Roger wasn't going home. He watched the coach arrive from Stubble Cross. It was to take the boys to the little railway halt six miles away and some of them would be heading for the London area. He wanted to be with them but his father had said "No".

The boys who were not on the coach mooned about in the courtyard by the road or wandered the empty, echoing corridors of the school. The place was dying for a few weeks, bereft of the life that gave it meaning. Cars arrived to take their quota of local boys off home to their farms. Fewer and fewer boys remained and Roger felt as bereft as the school.

He had been so excited at the thought of going home. But he wasn't going home. He was going to bloody Beddingford. His mother and his sister Margaret were already there, in the Quayside Hotel. Just imagine: Christmas in a bloody hotel. He bloodied and buggered his way miserably round the school and the school playing fields until mid-day. Then he went to the courtyard to wait for Miss Holly's nephew.

At last the car arrived with Roger's mother and sister aboard. He helped Mr Holly load his trunk onto the open boot and then they all set off for Beddingford, thirteen miles away. With the arrival of the car, Roger's spirits rose. He had been one of the last at school but now school was behind him.

Yet the Christmas holidays turned out to be a strange, dull time in that hotel. They saw nothing of Mr Wallace or Gerry or of Alfie and Eric away in the RAF. It was just the three of them and a few old fogies who lived in the hotel, and the food was as basic as school food. Nor was there all that much of it so Roger often felt a bit hungry.

Nor was there much to do. They visited Miss Holly a few times. They helped put up some Christmas decorations in the hotel. They went on the bus to the sea. Behind the bus and towed by it, there was a huge gas container. The bus ran on gas but it didn't have enough power to climb the hills. Every time they came to a hill they all had to get off and walk to the top and then get back on the bus again. At the sea they walked along the shore or climbed over the rocks or up on the hills. Roger visited the old coast guard station that he and Jimmy had used as their headquarters in days gone by, but nothing was the same. It all seemed dead and barren with the barrenness of winter, and it seemed to rain every day.

On Christmas Day they walked to the sea and they even had a quick swim just to say that they had done it. But having walked all the way there, now they had to walk all the way home. There were no buses.

Roger and Margaret often did walk all the way home. Their mother was so embarrassing. When buses came she pushed her way to the front of the queue to make sure they got on the bus. But when she got on she often found that the children had slipped quietly away. They were so ashamed of her, so they walked. 'Strange children,' she thought and took her seat without a moment's misgiving.

Much of the time they stayed in the hotel playing endless games of cards or monopoly or just reading. And they studied the other people there. It was that which led to the only excitement of the holiday.

There was one little old lady who seemed to be somewhat eccentric. Margaret nicknamed her 'Fuzzypeg'. Whenever they saw her she was always fully dressed in overcoat, and hat and gloves. Even in the dining-room she sat alone at her table in her coat and hat, with her gloves set neatly to one side of her place setting. The fact that she didn't like children and made it quite clear that she didn't feel that children should be allowed in the hotel only added to the children's interest in her.

"She's foreign," said Roger. "She must be. Only foreigners wear their hats when they have their dinner."

Margaret bowed to Roger's superior knowledge. She didn't know about foreigners and hats. But once Roger had established in his own mind that Fuzzypeg was foreign, it didn't take him long to make the next leap of identification.

"I'll bet she's German," he said. "That's why she's so horrible. She must be German."

Once again, Margaret agreed. If Roger said so, she was sure it must be so. She didn't feel that way about all Roger's dogmatic statements but on this occasion he was probably right.

"I'll bet she's a spy," said Roger.

That did it. They began to follow her everywhere and soon discovered that her room was at the top of its own staircase right up in the roof of the hotel.

"It's just right for a spy," said Roger. "I'll bet she's got radio equipment up there so that she can talk to the Germans."

He sat outside her bedroom door, trying to peer through the keyhole. Margaret wasn't too keen on that so she ran down to play cards with her mother. As Roger sat on the little landing he heard a tapping noise. 'Tap, tap, tap.' He thought she was probably sending messages in morse code though morse code had long and short taps didn't it. This tapping was very regular and very fast. (How was he to know she was typing? He'd never even seen a typewriter.) She must be an experienced spy, being so old. Perhaps she had been a spy in the first world war as well and had never been caught.

How could he catch her now? Should he tell the police? Or should he just try to catch her red-handed? He knew it was no good telling his mother. She would just pooh-pooh things.

In the event it was Roger who was caught outside her door. She reported him to the hotel manager. Roger tried to explain about her being a spy but the manager just laughed and warned Roger not to be a nuisance again.

With Christmas over, the New Year came and went and then it was time to take the decorations down. Roger overheard Fuzzypeg saying to the hotel manager, "Make sure they are all down by the twelfth night. It is unlucky if any of them remain."

He and Margaret offered to help take them down. When they had finished he crept up to Fuzzypeg's room and carefully pinned a strip of paper chain to it.

"That'll teach her. Serve her right if she does have bad luck all year."

At last it was time to return to school. Both Roger and his

mother felt quite relieved. The holiday had been rather a strain for her and pretty boring for him. Margaret felt differently. Unknown to any of them she was very unhappy at school and dreaded the thought of going back, but she never said a word.

Yet when Roger arrived back at school that seemed as bad as the holidays. All the excitement of his first term had gone. It was wintry, dark and cold and always wet. The rain never seemed to stop. Boys from London claimed that as soon as the train left Exeter on the way back to school the rain started to fall.

"Come to sunny Devon," they said,
"where it rains eight days out of seven."

And they sang:

"Up the hill we go
to the school we know,
to the college: to the college.

The sour milk we've drank
and the food that stank,
we'll remember: we'll remember."

Gloom seemed to descend literally like a wet blanket smothering them and hedging them in. Everything was cold, dismal, depressing and boring. They sat around the central heating pipes in the Assembly Hall, struggling to keep warm and irritating their chilblains.

Roger had never felt so miserable and home-sick in his life. He wanted to go properly home, not to Beddingford but to his own home and his own family and his old school and his old friends. The fact that everything had changed in the three years and more since he was last at home never entered his head. How was he to know that when he did finally go home nothing would be the same – not even his friends.

And although he had plenty of friends at Perspins and was with quite a lot of them in his dorm for that term, the large dorm twenty-eight, he still felt one on his own. The London crowd had come back to school on the train and some of them had met one another in the holidays. He wasn't one of them. The farmer's sons, so often related to one another, had come back from their farms. He wasn't one of them. He was friends with them all, but he always seemed to be on the edge of groups, never in the centre. He didn't ever altogether feel that he belonged.

That second term at school was the worst and the most miserable of all, yet even that term had its moments.

10

" 'It Un George"

At the end of January 1943 the magnificent defence of Stalingrad ended in a Russian victory and the surrender of a German army. Only the senior boys took much notice. They were pretty sure to be in the forces themselves before long.

But such things more or less passed Roger by. Perspins was largely untouched by the war. Even rationing had little impact on a school where feeding had always been pretty basic.

The biggest difference the war made was in the teaching staff. Teachers were older than they would have been in peace time and some of them were untrained. They didn't all know their subjects well enough to teach them and some of them were useless. They were easily side-tracked and there was no discipline in their classes at all.

One evening when the junior school was doing its prep in the Assembly Hall, Horace Wilcox was the master in charge. He was a middle-aged, balding bachelor who had had no teacher training at all. He taught art and woodwork. While he liked most of the boys as individuals, he had no experience of boys. As he looked out over row upon row of double desks, he felt intimidated by the sight of so many boys all together. They frightened him.

But tonight he congratulated himself. Prep was going rather well. It was true that there was rather more noise and chatter than there should have been, but it wasn't unbearable. And he hadn't noticed any really bad behaviour.

But then George Ellis put his hand up. George's elder brother had been expelled for knocking out the science master and his reputation had passed to George. That couldn't have been more unfair. Certainly George was big and strong but he was also unusually placid and gentle. Fifteen years of age, he was still in the second form.

Roger and his pals were delighted to have him there. If anyone in the class was being bullied, they just mentioned George Ellis and the bullying stopped. It was almost like saying, "My dad's the heavyweight champion of the world."

Horace Wilcox knew nothing of George. He only knew his brother's reputation and saw the size of the boy. He wanted nothing to do with him. So when George's hand went up, Mr Wilcox signalled to him to put it down again.

"Not now boy. Get on with your prep."

But that was the problem. George was trying to get on with his prep but he couldn't understand decimals and fractions. He sat and stared at his book for a while, deep in thought, and got nowhere. So he decided to try again. The teacher would understand decimals and fractions. He was a nice man. He would explain. So George put his hand up again. And for the second time he was told to put it down.

There must be a solution. He thought carefully. No one else could help him. The teacher must help, and for the third time he raised his hand.

By now some of the other boys in the hall were beginning to take an interest in what was going on. Mr Wilcox was beginning to worry. He flapped his hand.

"Put your hand down when I tell you and get on with your work."

"But zur . . ."

"Silence boy."

George was upset. He only wanted a bit of help with his work. Mr Wilcox would help if he understood. He was sure he would. But putting up his hand wasn't getting him anywhere.

He picked up his maths book, stood up and walked to the foot of the stage where the duty master's desk was. Mr Wilcox didn't notice until too late.

"What on earth do you think you are doing? Go back to your place at once."

By this time every boy in the hall was watching.

"But zur . . ."

"That's it boy. You tell 'n. Go on George." Voices began to be heard from different parts of the hall.

"Silence," shouted Mr Wilcox. "And you, go back to your place."

"Zur, I only want . . ."

"Go on George, you tell, 'im."

Feet began to stamp on the worn wooden floor. Desk lids banged. More and more voices were heard. And George, feeling confused, stood his ground.

Mr Wilcox came down from the stage and confronted the boy.

"I told you to go back to your place."

But George hadn't got so far to be easily rebuffed. Stubbornly he tried again.

"Zur, I only . . ."

The noise was increasing all the time – more feet, more desk lids, more voices, and then a new cry: "Go on boy. You tell un." And then, " 'It un one boy."

Sitting in the front row of desks, Roger was watching and listening in a mixture of fascination and horror. But he didn't join in. He liked George too well and felt for him. All this shouting was not helping George at all. And more and more boys were baying like hounds.

"Go on. 'It un George. Dap un down. Go on boy."

Mr Wilcox panicked. Grabbing a piece of paper he scribbled a note and called Roger forward.

"Take this to the Headmaster at once."

As Roger left the hall, he heard poor Wilcox almost screaming, "Silence. Be quiet all of you."

But by this time the boys were enjoying themselves too much and the din and chanting continued. Poor George stood totally confused, with the tears rolling down his face.

Roger stopped in the quad and read the note: "Sir, please come at once. These boys are uncontrollable."

He took it to the Head's study and knocked.

"Come in. What is it boy?"

"Please sir. Mr Wilcox sent me with this."

The Head skimmed the note.

"You've read it of course."

He didn't wait for an answer. He took his gown off the back of the study door, slipped it on and was gone with Roger almost having to run to keep up. As they crossed the quad, the din was incredible. The Head took the stairs up to the Assembly Hall three at a time, threw open the door and stood.

There was instant silence.

He walked into the hall closely followed by Roger. The Head turned and said quietly, "Go to your place." Then to all the boys, "Get back to your work. I shall deal with you all later."

He turned to Mr Wilcox and said, "I don't think you'll have any more trouble this evening Mr Wilcox." He looked at George's tear-stained face, paused and without asking any questions said, "Bring your books and come to my study."

The Head left and George followed. Once in the study he did his best to explain and the Head listened. He had a lot of sympathy for this boy who was so out of place. Schooling had done little for the boy and soon he would leave and go to work with his father and his brother on the farm.

He did his best to explain decimals and fractions but George couldn't understand. Then the Head took his exercise book and scrawled across it: 'The boy really has tried. Don't worry him. He leaves at the end of term.'

"There boy. When you hand in your homework your teacher will read that and know that you have done your best. You're a good lad but I'm afraid Mr Wilcox didn't understand. Go back to prep now."

"Yes zur. Thank you zur."

11

Academics All

Mr Wilcox felt humiliated. How was it that the Head inspired such complete awe when the boys took no notice of him at all? He wished he hadn't left his little carpentry business. But he'd barely been making enough to live on. The wartime need for teachers had offered him the chance of an income beyond his wildest dreams.

Dreams or nightmares? Miserably, he climbed the worn stone stairs to the Assembly Hall the following morning. He had those brats from form 2 to teach and that great ox Ellis. He wasn't looking forward to it.

He walked into the hall and around to the front of the stage to the master's table. There didn't seem to be as many boys as usual. So much the better. He handed out one sheet of paper to each boy, a box of water-colour paints containing one paint-brush, and two small jars of water per double desk.

"I want you to paint a river valley with a bridge over the river. Imagine that the time of day is just before sunset."

Roger was happy to do just that. He couldn't paint for nuts but it was a pleasant way to spend forty minutes. So he began work. He didn't even envy Bradders and his pals behind the curtains at the back of the stage playing cards. This was quite fun.

Joe Lendicott, sitting beside him, was another one who couldn't paint for nuts. He splashed some paint about any old how on his paper for a few minutes and then sat back with a long piece of string. He began to wind it around his fingers making a whole series of intricate loops.

"What are you doing?" whispered Roger.

" 'Tis called a cat's cradle – don't ask me why." He went on winding the string round his fingers. Then he said, "Yer, hold your fingers up close to mine. Now let's zee if us can transfer this yer onto you."

The first two or three times it all fell apart and they had to stifle their giggles and pretend to be painting, but at last they managed to transfer the cat's cradle across from Joe to Roger and back again.

Joe began to get bored again. "Give us your ruler," he said, "and ask those two over on the next desk for their's."

Roger knew what he was up to without asking. He dropped his paintbrush in the aisle, leaned across to pick it up and whispered, "Joe wants your rulers."

They grinned and passed them over. Joe leaned the other way and borrowed two more rulers. Six rulers, that should do it. He gave one end of the string to Roger, slid down under his desk and began to crawl back under the desks. He tied a ruler to the string, propped up a desk lid with a ruler and continued his crawl back. At each row of desks he repeated the operation until his string was exhausted and six desk lids were propped up with rulers. Then he crawled back to his own desk.

The hall was strangely silent as the boys waited in breathless anticipation. Mr Wilcox was busy marking another form's prep. He was very relieved that this was proving to be such an easy class to take. It was almost possible to forget that the boys were there.

Joe pulled his string. With a series of bangs the desk lids collapsed and the boys were hard put to it to stifle their laughter. Mr Wilcox nearly jumped out of his seat. He looked up but all of them were intent on their painting. There was nothing to be seen. Behind him, Bradders face appeared between the curtains. What had been going on? What had they missed?

Something made Mr Wilcox turn round. The curtains were swaying. He'd have sworn the noise came from the class but you never knew with noises. He jumped up onto the stage and pulled open the curtains.

Nothing. There was no one there. He walked all round the stage and behind the back-cloth. But he didn't look above his head to the spot where four boys were pinned back against the

73

wall on the narrow ledge used for getting to the lights.

He came back to his table. Might as well gather in the paint-boxes and call it a day. The bell would be going soon. He began to walk around the class. Roger quietly dropped his paint-brush through a knot hole in the floor and closed his box of paints. He did it every art lesson and Wilcox never seemed to notice that he was a brush short.

Wilcox looked at his work and at Joe's. "You don't seem to have got much done Lendicott but I must say I like your extravagant brushwork. That's what we need when we are painting, the courage to express ourselves. You don't seem to be willing to take risks in the same way Wallace. There's no boldness in your colour. On the other hand, you have tried to do as I asked. You do have a river and a bridge and a setting sun."

He walked round the class trying to be kind and generous in his comments and collecting the paint-boxes as he went. He came to Philip Jonas.

"Ah," he said. "Now that's more like it. Stand up and show your work to the whole class."

Jonas felt quite proud. He stood and showed his work of art. His class-mates looked at it with a complete lack of understanding. The river looked like a brown scar slashed across the paper, with white splodges scattered across it. The bridge was a mix of black and grey, yellow and purple, continued into the road on either side. There was no round red setting sun. Instead there were just vivid streaks of red and yellow lighting up dark clouds and marking the horizon. It looked horrible, a real mess.

The bell rang and they put their works of art into their desks and set off for the science labs. It was biology next with Mr Miner, better known as 'Digger'. They sat on stools at high benches with four bunsen burners per bench. Mr Miner issued each boy with a dead worm, a piece of cardboard from torn up boxes, a small knife and a handful of pins.

He drew a worm on the blackboard and took his metre ruler. Using the ruler, he pointed to the worm. "Stretch out your worms on your cardboard," he said, "and insert a pin at each end, securing it to the cardboard."

The boys did as he had told them. It was no use trying to mess about in his classes, unless you were on the back row, and even there you had to be careful.

74

"Now." He pointed at the blackboard again. "Take your knives and make a careful incision at one end of the worm and slice from one end to the other without cutting the skin which is against the cardboard. Be very careful. Do it now."

Some boys were more successful than others and a few had to be issued with a second and even a third worm before they managed it. But at last Mr Miner was able to continue.

"Ellis, collect up all the knives please and put them on my desk. We don't want any of you wasting your class carving your initials for posterity do we?"

George Ellis was glad to have been chosen to do something for a change, something he could do without strain or stress. He collected up the knives and placed them on Mr Miner's desk.

Again the metre ruler pointed at the board, where Mr Miner had drawn another worm sliced from one end to the other. "Now, holding back each side of the worm insert your pins from end to end. It will give you a chance to study the structure of the worm in detail. It only remains for me to tell you that the earthworm is one of the farmer's best friends. This humble creature does as much ploughing as any of your fathers with their teams of horses or their new tractors."

"Bollocks," whispered Joe.

"And it has been estimated that there may be as many as three million earthworms to an acre of pasture, all busily recycling nutrients so that the pasture is good for your sheep and cattle. Get on with your pinning boys. You don't need just to sit gaping. You can listen and work at the same time. My own view is that three million may be something of an exaggeration. I have seen estimates as low as one third of a million. When estimating always err on the conservative side."

"There's a hell of a lot of difference between a third of a million and three million," whispered Joe. "He doesn't have a clue what he's on about."

"Are worms good for the soil?" Roger whispered back.

"Oh yes," said Joe. "That bit's right. They eats dead rubbish in the ground and then shits. 'Tis like manure." Roger was finding it quite difficult to set his pins in. His fingers seemed to be too plump. Every time he tried to insert a new pin he seemed to knock the previous one skew-whiff. But he was slowly making headway. His worm was beginning to look like the skeleton of the hull of a ship. His mind began to wander.

He thought about ships and Nelson and Trafalgar, and U boats and convoys and Q ships in the First World War. And that led on to thoughts about his brothers Alfie and Eric in the Air Force and Gerry in the Army. He thought perhaps he would go into the Navy when he grew up. Surely the war would be over by then. But he would quite like to be in the Navy anyway, even in peace time.

The bell rang with his worm still unfinished.

"Leave your work on the benches and off you go for your break."

Free! Twenty minutes free. And then double maths. What a miserable prospect. They went out onto the parade and messed about with a ball until the bell rang again to summon them back to work. Bells, bells, bells, their lives were ruled by them.

12

Junior Colts

The rain came sheeting in from the Atlantic. Day after day it never seemed to stop: grey rain from grey lowering clouds on grey school buildings and a grey quad and grey parade.

There was no chance of getting outside in break times. Luckily the school library had masses of fiction to keep them going. Both Roger and Joe read as many 'Biggles' books as they could lay their hands on. Joe read Zane Grey's cowboy stories too but Roger preferred reading Leslie Charteris' books about 'The Saint'.

But boys can't sit reading all the time. They needed action. They lifted the master's table onto the stage and pushed the front rows of desks back to make space at the front of the Assembly Hall for football with a tennis ball. Soon there were ten of them going for it hammer and tongs with shouts and yells and the ball flying all over the place. No one noticed Mr Smart enter the hall by the back door. He quietly jotted down the names of all the boys playing football in his notebook and then he strode forward with his gown flying out behind him.

The game stuttered to a halt.

"Give me the ball. It is confiscated until the end of term. Then the owner can claim it back. I have the names of all of you who were playing football. You will report at 4.00 this afternoon to the prefect on duty and you will do the punishment run. It may help to get rid of some of your excess energy. You will also write one hundred lines and hand them in before assembly tomorrow: 'I must not play football in the classroom'. That is all."

He strode out of the hall.

"Bugger him." Bradders spoke for them all.

They put the room back in order, went to their desks and began their lines. Best to get them done. And after school they changed into their gym kit and reported to the duty prefect for the punishment run. There were about twenty other boys of all ages.

"You know the rules," said the prefect. "You've got to be back in twenty minutes or you do it again. And no cutting corners. I shall be out on my bike checking up on you all."

"No he won't," grunted Bradders, "not in this rain."

They set off on the road towards Beddingford for about half a mile and then turned right. Bradders was no longer with them. He had turned into a field at the first gate and was on a loop that would bring him towards the end of the run. Brilliant at a hundred yards, he was no long distance runner and he always skipped as much of the punishment run as he could.

But Roger and Joe were quite enjoying themselves in spite of the rain. Although the run was called 'the triangle' it was more of a two mile rectangle really. They ran along the road to the Squire's saw mills and then it angled right again.

On they ran, leaving more and more boys straggling behind them. By the time they reached the next right turning there were only a few of the older boys ahead of them. Nothing had been said but Roger and Joe knew that they were in a race with one another.

For most of that stretch of road they remained together but as the final turning for home came in sight, Joe stretched his legs and Roger had no answer. Tall and gangly, Joe seemed to move effortlessly away from him and Roger was finding it hard just to keep going. And then Bradders popped out of the hedge with a broad grin on his face.

"What's the matter Wallace. Puffed out? Got no stamina that's your trouble."

They turned right again and were in sight of the school.

"Nice sprint finish I think," said Bradders. "See if I can catch up with Joe."

Off he went. The prefect wasn't fooled but didn't say anything.

He marked the boys off. Two of them had done pretty well for new bucks. He must mention them to their house captains.

"Which house are you in Lendicott?"

"Alpha."

"And you Wallace?"

"Beta."

"Well run, both of you."

They ran into the tile house, washed and then rinsed off in the baths and dressed themselves. They felt quite chuffed.

"If us hadn't had to do those lines, I wouldn't have minded that punishment," said Joe.

"No, the triangle is quite fun really. But I wish I could run like you," said Roger admiringly. "I try to keep up with you but I can't."

It was almost tea-time. After tea they went back to their classroom and finished their lines. The following day was another wet one and it wasn't long before the desks were back and the master's table on the stage again for more football. It was too much fun to worry about punishments.

In one of the shorter breaks Joe took out his pocket knife and carved two notches at one end of the master's table.

"What are you doing?" asked Roger as Joe made his way to the other end of the table and carved two more notches in it.

"Making goals idn I," answered Joe. "There, us kin play penny football now . . . You got any pennies?"

Between them they managed to muster four pennies and a half-penny. One penny went into each goal, one showing heads and the other tails. The ha'penny was the ball on the centre spot where Joe had cut a line right across the table. The other pennies were their outfield players. They tossed for first kick and then took it in turns, using broken rulers to shove their players about.

Soon Bradders was watching and commenting and it wasn't long before he was joined by another of their best pals, Nobby.

"Can we join in?" asked Nobby.

"You got any pennies?" asked Joe.

The two boys fished in their pocket and produced a penny each.

"Right," said Joe. "Nobby is on my side and Bradders, you play with Rog."

They were still playing when the bell rang. It was the Head's weekly lesson on citizenship. They went to their places and in swept the Head. He took one look at the table.

"Which boy has been carving up the master's table?"

Joe went crimson and rose to his feet. "I have zur."

Roger, Bradders and Nobby also stood up and all claimed, "I have sir."

"Hm. Not much carving for four boys." He looked at the table again. "Penny football I suppose. Report to my study after school."

When they reported to the study he had all four of them into his study.

"Whose knife was it?"

"Mine zur," said Joe.

"Hand it over. You can claim it back at the end of term. In future mark out your pitches with chalk."

"Yes zur."

"You three wait outside."

Bradders remained inside while the other three went out to wait their turn. As always, Roger cursed his surname. He would be last. They heard the cane and Bradders' muffled "Thank you sir." Out he came raising three fingers. So they knew what they were in for. Nobby was next, then Joe and Roger last of all. But it was soon over. They were all well used to canings by now. And this one was soon forgotten when they were told their names were on the notice-board.

It was Dave Shaw who met them with the news. He was another of their close friends. "Hey you lot, come and look at this. We're all in the Junior Colts for Saturday's game at Sparta."

"Never. You're kidding."

The Junior Colts was for boys under thirteen. It was normally the preserve of form 3 where voices were beginning to break and boys were growing fast. But Dave was right. Six of them from form 2 had been chosen, the four who had been caned, Dave himself and little Andy who was such a lightning hooker.

The boys looked at the list in amazement and then Roger noticed his position and disappointment set in. Apart from Andy he was the only one in the scrum and he was in the second row. He hated it in the second row. He was too small for the second row and too fast for the scrum. He was as fast as Joe or Dave. Why couldn't he have been in the threes?

Mr Wilcox was passing. He saw the boys and stopped. He knew nothing about rugby but he was their coach. "Well done you boys. Let's see. Yes. All five of you have been picked. The

Spartans are a tough side to beat. We'll expect you threes to score lots of tries you know. Ah. And you Wallace. Picked for your dribbling skills. The Head insisted on it. He's seen you practising. Well done all of you."

He walked on. He had found it quite an effort talking to the boys like that but perhaps they would like him better if he showed an interest in their rugby. Frightful game though. He wished he wasn't involved.

All week the boys' excitement mounted. The Junior Colts only had two fixtures a year, both of them against the Spartans. None of them had been picked in the autumn for the home match when the Spartans had wiped the floor with all four Perspins teams. But now they were in the team and playing away. That was a bonus. A journey away from school.

"Why do they call them Spartans?" Roger asked Dave.

"Their school is just as tough and bare as ours, and all they ever seem to want to do when they leave school is go into the army. Of course, a lot of them are the sons of army officers."

"Then we'd better be Athenians," said Roger.

"Why's that then?" asked Joe.

"Because they had much more imagination than the Spartans. We'll beat them with brains and skill."

The others scragged him for being such a twit. But when he went out in the driving rain onto the rugger pitch to practise, they were all there with him, though they practised passing and running while he dribbled up and down the field with little Andy. He couldn't help admiring Andy. He was so small but he was all bone and muscle.

Saturday came and they joined the Colts, the under fifteens, on the coach along with Mr Wilcox and Mr Smart. It was a pity Smarty had to come. He wouldn't let them stop in Beddingford on the way home for an hour or two, and they wouldn't get much fun on the coach either.

The coach passed through Beddingford and over the bridge with the twenty-four arches before turning east towards Exmoor. It skirted a second town, drove a few miles through country roads and brought the boys to Sparta. The front of the school looked quite smart with a drive and statues and a pair of lions at the gate. But once inside it was as harsh and rugged as their own school and the changing rooms were just as primitive.

Muted excitement had kept the boys pretty quiet on the journey and they were still quiet as they changed. Roger felt that he wanted to be sick. His stomach was turning over and over.

Both matches were to be played at the same time. Out they ran into the pouring rain. The pitches were quagmires. They took their position on the field and looked at their opponents. They looked huge. Opponents always did. They were already soaked before the whistle blew.

Dave kicked off for Perspins and at once the scrum's fears and collywobbles melted away. They hurled themselves forward after the ball, tackled, ran, kicked, fell, tried to pass. But the ball was too wet. No one could hold it. Every pass seemed to end in a knock-on and a scrum down. Roger clung to the other boy in the second row, his head gripped firmly between the thighs of the front row. Strewth, little Andy was bony! Roger wished he had a scrum cap. Steam rose as the two scrums heaved at one another and again and again collapsed in the mud.

Outside the scrum the threes shivered miserably in the rain. Dave tucked his hands into his armpits to try to keep them warm and dry. He seemed to be about the only boy on the field who managed to hold a pass and every time the ball came to him he kicked it upfield. There was no point in passing it out.

To and fro the battle raged with neither side getting the upper hand. Neither side looking like scoring. The half time whistle blew.

"Turn right round," shouted the ref. "No point in standing around getting cold."

"I couldn't get any colder," grumbled Bradders.

"No, I've hardly seen the ball yet," responded Joe from the wing.

Roger's game had been too hectic for him to notice but now as he heard their grouses he was glad he was in the scrum. The battle continued, on and on in the driving rain and the mud. Would it never end? The Spartans drove Perspins back towards their line again and again, but again and again Dave kicked for touch and earned some respite. And the forwards kept managing to break through the Spartans, taking the ball at their feet.

Five minutes to go. The Spartans broke free, flung the ball out to their inside centre. The boy was frozen from wet and inactivity. He grabbed at the ball and it squirted out of his hands. The whistle blew.

"Scrum down. The ball went forward. Perspins' put in."

Perspins were back on their own twenty-five. The scrums locked and the Spartans began to push Perspins back. The scrum half popped the ball into the channel between front rows. Andy swung on his two props and whipped the ball back. The scrum half took it firmly and passed to Dave whose kick soared forward almost to the Spartans twenty-five yard line. A moment's respite from the relentless pressure.

"Spartans' throw. Straight lines. Five yards back."

The whistle blew. The Spartans forwards tapped the ball back to their scrum half – stupid in those conditions. The ball stuck in the mud. Roger and Andy burst through the line and kicked. Now, onto the ball and dribble, the ball kept close between ankles and knees. A solitary voice, "At your feet Perspins."

Other forwards were coming up in support. The Spartans' full back ran to dive on the ball but as he dived Roger punted. Close to the action, Dave had been waiting and watching. Now he sprinted as the ball ran over the try line. He fell on it. The whistle blew. Try. Three points. Dave missed his conversion attempt so the score stayed at three points.

Back came the Spartans like angry tigers from the kick-off but time was up. The final whistle blew. Perspins had won. It was unheard of.

They ran off to the baths. The threes were so cold that they couldn't stand the heat of the water. The Colts came in ten minutes later, beaten as usual. It made the Junior Colts victory all the sweeter.

A very Spartan tea followed and polite speeches from the team captains and then the coach back to school in the early evening darkness with the rain still coming down in torrents. The Spartans had beaten both the 1st and 2nd XVs so the Junior Colts felt excessively proud of themselves. It had been the one highlight in a miserable term. And when term ended the new bucks knew that they had taken one step further forward towards becoming Perspins boys. After Easter they would be 'old bucks'.

13

The Pride and the Pain of War

Roger, Margaret and their mother had spent the Easter holidays in the hotel in Beddingford again. Right at the end of the holidays Gerry came down in his army uniform. His mother had never seen him look so smart, tall and slim as he was. She felt very proud. When the two youngsters went back to school, Gerry took her home before going back to his training.

Back at school Roger couldn't help swanking about his three brothers. He went on and on about them and the others grew sick of hearing about them.

"Oh shut up about your brothers Wallace," Bradders said one day. "Anybody'd think they were winning the war all on their own."

"All I'm saying is . . ." but Roger got no further.

"You're not saying anything," Bradders interrupted and pushed Roger out of his desk. Nobby joined in and the two of them held Roger down no matter how hard he struggled. "We're sick of hearing about your brothers: Alfie this and Eric that and Gerry the other. So shut your gob about them right."

Roger didn't answer. These were supposed to be his friends. If he couldn't talk to them about his brothers who could he talk to.

They let him up and he ran out to the cricket pitch and started to walk round it, tears coursing down his face. "Rotten school. Rotten war." He wanted to be at home, his real home with all his family and his old friends. Slowly he calmed down. He could hardly remember most of his old friends. What would it be like to be back at home he wondered. And then he thought, if Bradders and Nobby were sick of hearing about Alfie and Eric and Gerry, he'd better shut up about them. In fact, he'd never speak of them again. Not ever.

But that didn't stop him feeling proud of them. His mother had told him that Alfie was flying on bombing raids over Germany and Eric was flying his Hurricane in North Africa. Gerry was still training of course but his turn would come. Roger's heart swelled with pride. He still saw the war the way the Head did, the way Eric did too, with jingoistic patriotism.

The Head was too young to have been in the First World War and he was too old for this one, so he knew nothing of war's reality. His teaching of history was one long propaganda exercise but because he believed it, he taught it with uncritical sincerity and boys who swallowed his teaching felt that the British were superior to any other nation on earth. That was especially true now that the German army in North Africa was on the run.

Eric had entered the war feeling just that way. Although he had seen some pretty awful things, nothing seemed to quench his enthusiasm. His letters home bubbled with excitement: 'I had another kill last week, so that makes three I've downed. The army is still doing well in spite of the heat and the dust. It makes you proud to see how the Empire has rallied round. We've got Australians, New Zealanders, South Africans and Indians all fighting for us, as well as Czechs and Poles. It makes you feel that the whole world is on our side. I'm looking forward to meeting my first Yanks.'

Eric still saw his country as the mother country ruling the Empire in righteousness, bringing justice, peace and prosperity wherever she ruled. To him, Britain was always on the side of right and right always won in the end. The Head shared those views precisely, and taught them.

It would take another generation before history was seen in a rather different light and the pendulum of bias swung too far the other way.

Eric was fighting like the knights of old, for God (who was British of course), for goodness and for the right. Even now when the realities of war and injury and death, heat and dust and exhaustion were all too clear, he still clung on to his idealistic vision. When he climbed into his Hurricane he was still in his own mind one of the noble knights of the round table rising into the sky to do battle with an evil foe.

He had notched up his first kill at El Alamein and there had been two more since. Now as he flew with just two other planes the adrenalin flowed again at the sight of a small group of Messerschmitt 109s flying below, unaware of their presence. He was ready when the command came to attack. He peeled off in his turn. A steep dive brought the three Hurricanes down in a perfect position. Not until it was too late did the Germans break formation and take avoiding action.

Two of them went down in flames and Eric peeled away with that sense of triumph he had known before. The three of them set course back to base to refuel and fly again. But above them another squadron of ME 109s had been too late to help and was now poised for vengeance. Eric never saw death coming out of the sun. The other two Hurricanes got away but for him the war was over and life with it.

He would know nothing of the posthumous DFC which brought such comfort to a grieving father and no comfort at all to a heart-broken mother.

Alfie was sent home on compassionate leave and he and his mother travelled west to break the news to Margaret and Roger.

Mrs Wallace went to see Margaret and Alfie cycled out into the country to see Roger. The Head was expecting him but Roger knew nothing of his visit. When the note came telling him that he was wanted at the Headmaster's study he wondered what he had done wrong. The note also informed the form master that Eric had died, and asked him to pass the information to the class after Roger had gone.

Roger made his way to the study with its now familiar smell of old leather. He knocked and a voice said, "Come in."

He went inside and was astonished to find Alfie standing there. He flew into Alfie's arms. Alfie was very thankful that the Head had left them to meet alone. He was pretty embarrassed by his brother's show of affection – and not a little pleased as well.

"What are you doing here?"

"Mum asked me to come. I've got some bad news I'm afraid."

"They haven't been bombed?"

"No. Nothing like that. It's Eric." He didn't know how to go on, and for a little while he felt too full to go on.

"He's been shot down by German fighters."

"Is he still alive?"

Alfie shook his head. The two boys stood for a little while and then Alfie started to try to paint a picture of Eric as a hero. He didn't find it easy. His heart was sick with the deaths of so many of his friends, and so many more crippled or in prisoner of war camps. There were no heroes. Only fools fighting other fools and going to an early grave. He hated the whole thing — yet he still felt that it had to be continued now until it was all over.

But he must let Roger know nothing of this. His brother was ten years younger than he was. He must be given a comfort Alfie could never enjoy.

"We don't know very much yet but it sounds as if Eric was a really good pilot. He shot down four enemy planes before they got him. He was in that battle of El Alamein and he's been up with the army ever since."

Roger felt so proud but so full of pain as well. And there was Alfie in his uniform with his sergeant's stripes. He invested him with the same glory Alfie had painted for Eric. What wonderful brothers they were. And now Gerry was in the army too. He clung to Alfie again and wept tears of grief and pride together.

There was a knock at the study door. The Head came in.

"Well young Wallace. You've had bad news. Your brother has died for his country. You can't do much better than that. You are excused classes for the rest of the day. Show your brother round. He'll be sleeping in your dorm tonight."

"Yes sir. Thank you sir."

The two of them wandered through the quad and across the parade into the cricket field. It was a huge field and they drifted slowly round it. As Alfie looked at his brother he felt Roger's pride and it worried him. Roger seemed to be looking at things just as Eric had done. Was this the time to try to put him right?

"What's it like, flying over Germany?" asked Roger.

"You're not supposed to know that I do. But if you really want to know, it's horrible. First there's the long flight in the darkness. Then as we get near to our targets, there's anti-aircraft fire and fighters. Then we drop our bombs and turn tail and head for home as fast as we can go. Don't let anyone kid you young Rog. War is a nasty business and the sooner it's over the better. I don't want to get killed like Eric."

Perhaps it was because of Eric's death, perhaps it was just

Alfie's own depression and fear getting across to him, but for the first time Roger glimpsed the fact that war was not the romantic thing he had always seen.

The insight soon faded. He would be many years older before he asked which took more courage, to fly in brief combat in a Hurricane as Eric had done, or to make the long journey to Germany and back night after night. And it would be even longer before Alfie spoke freely and frankly of his nightly terror and his thankfulness when he was finally grounded.

He began to turn the conversation off the war and onto the school. It was his first visit and he wasn't very impressed by what he had seen. The buildings seemed pretty old and dowdy. But this was a good cricket pitch.

"I wouldn't mind a game here," he said. "Are you any good at cricket?"

"Not much. I'm better at rugger and cross country. They don't let me bowl very often and there's no fun batting except when you're in. Cricket is all waiting around. Fielding you wait for someone to hit the ball where you are, and then if it's a catch you're scared you'll drop it. And batting is just waiting for your pals to get out so that you can go in."

"You'll have to get better at it. Then you'll enjoy it more. This looks a pretty good pitch to me. Gosh look at that roller. How do they use that on the pitch? It's huge."

"Oh that's one of our summer punishments. They have sixteen boys on punishment pulling it up and down the pitch for half an hour. Once you get it going it isn't difficult, just boring that's all."

"Where does that path go?"

"Down to the swimming pool. Shall we go and look."

So the two walked through a couple of fields and past the school farm down to the pool. Although it was early in the year, the sun was warm.

"Come on young Roger. Let's have a swim."

"But we haven't got costumes or towels."

"Oh don't worry about that. Come on. Get your clothes off."

Roger felt shy all of a sudden. His brother stripped out of his uniform and laid his clothes on the ground. Roger undressed more slowly. He hadn't seen his brother naked for a very long time. Black curly hair, hairy arms and legs and chest, and rippling muscles, and hair in places where Roger had none. He suddenly

88

felt that he was still a very little boy.

Alfie dived in and while he was swimming away from Roger, Roger whipped off the last of his clothes and dived in out of sight. He had never swum in the nude before. He liked it. Soon his shyness and youth were forgotten. The two splashed and swam and dived and then ran round and round the pool to dry off reasonably well before they dressed.

"Strewth that was cold. Water looks pretty foul too. Use your vest as a towel. We'll dry them tonight."

They were back at school in time for lunch and then walked down to the village where Alfie bought a loaf of bread straight out of the baker's oven. As they wandered on enjoying the smell and the crusty crust and the hot, doughy middle, Eric's death receded and they felt a warmth of companionship such as they had never known before.

The next day the first eleven had no match so they were down to play the Staff. The Head asked Alfie if he would turn out for the Staff. He opened the bowling and in six pretty wild, fast overs he took three wickets. The school team was in trouble.

But against the amiable bowling of elderly teachers they soon recovered and began to pile on the runs. Eventually at 112 for 8, Alfie was brought back. In one over he had the last two batsmen out: 112 all out.

Now it was the turn of the Staff to bat. Out came the Head swinging his bat around his head, stretching his shoulders and generally showing that he intended to knock up a good score. With him was 'the ancient', the oldest and fattest member of staff. His bat looked tiny as he waddled out to the crease and took guard.

But appearances are deceptive. It soon became clear that 'the ancient' had been quite a cricketer in his time. He scored freely and hardly gave the Head a look in, keeping the bowling very much to himself. On the rare occasions when the Head did face he made some very impressive strokes, but mostly missed the ball. It wasn't long before he was out, bowled middle stump. The sportsmaster followed him and the score began to rise fairly quickly. But then 'the ancient' was given out, leg before wicket. He clearly felt that the umpire was wrong, but with thirty-three runs he was fairly content.

Alfie took his place and a few balls later the sportsmaster was out, caught on the boundary. Fifty-eight for three. As he passed Alfie on his way back to the pavilion he said, "It's all up to you now. None of the rest of the staff can bat."

It was just the kind of challenge Alfie loved. He was a pretty good batsman, if a bit on the rash side. He fancied himself as another Denis Compton. So he started dancing down the wicket, whipping the ball away in all directions, or taking sneaky little singles. He soon had the members of staff at the other end puffing and panting with the exertion of running between the wickets, but none of them stayed long.

Soon the score was sixty-seven for four, seventy-five for five, seventy-five for six when old Smarty was out for a duck. Roger and his pals cheered the fall of every wicket. "Down with the Staff. Up with the School." Although Roger found himself torn. Alfie was in the wrong team really. He wanted Alfie to win — on his own if necessary — but he certainly didn't want the Staff to win.

Seventy-eight for seven and more cheers from Roger's group. Alfie worked hard to keep the bowling, trying to score singles at the end of each over. Ninety-two for eight. The match was getting too close for comfort. The fielders crowded round the members of staff when they were batting and then moved right out for Alfie. One hundred and eight for nine. Five runs for victory. One wicket to fall and tension mounting all the time.

'Puffer' Sanderson came in with his empty pipe in his mouth. He took guard, put his pipe in his breast pocket, looked around the field and carefully blocked the remaining balls of the over. It was clear at once that he had played cricket before. That was a relief, thought Alfie. The tension was getting to him. He mustn't lose his wicket now.

On the boundary the watching boys fell silent. Roger could hardly bear to look. The school had brought back their best bowler. Alfie took fresh guard and watched the first four balls carefully, playing defensively to each one. He hit the fifth for a shortish single, called and ran. But 'Puffer' couldn't run. He'd lost a lung in the first world war and Alfie didn't know. 'Puffer' put his pipe in his mouth, and began to walk down the pitch. Alfie arrived, turned to look and stood aghast. The fielder hurled the ball to the wicket keeper and 'Puffer' was out by almost half a pitch. He quietly carried on walking towards the pavilion. The school had won and cheers rang round the field. Alfie ran to 'Puffer'.

"I'm so sorry sir. I didn't realise . . ."

"Don't apologise, Wallace. Best thing that could have happened. It's always good for the school to beat the Staff. You weren't to know I couldn't run. Anyway, it's thanks to you that we've managed to make a match of it."

Roger ran shyly over to his brother.

"You were smashing. Forty-three not out and five wickets."

He was so proud – even more so when he heard his pals talking about how good his brother was. But the crowning moment came when the school cricket captain came up to him and said, "If you become half as good as your brother it won't be long before you get into the Colts."

Roger made up his mind. He would work at his cricket. One day Alfie would see.

That evening there was a film in the main hall and it only broke down three times, so that was pretty good. Another night together and the following morning after breakfast: the two of them went to see the Head.

"I've just come to say 'good-bye' sir, and to thank you."

"You're off then. Glad you were able to come. You did well for us on Saturday."

"I enjoyed it. It was nice to get back on a cricket pitch sir. It was my first match this year."

"All the best when you get back on duty. Give 'em hell. Oh, and my sympathies to your parents."

"Yes sir."

The two shook hands and the two brothers went out to the cycle sheds. Alfie collected the bike he had borrowed and the two walked out to the road. Alfie put his hand in his pocket and pulled out a shilling.

"Here. Put this in your pocket." He ruffled his brother's hair. "See you sometime."

He pushed off, swung his leg over the saddle and was away. As he cycled round the curve in the road that would take him out of sight, he turned and waved. He felt choked. Would he ever see Roger again he wondered. No use thinking like that. But Eric had bought it. Would he be the next?

Roger had stood and waved. The tears were pouring down his

face. He was so proud of his brother. He pulled out his hankie and wiped away the tears. Then he turned off the road into the rugger field and walked round it in the sunshine, trying to pull himself together before going back into school. It was nearly chapel time. He put the handkerchief back in his pocket and felt the shilling. A shilling! What he could do with a shilling.

He could go down to the village again and buy bread. He could go twice. Two loaves at fourpence halfpenny each. He would still have threepence to spend. Or perhaps he would spend all of it on his sweet ration. Usually he shared his sweet ration with Joe. Joe supplied the money and he supplied the coupons. But this time he was rich. On the other hand that bread *was* super. . .

Spending his shilling in his mind he was soon lining up with the other boys for chapel. There was an awkwardness between him and his friends. They had scragged him for talking about his brothers and now one of them was dead. They didn't know how to handle it.

That afternoon they all walked together as usual but the awkwardness persisted. In school there was no real problem. They got on with their usual lives and nobody mentioned Eric. But free time was different. Roger found that he was quite often left alone and he began to spend time with other boys, Philip Jonas for one and poor old Parsons who was still being teased and tormented by the form bullies.

Once again Roger felt that he didn't completely belong in any group. He had so many friends and yet he never fitted with one group to the exclusion of others the way some boys did. Some of them seemed to spend all their time with one another.

And then the Head announced that the Allies had won the war in North Africa and that the German and Italian forces had surrendered. It was May, only a few weeks after Eric had been killed. Roger felt both proud and sad. Eric had done his bit towards winning that victory. But he didn't really know Eric all that well. He'd hardly seen him since the war began and there was eight years difference between them. Now he never would know him. He wondered if Alfie would survive. He wanted so much to grow up to be a man like Alfie.

14

Punishments and Pleasures

It was a stupid argument – all the more so because it was so early in the morning.

"Alpha's best," said Joe.

"Beta," retorted Roger.

"Alpha."

"Beta."

"Alpha," with a swing of his pillow.

"Beta," standing to get a better swing.

In no time the two boys were standing on their beds swiping one another with their pillows and grunting "Alpha", "Beta" with each blow. Soon all the dorm was awake and boys were watching with delight.

A slipper whistled across the room and missed. Saunders, the dorm prefect, had thrown it. "You two, cut it out." And then he said, "Take your tooth mugs and borrow two more and go and fill them with water."

When they returned he said, "Take off your pyjama tops and go and stand on two buffaloes facing the kitchens."

They clambered onto the buffaloes and looked down across the courtyard to the kitchens.

"That's it. Feet apart. Raise your hands with the tooth mugs in sideways as if you were being crucified because you'll soon feel as if you were." He paused while they raised their arms. "Now Bradders, go and pull their pyjamas open so that the kitchen staff can see their cocks. Give them a thrill while they get our breakfast ready."

Bradders was delighted. He pulled open their pyjamas as wide as he could and then, because he could get away with it, he grabbed each of their cocks and pulled.

"Sod," gasped Joe and quick as lightning he poured some of the water from one of his tooth mugs onto Bradders. When Roger saw what Joe was doing, he followed suit.

Bradders ran for it.

"Keep your arms up." It was Saunders again. "You can stay like that until the bell goes."

It was easier said than done. Joe was managing better than Roger. He was tougher. Sweat broke out as they fought the pain and struggled to keep their arms up. Roger's began to fall.

"Up, I said."

He jerked them up again. But he couldn't keep them up much longer. It was murder. And then the bell rang.

They got down and made their way to the wash-room.

"Sorry," said Joe and then he added with a grin, "but Alpha is best."

"Rubbish. Beta's better."

"Alpha," with a punch.

"Beta," and a punch returned.

"Alpha," beginning to wrestle.

Roger knew he couldn't beat Joe. "There's Bradders," he said.

Joe looked. "Dirty sod." He turned from Roger and swung his fist at Bradders. Roger joined him. Soon the three boys were writhing and wrestling on the wash-room floor. Saunders came in.

"Cut it. Not been punished enough eh? As it's Sunday each of you can write out psalm 119. Don't try to miss bits out because I shall check. I'll give you to Wednesday to finish it."

They washed, dressed, made their beds and went to find their Bibles.

"Bloody hell," said Bradders. "We shall never finish this. There's a hundred and seventy-six verses. Christ almighty. It's all your fault Wallace, saying Beta is best."

Roger just managed to bite back the words, 'Well, so it is.' Both Bradders and Joe belonged to Alpha. Instead he just said, "Oh shut up Bradders. You shouldn't have pulled our cocks. I'm going to start writing."

All three of them started and wrote until it was time for

breakfast. The bell rang just as Roger wrote, 'How can a young man keep his way pure?' Never mind 'pure'. How could a young man keep out of punishment? That's what he wanted to know.

At every spare moment in the day they went on writing. After lunch when they all had to write home, their letters home were skimped so that they could get on with the psalm.

"Yer, look at this," said Joe. " 'I have more understanding than all my teachers.' That's true any rate."

Not until it was almost bed-time did they reach the verse which said, 'Redeem me from man's oppression' but there were still forty-two verses to go. Luckily for Roger, he had enjoyed some of the best moments of his life that afternoon. He had been so engrossed in the psalm that he had been late leaving for the Sunday afternoon walk, which meant that he went out on his own.

It was the kind of perfect day that makes May so special. The sky was pure blue with white clouds strolling quietly across it. The sun was warm and the whole countryside seemed fresh and new. Once out of sight of school, Roger stuffed his cap into his pocket. He passed a roadside house.

Rowena lived there. He was sweet on Rowena but he knew she wouldn't be there. She would be out with the other two village girls who came to chapel. They would be managing accidental meetings with boys out on their walks. Roger felt jealous and walked on.

He left the road for the fields. By a roundabout route he circled the rugby pitches and strolled down close to the back of school farm. Soon he was in open fields he'd never walked before. He passed through a wide valley with woodland on either side and fields with sheep and cattle.

He felt wonderfully at peace with himself. He came to an empty field and lay on the grass close to the hedge, basking in the warmth of the sun. He closed his eyes and then he heard a cry. It was unmistakable. Even he knew what it was. He opened his eyes and there, high overhead he saw a buzzard circling. It looked so effortless, floating up there slowly soaring round and round. He closed his eyes again and dozed. When he opened his eyes there was no sign of the buzzard. He searched the sky but it had gone.

Then he noticed movement on a tall old oak tree which stood alone in the centre of the valley. As he watched he realised that he had found the buzzard's nest for there were two of them there.

One flew off and climbed to begin circling again. The other settled down. Was it sitting on eggs?

Roger got up and walked across the field to the tree. He was very excited and a bit nervous too. He didn't know much about buzzards. If he climbed up to have a look would they attack him?

But he had to have a look. He just had to. So he began to climb, carefully, slowly and quietly. He moved away from the trunk of the tree a bit and climbed through the branches. The top of the tree was flat, almost as if the top had been sliced off. Roger's head and shoulders rose above the branches and the buzzard that was on the nest. She hissed a bit as she watched him anxiously, but she made no move.

Roger stayed quite still. She was a large bird with piercing eyes and the strong hooked beak of a predator. Her nest was a fairly rough construction mostly of sticks lined with leaves and grass and bits of sheep's wool. She seemed to come to the conclusion that Roger did not intend to harm her and she settled herself more comfortably. She must be sitting on eggs.

"I wonder if she'd let me see them," thought Roger. "Hens do. They let me take them from under them."

Very gently he reached out his hand. Again she hissed. Would she go for him? That beak was pretty powerful. He stretched forward until he was touching her. She never moved. With the utmost care he slid his hand under her warm body. Eggs. He could feel them. The mother was getting suspicious and anxious again. She moved her body slightly and he saw two greenish coloured eggs looking a bit dirty with brown blotches.

For the briefest moment he was tempted. Some of his friends had collections of birds' eggs. What a trophy a buzzard's egg would be. But then he looked at the mother bird and drew his arm quietly back. For a little while longer he just stayed and gazed at her. He might never be this close to a buzzard again. He felt that he ought not to climb to the nest again however much he wanted to. And he mustn't tell anybody about it. They were his own secret pets. He would come and watch from the field sometimes but he would leave them in peace.

Quietly he withdrew and climbed back down the tree. He hadn't realised just what a size the tree was until he started to climb down. Back on the ground he found that he was trembling but was it excitement or nerves? When the trembling stopped he found that he was almost glowing with the happiness of his afternoon. Nothing that summer would be quite so special.

He guessed it was time to be getting back to school so he set off back the way he had come. As he came out onto the road he saw a lone figure walking towards him. Rowena! It must be Rowena. Oh dear, so he was late. He began to hurry and then slowed as he met her.

"Hello."

" 'Ello boy. What's your name then."

"Roger," he said shyly. "Roger Wallace."

"Roger." She sampled it. "That's a nice name. Mine's Rowena."

"I know," said Roger.

She smiled, pleased at the thought that he knew her name. He must be interested. But she couldn't think of anything more to talk about. "You'm late back," she said. "If you don't rin vor it you'll miss your tea."

"Yes," he said. But he didn't want to run for it. He wanted to stand there and stay with her for ever.

"Git on with ee then, and don't forget to put your school cap back on."

"No." He pulled it out of his pocket. "Thank you. See you in chapel." And he fled, his spirits sky high. He had spoken to Rowena! He had been with her all on his own. It almost drove the buzzard's nest out of his mind, such is the power of woman.

e

15

Swimming

That summer justified the old saying about school-days being the happiest days of your life. Roger played a lot of cricket and enjoyed himself on the athletics field. It took him a while to decide which races to concentrate on but gradually he settled for the longer ones, the 880 yards, the mile and his favourite, the cross country. The two mile triangle punishment run kept him in good training for that.

But perhaps best of all that summer was the swimming. Twice a week his class was marched down to the pool for their turn. The thick green colour of the water never put them off. They just revelled in the fun of it all.

One June night Roger couldn't sleep. It was far too hot and stuffy and none of the dorm windows was open. He got out of bed and quietly opened the nearest window. It was a beautiful night with a fullish moon and myriads of stars in a cloudless sky. Suddenly Roger thought it would be super to go for a swim. He whispered, "Is anyone awake?"

Joe, Bradders and Dave all answered him.

"I'm going for a swim. Anyone coming?"

"Yeah."

"You bet."

"Cor."

There was no hesitation. They woke Nobby and all five crept from the dorm to the washroom and collected their towels. "What about costumes?" asked Dave.

"If we use costumes, we might get caught drying them. My

brother Alfie and me went in in the nude when he was here. It's smashing."

So they sneaked across to the parade and ran over the cricket field down past the farm to the pool. Everything was so still. The moon shone on the pool. It was magic. They slipped quietly into the water. There was no diving or shouting or splashing. They didn't want to wake anyone at the farm who might report them. They just swam and talked quietly to one another and then headed back for school, where they slept like logs.

That swim was the first of many, but one night as they drew near to the pool Joe hushed them, "Sh. Listen. There's somebody already there."

It was true. As they listened they could hear voices. At one end of the pool there was a bank boys changed on and lay in the sun. Joe led the others behind the bank and they crawled to the top and peeped over.

"Gyaw. Look at they."

"Just wait till we tell the rest of them back at school."

"But we won't get a swim."

"We will if we wait."

"Just look at her tits."

"Her idn bad is 'er."

The cause of all the excitement was the Headmaster and his wife, the sportsmaster and his wife and daughter, all swimming in the nude. The daughter was roughly the same age as the boys and very much aware that with so few girls around, she was the object of a good deal of attention. But she might not have been quite so pleased if she had known about this night's attention.

The boys couldn't take their eyes off her. Joe whispered to Roger, "Just look at Bradders and Nobby. They'm like two randy gurt booyulls."

Both of them were holding themselves and gawping hungrily at the sportsmaster's daughter. Roger made no comment. Why did things like that happen to Bradders and Nobby and not to him? And why was Bradders so hairy? He wasn't. He felt inadequate, unformed and incomplete somehow. So many of the boys seemed to have left him behind. He wondered if there was something wrong with him but he knew he wasn't the only one. Dave wasn't like a bull. And he did have one or two hairs. He had counted eleven only a few days before when he was in the bath.

The swimmers dried themselves, dressed and left, and the boys took their places in the pool. They had a good swim but it was the last time they risked it that summer. Not even the chance of seeing Dorcas in the nude again could tempt them. They knew that there would be all hell let loose if the Head caught them watching. But at least they could picture her and talk about her and dream of her at night or in the classroom.

But night dreams and day dreams were no substitute for midnight swims. As it happened it was Roger who stumbled on a partial substitute.

It was on one of their Sunday afternoon walks. The usual five were out together one hot, lazy summer afternoon. They had worked their way across to the squire's lake and gone out in the rowing boat that was always there. But someone saw them so they rowed to the far side of the lake away from the big house and ran for it. It was easy enough to get away because the squire never bothered very much.

Quite soon they were in the woods. They stopped running and strolled in the woods for a while, getting further and further from school. They drifted down towards the stream that ran out of the lake. It had a series of dams leading down to a mill the squire used occasionally. The boys often caught fish by draining a stretch of stream between two of the dams. But this Sunday they just wandered idly along with nothing in particular in their minds.

A little off to one side of the stream there was a high hedge. Roger had never taken any notice of it before. But he suddenly realised that it only ran for quite a short distance, and that it was carefully looked after. Most hedges were only cut when it was necessary. As he looked at it more carefully he saw that it wasn't just one hedge but four, making a rectangle.

"Here. Have you ever noticed that hedge?"

"No. What about it?"

"It's not like ordinary hedges. See."

"So what?"

"I just wondered what was the other side. Whatever it is, it's all closed in."

"Oh yes. You could be right."

"Let's go and see then."

So they crossed the stream and made their way to the hedge, and then followed it round until they came to an opening. They crept through the opening keeping a good look out. They didn't want to get caught.

"Cor."

"Look at that."

"Whose do ee think it is?"

"Must be the Squire's. He owns all this land and the dams and that."

"Wonder how often he comes here?"

In front of them was a small swimming pool. Unlike the thick green water of the school pool, the water here was pure blue and the pool was tiled in blue marble. In the warmth of the sun it looked perfect.

"How about it then?"

"Nah," said Bradders.

"Why not? Even if we are caught we shall only get scatted."

"I reckon t'would be worth it," said Joe.

Roger and Joe were already stripping off and it wasn't long before all five of them were in. After their swim they messed about in the sun for a while until they had dried off enough to put their clothes back on. Dave had a watch and warned them that they had left it a bit late to get back to school.

They ran across the fields to the road and most of the way back to school. They swore that they would keep the secret of the existence of the pool to themselves. It was one promise they almost managed to keep. Very few other boys ever got to know about the pool, and those were only their closest friends.

For the whole of the rest of his school-days, hot Sundays saw Roger heading straight for the Squire's pool. If the Squire was ever aware of his uninvited guests he never let on. But he was a decent sort of cove. He didn't even report the fact that boys had been using his boat on his lake.

16

Scout Camp

That perfect summer term became complete when Roger went to his first scout camp towards the end of it.

When he had been an evacuee in Beddingford he had been thrown out of the scouts in disgrace but at Perspins he was able to begin again. There were two scout troops and he was in troop 2.

The 'Swift' patrol was made up entirely of young boys with the exception of Cardew, the patrol leader. Because Roger had already been in the scouts he soon passed a lot of his tests and he was made the 'second' to Cardew.

The scoutmaster was Mr Emerson. The new boys didn't know him very well. He was deputy head of the school and most of his teaching was done with older boys. He had taught form 2 art briefly because of a teacher shortage, but now they only saw him outside the classroom.

Roger had felt an immediate respect for the man, in spite of his funny ideas about colour. He rarely punished anybody – rarely needed to – and never seemed to have to raise his voice. Somebody had once said that he was 'as wise as Odysseus' and that had led to him being called 'O.D.' Roger rather liked Odysseus and he found that he liked and respected O.D. too.

O.D. was a small, brisk man who had been a major in the First World War. He was now captain of the local home guard. Knowing that many of his scouts would end up in the armed forces, he did his best to prepare them. He wanted them to serve with distinction but he also wanted them to survive. His discipline was both strict and fair but his emphasis was always on the flexibility of scouting. He hated the rigidity of much military thinking and urged his boys to use their own initiative. He taught them to restrain their natural enthusiasm and impetuous instinct in favour of patience, silence and invisibility.

Scout camp was the climax of the scouting year. In 1943 the shortage of petrol meant that it wasn't possible to take the camp far from the school. The boys loaded a lorry with their equipment and a few rode on the lorry to help unload. The rest set out from school in their patrols and travelled at scout pace the two miles to their site. It was on a piece of open ground between the squire's saw-mills and a long stretch of woodland. A small stream ran below the site and supplied all their water.

The tents were ex-army bell tents dating from the first world war. It was quite a work of art getting them up, but the boys had practised at school and were well organised. Within a matter of about ten minutes the tents were all standing. A few minutes more saw them all pegged out and the guy ropes steady.

With care you could fit twenty-two people into each tent but there were only eight boys to each patrol so there was plenty of space. Before they laid their ground-sheets on the ground quite a lot of boys took hooks down to the stream and cut themselves armfuls of reeds. With these they made themselves mattresses to give themselves a bit of comfort.

They laid their ground-sheets on top and then made their beds military fashion with their three blankets and sheet interlocking and folding to make a bed similar to a modern sleeping bag. When their tents had been inspected it was time to mark off patrol dining areas and to put up bivouacs for dining shelters together with dining tables and benches. Meals were to be eaten properly, sitting up to the table!

While four of the boys were busy with that, two more were marking out the cooking area. In the Swift patrol this was Joe's forte. In preparation for the camp he had made an oven with two biscuit tins. Now he dug out a channel for the oven fire, set the oven on bricks and above it made a tube from an old piece of metal to serve as a chimney. Then he fetched mud from the stream and built it all round the oven with a thickness of three to four inches.

While he was working, Bradders had prepared another area for an open fire with a stand and cross beam big enough to carry two dixies. Then he had gone off to begin the endless task of collecting firewood stacked neatly in three piles of varying thickness.

Meanwhile Philip Jonas had carefully paced out twenty-five yards and dug two cesspits, one for dry waste and one for wet. Once those were completed and covered with bracken, he went off with one boy from each of the other patrols to dig the latrines well away from the main camp. They dug a deep trench, and on one side of it they set up a bar for boys to sit on, a silver birch cut specially for the purpose. Then they surrounded the whole area with canvas to give proper privacy.

That done they moved off to a clearing in the woods and prepared a camp fire area, dragging old fallen trees into a circle to make seats and collecting vast quantities of firewood. Two of them laid the core of the fire and then built a large bonfire ready for a camp fire evening.

Mr Emerson watched with satisfaction, inspecting each piece of work as it was completed. The boys knew what they were doing and were working well. The term's training was standing them in good stead and the older boys, who had done it all before were giving a good lead. He took a running jump at one of the bivouac frames and swung on it. It was a favourite trick of his. Badly built and the whole thing would collapse, but this one hardly moved. Made of wooden poles lashed together, everything depended on choice of ground, depth of the poles in the ground, and the skill of the boy who had done the lashings. On this occasion it was Gordon Rew of the Eagle patrol and Mr Emerson was quick to praise his work.

The camp was looking good. The boys had done splendidly.

Once he had inspected a patrol's dining area, Mr Emerson issued each patrol with its rations. Joe stowed these away in two raised cupboards made from small tea chests. He wasn't all that impressed with what he was given. If they were to eat well he would have to do something to supplement the rations. (In point of fact, Mr Emerson had scattered farmers' sons through the patrols for precisely that reason. With their practical background and country skills he knew they would soon get busy.) Joe took Roger and Bradders with him and led them away from the woods onto neighbouring farmland. He showed them where there were potatoes growing and another field where there were turnips. They pulled a few turnips and dug some potatoes and left them in a bucket in the hedge. Then he set half a dozen wire traps for rabbits. After that he cautioned silence and led them down the lee side of the hedge out of sight of the farm.

"D'ee zee thick barn," he whispered. "There'll be hens in there I reckon. Us'll have to be careful not to disturb the dogs, but us should get a few eggs if us comes yer when 'tis dark — and perhaps us'll 'ave a chicken too one day."

Back they went to the camp and Joe set to and prepared a stew with plenty of potatoes and turnip and with dumplings. He cooked the stew in a dixie on the open fire and followed it with cocoa (a dixie of water was always kept on the boil).

Joe put some wood in a third dixie and hung that to dry out over the fire while they were eating. Then he stored it in the oven.

"What are you doing that for?" asked Jonas.

"If it rains us'll have some dry wood for lighting the fire tomorrow morning."

While he spoke he drew the embers of the fire together, surrounded them with stones and then covered them carefully with earth.

"If we're lucky these embers will still be fit in the morning and us'll get the fire gwain easy."

It wasn't long before they were all thankful that Joe had taken such care. They were no sooner in bed that night than it began to rain. Cardew, the patrol leader, had been to camp before. As soon as the rain began he said, "Pay attention all of you. Be very careful not to touch the tent. As long as you don't touch it, it will stay dry, but wherever you touch it water will come in."

Mr Emerson did his rounds and repeated Cardew's warning in every tent. The patrol leader put out the candle burning in a jar hanging from the tent pole and after some fairly desultory conversation the boys were soon asleep. But the rain was not. It continued to pour down and the canvas of the old bell tents grew heavy with water. Mr Emerson sat in his tent and waited with foreboding. He was just beginning to feel that everything would be OK and that he could turn in when he heard the noises he had been dreading. There were muffled shouts and cries.

The boys in the Swift patrol were woken by them and Cardew knew at once what they were.

"Nobody move," he shouted.

Outside the rain was still driving down.

"Now. Bradders, light the candle – and don't touch the canvas."

He shone a torch and Bradders got the candle alight. Then Cardew said, "I want each of you in turn, starting with Jonas by the door, to bring your beds over to this end of the tent. And make sure you don't touch the canvas. I want all eight beds this side."

While he was speaking he was also dressing.

"What we are doing is making room for another patrol. Those shouts mean that one of the tents has come down in the rain. You will all stay here while I go to help."

At that moment Mr Emerson poked his head in: "Oh, well done. You are all ready to receive guests I see. The tent pole has gone through the top of the Eagles' tent. We'll get them all across here."

He and Cardew made their way to the Eagles' tent which was just a crumpled, wriggling mass of canvas. Two or three other patrol leaders also arrived. They held the tent door open while boy after boy crawled out, dragging his bedding with him.

"Blankets INSIDE groundsheets. Good lad. Off you go to the Swift patrol tent and DON'T TOUCH THE CANVAS. You go too Cardew. Organise things your end."

One by one the boys dashed through the rain to the Swift tent.

They stood by the tent pole while Cardew handed them towels and allocated spaces.

"Make your beds as carefully as you can. Keep the wet bits of your bedding away from your bodies and away from the dry bedding."

He gave each boy plenty of space and soon after they were all settled Mr Emerson arrived with a box of extra blankets that were dry. In a surprisingly short period of time all was quiet again, except for the sound of the rain lashing down.

"If any more tents go tonight, we stay put. O.D. won't expect any more help from us. So get to sleep again if you can."

"Yes, but Cardew," said Jonas, "what happens if our tent goes?"

"It won't. Why do you think I chose this tent? But if I'm wrong just stay as still as you can and leave everything to me."

Cardew wasn't wrong, although one more tent went during

that first night and neither Mr Emerson nor his assistant got much sleep. The boys of the Swift and Eagles patrols slept through it all and when they woke in the morning the sun was shining on a sodden landscape of wet grass and dripping trees. Thank goodness Joe had put some wood in the oven to keep dry.

After breakfast the mornings were spent on the camp chores: tidying up the tents and lifting their skirts to allow fresh air in; washing up, preparing food and collecting and chopping firewood. Joe checked his rabbit traps and usually brought back a couple to skin and clean ready for cooking for lunch.

The two patrols whose tents came down in the storm were issued with fresh canvas, needles and thread and set to the task of repairing their tents. Mr Emerson supervised but he made them do the actual work themselves. Later that day their tents were standing again, to the supporting cheers of the whole troop.

The second night their patrols spent with their hosts while their own tents dried out, but on the third night they went back to their own tents.

In the afternoons, Mr Emerson led the troop in something called a 'wide game'. Mr Emerson used these wide games as military training exercises. Roger enjoyed the stalking exercises where they had to get as close to Mr Emerson as they could without being seen. He had plenty of patience and was ready to lie still between every move, so he achieved good results every time.

One of the wide games brought them close to a fairly wide, shallow, fast-running stream – almost a river really. Joe took a good look at it and said to Cardew, "Do ee think I could be excused this afternoon's wide game?"

Cardew looked at Joe and then he looked at the river. "Do I want to know why?" he said.

"Shouldn't think so," said Joe.

"Do you want Wallace to stay with you?"

"Might be useful," Joe said.

"See you both back at camp then – oh, and don't get caught."

"If us do, you don't know nothin' about it anyway."

The patrol went on its way leaving Joe and Roger behind.

"What are you up to?" asked Roger.

"You'll soon see," said Joe. "Just keep quiet and stay still."

He took off his shoes and socks and then took off his shorts as well. He tucked his shirt into his underpants and waded out into the stream. There were rocks in the stream forming dams and rapids, but on the upstream side of some of the rocks the water was still.

Joe waded out to one of these and bent low over the water. He lowered his hands into the water, just below the surface. Roger was not too sure what happened next, it all happened so quickly. There was a splash, Joe seemed to bend even further forwards and his hands came up holding a fish.

He threw it onto the bank and said, "Take'n further up the bank and cover'n over where he'll be safe."

Roger did as he was told and came back to find Joe bent over again with his hands in the water. About three quarters of an hour later Joe could stand it no longer. His feet were frozen but he had caught four trout. They would make a useful addition to the evening food supplies.

"You're brilliant," said Roger, "absolutely brilliant."

"Yes I be idn I?" answered Joe. "Keep rubbing my feet with your scout scarf. They'm almost dead."

"Did old Sam teach you to catch fish like that and to do all the other things you do, like catching rabbits."

"Old Sam? What our farm labourer?"

"Yes. He taught me a few things before the war."

"I s'pose he did teach us a few things. He was quite fond of a bit of poaching. But Dad taught us a lot too. When you live in the country you learn to live off the country as much as you can."

The two of them made their way back to camp, checking Joe's rabbit snares on the way. A pheasant was caught in one of them. Joe's scout hat covered it beautifully while he caught and killed it.

"Us idn doin' bad, I reckon," said Joe. "Rabbit pie, trout and now pheasant. I reckon I shall get my cooking badge after all this."

But they had to be rather careful to cook the trout without Mr Emerson getting to know; and they plucked the pheasant well away from the camp and buried the feathers. It tasted all the better for the secrecy involved, though one pheasant shared out between a whole patrol didn't leave much for each boy.

17

The Wide Game

During that particular camp there was one wide game which Roger enjoyed more than any of the others. It was one which gave the Swift patrol the most interesting task.

A large area of the Squire's land was sub-divided between the other four patrols. They were the defenders. Their task was to spot the Swift patrol; follow them without themselves being seen; and at the same time, co-ordinate all the defence patrols in such a way that they would be able to prepare a trap where the Swifts would be captured or 'killed'. This they were to do by using semaphore signallers posted on the hills. Their chief handicap was that they didn't know the target the Swift patrol was aiming at.

The Swift patrol was given a secret starting point and a target which had to be 'blown up'. It was required to pass through some part of every patrol's defence area but it could follow any route it chose.

Cardew divided his patrol into two. He took four of the boys with him, but put Roger, Joe and Philip Jonas as a separate group. They were to follow the first group. If the first group was seen and followed they would take no action to save their friends. They would simply make alternative plans and try to reach the target on their own. This gave the patrol two chances of success instead of one.

Cardew led the patrol into a narrow stream – more like a ditch really. It was completely overgrown with brambles and undergrowth so the patrol was able to creep along it almost as if they were in a tunnel. They moved slowly along for a good half a mile and came out in a stretch of fairly thick woodland.

"Keep off the paths and move from tree to tree. When I move, you move."

It was hard going, and quite boggy in places. Sticks breaking underfoot made it virtually impossible to move silently, and everywhere there were those ruddy brambles tearing at their legs. Shorts and socks were no protection at all.

A couple of hundred yards behind, Roger, Joe and Philip followed, keeping close watch. It was Joe who saw the 'sniper' hidden at the top of a tree. He had seen the patrol and in his excitement failed to count its numbers. From his perch in the tree he waved to his signaller up on the hill showing which way the patrol was heading. Then he climbed down the tree and began to track the Swifts. Roger said, "For the moment, we'll track HIM. It will take them some time to get people together and they'll all be rushing to get well ahead so no one will be watching for us."

So, right through the woods, Cardew led his group, followed by the sniper, who signalled out from time to time to his fellow defenders. And he was followed in turn by Roger, Joe and Philip. It wasn't long before they discovered what the defenders' strategy had been.

They had set three lines of boys. 'Snipers' on the outer edges of the defence areas and another line of 'snipers' in the central woodlands. And between them, on the hills, they had set their signallers. The 'snipers' from the perimeter were now running hell for leather to the collection point where the final trap would be set, depending on the route the Swift patrol followed. As soon as they had been passed, the signallers were doing the same. Meanwhile the 'snipers' in the woods were joining one another in a following group behind the Swift patrol. This meant that the outer fringes of the defences were now completely emptied of defenders.

It also meant that Cardew and his group were now aware that they had been seen and were being tracked. There was no point in secrecy or silence any more. Only speed could get them to their objective before the defenders were massed in their way – speed and a bit of cunning.

Cardew suddenly switched route and led his patrol, still pretending to try to keep under cover, off towards the Manor

House. The defenders took the bait. They had guessed that the Manor House might be the target. Now they knew – or so they thought. Semaphore signals went from hill to hill and the defenders moved to set the trap. Roger took Cardew's move as his own cue: "The right hand flank will be clear of defenders now so that's the side we'll take, and we shouldn't need to be too careful about being spotted."

The trio swung away right through the woods, and then along their edge and around a wide sweep of fields until they approached their real target, the saw-mills.

As they drew near Philip said, "Roger. It was pretty obvious that this might have been one of the targets. They might have left a group of defenders there just in case."

"I hadn't thought of that. You're right. We'd better switch to stalking tactics, spaced wide."

So the three began a slow advance on their target. Meanwhile, half a mile from the Manor House, Cardew suddenly changed direction again and took his group at full tilt towards the saw-mills. There was no attempt at taking cover now. The defenders at the Manor House set off in pursuit and semaphore signals were flagged from hilltop to hilltop to the saw-mills: 'Attackers coming. Bridleway One. Head them off. We follow.'

The trap was set and was inescapable now. Twelve boys streamed out from the saw-mills to lay an ambush at the top of Bridleway One. Joe was the first to see them going. He wriggled over to Roger and told him and they signalled to Philip to join them. The saw-mills lay defenceless before them. They ran in and found Mr Emerson.

"We've blown up the saw-mills, sir."

Down on Bridleway One, Cardew and the others were being bombarded with mud grenades. Mr Emerson's whistle summoned them all back to the saw-mills and for the first time they realised to their dismay that they had only trapped part of the Swift patrol.

The target had been 'blown up'.

"Well done you three," said Cardew.

Mr Emerson had been following the progress of the whole exercise and was well pleased. He felt that both sides had come out of it with a good deal of credit, and he said so.

The camp continued for a full two weeks before all the final clearing up and the return to school. Mr Emerson made a final inspection. Apart from the wear and tear of two weeks of boys, which nature would soon hide, there must be no sign that they had been there. The troop paraded and Mr Emerson stood before them with a tray.

"See this?" (a piece of frayed twine about four inches long). "It was left where the Eagles' bivvy stood. These two pieces of reed were on the ground by the Seagulls tent area. And here's a broken tent peg which someone threw carelessly into the woods." (So it went on). "No patrol is perfect. The enemy knows that you have been here." (He paused.) "But it has been a first class camp. Fine show. Dismiss and march in your patrols back to school."

And so back to school and within a few days, home for the summer holidays.

18

Summer 1943

At long last Roger's father gave way. The bombing was so reduced that he decided that Roger and Margaret could come home for the holidays. So Roger joined the boys on the coach to the tiny station six miles from school. When people saw the boys getting onto the train, they moved to leave the boys with compartments to themselves.

It was a long time since Roger had been on a train and the journey to Waterloo was a long one. He was soon bored. Some boys seemed to love trains and train journeys. He was not one of them.

He leaned out of the window and got smuts in his eyes. The compartment itself was grubby and dusty. Boy though he was, he soon felt that he would need a good bath when he arrived home.

Conversation was desultory and Roger gave himself up to a book and to his thoughts and feelings. He had been so excited when he heard he was going home. Now he hadn't even got there and he was bored stiff. What was it going to be like? As they approached Waterloo his excitement returned.

They all piled off the train, separating as their parents met them. Roger's mother was there. She took him in her arms, she was so thrilled to see him. He wished she wouldn't do that, not in front of the other boys. It was embarrassing.

They crossed to the other side of Waterloo and took a local (electric) train. For the first time Roger began to find the journey interesting. Everything was so built up. Row upon row of houses and chimney pots. He laughed and said, "I've never seen so many chimney pots in my life. It's a good job we don't have to count them."

"Funny boy," his mother thought. It was going to be strange having the children home again. She wondered how they would be. Would they settle?

By now Roger was noticing the bomb damage: sometimes individual buildings, sometimes a whole row.

"Gosh. There is a lot of damage isn't there."

"Yes dear there is. Now perhaps you can begin to understand why your father would never let you come home."

"Is the bombing all over now we are winning the war?"

"It's not all over, but it isn't anything like it used to be."

They got off the train and caught the bus to the end of their road and then they walked home. They had left Roger's trunk at the station for his father to collect.

It felt strange being home. Everything was just as it used to be. The small front garden was full of roses, his dad's pride and joy. The house was just the same but quiet somehow with no Alfie or Eric or Jerry. And Margaret was still not home either. They had to go back up to London the next day to meet her.

Roger ran upstairs and straight up the next flight to the playroom in the attic. He went to his old toy cupboard. There were so many things he wanted to see again. But his toy cupboard was bare. He couldn't believe it. Where were all his things? Where was his toy dog? Where was his teddy? Where were his cowboys and Indians, his farm, his soldiers? Where were his books?

He ran downstairs to his mother. "All my things have gone."

"Things dear?" She knew what he meant but what could she say to him. She needed time to think. "Things dear? What things?"

"All my toys. My dog and my teddy."

"What does a big boy like you want with a toy dog or a teddy?"

"They were *mine*. Where are they?" He was accusing now and his mother was uncomfortable.

"You know, it is impossible to get toys nowadays with the war and the bombing and all that."

"That's why I want them. Where are all my toys?"

"So many people have been bombed out and left with nothing. Their poor children lost everything. They didn't have any toys to cuddle or to play with."

"You've given them away haven't you. You've given my toys away. And you didn't even ask me. They were *mine*. You had no right to give them away." He burst into tears and ran out of the room.

He knew he was being mingy. He knew he was being silly too. His mother was right. What did he want with a stupid old dog and a teddy bear. . . But he did want his dog and his teddy. All right, so he was twelve years old. But that didn't stop him wanting his old things. And if he had them he might have been willing to give them away. But he hadn't been asked. It wasn't fair. It wasn't right. He went into a sulk. He walked out of the front door and slammed it behind him.

His mother watched as he walked, unthinking, with his hands in his pockets, across to the park. It was instinctive.

"Oh dear," she thought. "What a home-coming." It had never entered her head that those old things would mean so much to him. But at least he had slotted back into something of the old life-style. Like all the other boys, if he wasn't at home she could be sure that he would be in the park.

As Roger walked into the park, it seemed to have shrunk. It wasn't even as big as the sports' fields at school. He walked slowly all round the perimeter path. A couple of teenagers were playing tennis on the park courts. Three more were messing about with a football. He didn't know any of them. He strolled over to the footballers.

"Can anyone play?" he asked.

"If you don't mind playing in goal," one of them answered.

"No, I don't mind."

So he joined them – not just for an hour there and then but for an hour or so almost every day of the holidays. It was to be by far the best part of the holidays. More than anything else, it kept him from getting bored stiff. But in spite of it, it wasn't long before he was wishing himself back at school.

That evening his father came home from work but as soon as the meal was over he settled down to some office paperwork. Roger and his mother played cards. And every evening afterwards (except Sundays) he and his mother and Margaret played cards or Monopoly. They were quite content. It was the day-time that was difficult. He and Margaret had grown apart. She spent her time

115

with her mother. She even did a bit of cooking. Roger went over to the park or wandered off on his own.

He walked to his old school. It hadn't changed. But because of the holidays there was no one there. It didn't seem so far away. Distances had shrunk. He went to see Jimmy Smith. Jimmy was tinkering with his Dad's old motor-bike.

"Does your Dad let you do that?"

"Course ee does. Ee 'elps me. He showed me 'ow to take it apart and put it together. An' if ee can get a bit of petrol ee takes me out on it. And sometimes ee lets me drive it."

"But you're not old enough."

"That don't matter, not if you don't get caught, and there ain't many coppers about."

"But you're not big enough."

"I can reach."

Roger watched for a while, and then asked, "Is that what you do all the time, just mess about with your dad's motor-bike?"

"Sometimes I go up the garridge and 'elp the mechanics up there."

Roger still liked Jimmy but he had no interest in engines and no skill in that direction either. Some of the boys at school were never happier than when they were tinkering with their father's cars or tractors. He was afraid to touch such things for fear that he would break them or lose a part that was essential. If he tried, he would be bound to muck things up.

"I'll be off then," he said.

"Yeh. See yer."

It was obvious to Roger that it didn't matter to Jimmy whether he saw him or not. It had been pleasant to meet each other again, but they no longer had anything in common.

On Sundays they went to chapel and visited their grandparents and their uncles and aunts. Everybody seemed to have shrunk – especially his favourite grandmother. She welcomed him as if he had never been away. She made no fuss at all but he knew she was pleased to see him – and Margaret, of course. He gave her a hug because he felt he wanted to. He was happier to see her again than anybody.

So many of the uncles and aunts just made him sick. How they did go on. Fuss, fuss, fuss. He hated it.

"My hasn't he grown? What a big boy you are now. I suppose

we shouldn't call you a boy. A real little man aren't you. You'll be in long trousers soon. And look at Margaret, quite the lady. Isn't she growing up to be a beauty?"

On and on they went, and it wasn't even true, or so Roger thought. He hadn't grown much. Margaret was as big as he was, well almost, even though she was so much younger. It wasn't fair. Everyone else grew but he never did. At school his pals had all left him behind. He was even still singing soprano in the school choir.

One night the siren went. His father looked up from his paperwork and then just went on working. His mother made no comment. They just went on playing cards. There was plenty of noise as the guns tried to shoot the planes down and as the bombs fell but it was obvious that people had got so used to it all that they didn't take much notice any more. It wasn't a big raid after all, and before long the 'all clear' sounded.

When Roger went over to the park the following morning one of the boys showed him a chunk of shrapnel he had found.

"I've got a smashing collection at home."

"Can I come and see it? We don't have bombing where I am at school."

So he went and saw a host of bits of metal, shell cases and even small pieces of the wreckage of planes. How much he had missed. He felt quite envious. On his way home he went to see where Rachel Pollard had lived. She had been a smashing kid. Now she was dead and her house was just a heap of rubble. Like Eric, he would never see her again. He thought about all the people he had known and liked at school before the war. Had any others died?

The more he stayed at home, the more he felt that he didn't belong there. It was strange. He seemed to feel that way everywhere. He wasn't really a townie any more, not like Jimmy Smith. But he wasn't a country boy like Joe either. Margaret had found a Judy Garland record amongst the collection at home. On one side Judy Garland sang a song about being 'Sweet Sixteen'. On the other side the song was about being younger than sixteen and Margaret never stopped playing it. Roger almost knew the words off by heart. Margaret played it so often that Roger thought it must describe how she felt. He didn't ask her. But it certainly described how he felt: 'Hide yourself behind the screen, You shouldn't be heard, you shouldn't be seen, You're just an awful IN-BETWEEN.'

When the holiday was over his mother came with him to Waterloo again. But he told her that she mustn't kiss him or cuddle him at Waterloo. So they hugged at home and although Roger was quite glad that the holiday was over, he still felt that he didn't want to leave his mum. He giggled to himself. She would have been horrified to know that he thought of her as his 'mum'. 'Mum' was such a common word. She insisted on being called 'Mother'.

Their actual journey together passed almost in silence. But as they drew into Waterloo Roger said, "I'm a Perspinian now."

"Yes dear. That's nice for you isn't it." She hadn't the faintest idea what he was talking about. He had been at that school for a year already.

"There'll be a new lot of 'bucking new snips'," he mused. "You see mother, you're not regarded as a proper Perspinian when you first go there." And then he added proudly, "But I am one now."

His mother still didn't understand, but if it made him happy to go back to school it was obviously all right. They crossed to the other part of the station. Bradders and some of the other Londoners were already there and Roger joined them. His mother chatted to some of the other parents and waved as the train drew out of the station. She felt almost redundant. The boy didn't seem to need her any more. Thank goodness she still had Margaret.

19

A Bit of Bother About Beds

Back at school, Roger checked his dorm. He had been moved again to Dorm 20 right up on the top floor above the staffroom.

He took his trunk and began to manhandle it up the stairs. He rested outside the staffroom before heaving it up, end over end, to the very top. It suddenly struck him that there didn't seem to be any rhyme or reason to the numbers of the dorms. He had already been in 16, 28 and 23. He wondered how the dorms had got their numbers, but it was only a passing thought.

He found a spare bed and buffalo and unpacked his trunk. As he looked round the dorm, a small one with only twelve boys in it, he wasn't very pleased. Only Dave of his best friends was there and there were one or two of the boys he didn't like. Opposite him poor old Parsnips was busy unpacking his trunk. Roger reckoned that he wouldn't be very happy to be back again. All through his first year he had been tormented by the form 2 bullies and now they were all in form 3 together.

Roger took his trunk down the stairs and out to the tower to be stored. Then he made his way to his new classroom. Joe was already there and had bagged a double desk for the two of them. They were beside a window that looked out at nothing in particular – but at least it looked out. It would give them something to gaze at when lessons were boring.

The trouble with this classroom was that it was right under the staffroom. Just imagine, his dorm above the staffroom and his class below it. Messing about was going to be difficult this year.

He decided to go back up to the dorm. At the bottom of the

stairs he found Parsons struggling with his mattress. "D'you want a hand?"

"Yes please."

"How did it get down here?"

"Wilkins and Cooke dropped it down."

"Well, we'd better get it up again."

So the two of them began the long haul up the stairs. As they reached the staffroom landing, Mr Smart was waiting for them. He ignored Parsons. "Well, well, well. Welcome back Wallace! I might have known. You're starting the new term as you mean to continue I suppose."

Roger was puzzled. "Sir?" he queried.

"What is that mattress doing down here?"

"It fell down the stairs sir."

"Ah yes: leapt off the bed, bounced out of the dorm and fell down the stairs. Is that what happened Wallace or did you throw it down?"

Roger coloured angrily. "No sir. I didn't throw it down. I wasn't there sir. I found Parsons trying to carry it upstairs and gave him a hand sir."

"Oh very noble of you I'm sure," said Mr Smart sarcastically. Then he turned for the first time to Parsons. "Is that true boy?"

"Yes sir."

"Hm. So somebody else threw the mattress down." He didn't wait for an answer. He leapt up the stairs to the dorm and confronted the boys who were there. "Which of you threw Parsons' mattress downstairs?"

There was no reply.

"Come now. Either the guilty boys own up or I scat the lot of you."

There was still no reply. All four of them had been in on it, though it was Wilkins' idea. So, as Parsons and Roger arrived at the top of the stairs, the four of them followed Mr Smart to the staffroom for their first scatting of the term. At the first opportunity afterwards, Wilkins hissed at Parsons, "I'll get you for that you dirty little sneak."

And on Sunday he took his revenge. The beds had iron bedsteads with metal, linking springs. But almost all of the beds had springs missing and that made them slack to sleep on.

Instead of going on their Sunday afternoon walk, Wilkins and

Cooke made their way up to the dorm armed with an old fashioned metal key each. They got under Parsons' bed and began to unloose spring after spring, taking them to their own beds to fill up the gaps. By the time their own beds were complete, there was a large hole in the middle of the springs on Parsons' bed.

That night, when Parsons went to bed his mattress sagged down through the hole until it was almost touching the floor.

"What's the matter with your bed, Parsnips?" asked Roger.

"I think some of the springs have gone," he replied.

"That'll teach you not to sneak on other people," laughed Wilkins nastily. "Sleep well."

"He didn't sneak on you," said Roger. "He didn't say anything about you at all. But old Smarty's not a fool. You shouldn't have thrown the mattress downstairs."

"Oh shut up Wallace unless you want a thumping."

Roger didn't want a thumping and both Wilkins and Cooke were a good deal bigger than he was, so he kept quiet but he was seething.

The following morning at the end of the morning break he took Parsons to one side. "Come on Parsnips. Come up to the dorm with me."

"But we're not allowed up the dorm in break time."

"Never mind that."

"But we'll get caught as we go past the staffroom."

"So we won't go past the staffroom. We'll go the long way round." He led Parsons up a different stairway, through two other dormitories to their own. "Now," he said. "Give me a hand with your bedding. We'll put it on the next bed."

"But what . . ?"

"Come on. We haven't got much time." So they heaved Parsons' bedding off his bedstead. "Now do the same with Wilkins'."

"Oh but I don't think . . ."

"Shut up and do as I tell you."

Parsons caved in. They took Wilkins's bedding off his bedstead and then the two of them switched the bedsteads. They put Wilkins' bedding back on the bedstead with the hole in it and Parsons now had just about the best bedstead in the dorm.

"Make sure you get up here early tonight. We want to watch Wilkins when he comes into the dorm. You know what he

f

always does."

Parsons did know and he giggled. Then he stopped. "There's going to be all hell let loose when he finds out."

"Well you keep out of it. You don't know anything about it. I'll deal with Wilkins." Roger spoke with a bravado he didn't feel but it was time someone stuck up for poor old Parsnips.

That evening the two of them were the first into the dorm. They made a pretence of getting ready for bed but they were both feeling anxious and tense. Wilkins arrived at the top of the stairs and began to run. He ran straight into the dorm and leapt onto his bed, ready to spring up into the air. Instead, his mattress went straight through the hole in the springs and he fell forward awkwardly. Everybody burst out laughing – even Cooke. But Wilkins wasn't laughing. He picked himself up and swung round on Parsons.

"Parsnips," he roared. "You've done it this time."

"It wasn't Parsnips," Roger said quietly. "It was me."

"Bloody Wallace." He turned on Roger and then went for him.

But Roger was expecting it. He threw himself at Wilkins with all his force, pummelling away at Wilkins' chest and stomach as hard as he could go. In the confined space of the dorm, Wilkins couldn't make as much use as he wanted of his extra size and Roger was like a mad thing. Cooke wondered whether to join in but boys from the opposite dorm were flocking across and some of them were Roger's friends. Soon there was quite a din as rival supporters shouted their favourite on.

Wilkins managed to get Roger down onto the ground where his superior weight told, but he still didn't have room to lash into Roger properly and Roger was like an eel, wriggling furiously away underneath and still punching up at the boy above him. He was hurting Wilkins more than the bigger boy had ever been hurt in his life.

And then suddenly everything went quiet. Wilkins looked round to see why and came face to face with Mr Smart. He scrambled to his feet and Roger did the same. They stood side by side. Roger only just reached up to Wilkins' shoulders.

Mr Smart's first instinct was to scat both of them, but then he saw the disparity in their sizes. It would do young Wallace good to have a thrashing and Wilkins was just the boy to give him one. The more complete young Wallace's humiliation the better. And then he noticed Wilkins' bed.

"Whose bed is that?"

"Mine sir."

"And I suppose Wallace is responsible for the lack of springs?"

As quick as a flash Roger replied, "Oh no sir. Wilkins took the springs out himself."

"A likely story. You Wilkins, will go to see Mr Battersby in the morning and ask him to replace your bedstead."

"Yes sir."

"That deals with that little matter. Now. You know that fighting is not allowed in dormitories."

There was a murmur of acknowledgement.

"The proper place for fights to take place is behind the gym. You all know that. I see that there are boys from two dorms here. You will all get dressed and go down behind the gym. There, these two boys can continue their fight to the finish. You have half an hour and then I shall give you a further quarter of an hour to get yourselves to bed. Is that understood?"

"Yes sir."

"Then get a move on."

The boys dressed quickly and sped to the back of the gym. There hadn't been a proper fight down there for ages. Poor old Wallace was in for it now they reckoned. Roger reckoned so too but he didn't care. He would make as good a fight of it as he could. And if he could hurt Wilkins a bit he would. It was time someone stood up to the rotten bully. He made his way to the back of the gym where the boys had formed a circle. He stood inside the circle and waited for Wilkins to arrive.

Some of the older boys had heard what was going on and they joined the circle so that before long half the school was there. And still they waited for Wilkins to come. But Wilkins knew that this would be a boxing match. He wouldn't be allowed to wrestle Roger to the ground and sit on him and pummel him into submission. The two would have to stand and slog it out. He wasn't too keen on that. Roger had hurt him when he had come at him fists flying.

Wilkins and Cooke made their way down the stairs and across the quad and then Wilkins turned to Cooke and said, "Go and tell Wallace I'll let him off this time."

Before Cooke could respond, he had turned and was heading

back up to the dorm. Cooke hesitated. "Crikey. Wilkins was funky." He dithered. Should he go and tell people or not.

Eventually he decided that he had better go.

By the time he arrived people were getting impatient and there was a good deal of noise. As Cooke joined the crowd and made his way through the centre of the ring more and more people asked him, "Where's Wilkins? Why is he keeping us waiting so long?"

They fell silent.

"Wilkins is not coming," said Cooke. He felt sick. He was blowed if he would ever support Wilkins again. "He said I was to tell Wallace that he would let him off this time."

There were hoots of laughter, jeers, yells of "cowardy custard", "the dirty funk", "fancy being scared of Wallace". But Roger felt nothing but relief. He found that he was trembling from head to foot. And then quite suddenly, he felt sorry for Wilkins. He knew that Wilkins would never live this down.

They made their way back to their dorms. Wilkins was already in his bed with his bum almost touching the floor. He said nothing and nobody spoke to him either. They all felt a bit flat. It was as if Wilkins had not only let himself down, he had let them all down. Without quite understanding why, they felt tainted – all except Parsons.

As he got into bed that night he knew that his long nightmare was over. Wilkins and Cooke would never bully him again. He might even begin to enjoy school now.

Down in the quad, Mr Smart drew one of the senior boys to one side. "How did the fight go between Wallace and Wilkins?" he asked.

"Wilkins funked it," said the boy, "so there wasn't a fight at all."

Fury swept through Mr Smart's whole being. That nasty little brat had got off scot free. 'Except, young Wallace,' he thought, 'that I shall remember. One of these days you'll come a cropper I promise you.'

But it was almost the end of term before he did.

20

Tatey Pickin'

They had only been back at school for a couple of weeks when form 3 was sent out of school for the day. They dressed in a mixture of scout and rugby clothes with extra layers for warmth.

"What's it all about?" Roger asked Joe.

"Us be gwain tatey pickin'," Joe answered. He didn't sound very thrilled at the prospect.

"What's tatey pickin'?" asked Roger.

"Spud digging," answered Bradders. "It's part of the war effort and it gets us off school all day." He and the other town boys who didn't know what they were in for were delighted.

The coach arrived soon after Assembly and took them a few miles away to the farm where they were to work. They piled off the coach carrying a pack of sandwiches each and walked up a muddy farm track into the yard. Two great carthorses were standing there harnessed to their carts and the farmer told the boys to climb into the carts. He hoisted Roger and one or two of the others onto the back of the carthorses. Roger reckoned this day was going to be a bit of all right.

They bumped further along the lane, lurching from side to side. Roger's horse crapped a load of turd and the smell rose to greet the boys.

"Pyaw."

"Phew."

"Ugh."

And a cart-load of giggles.

The second horse was anxious not to disappoint his load of

boys so he let loose with a string of farts and the comments that followed were almost as ripe as the smell.

Out in the field, the farmer got down to work at once. He told the boys to stow their sandwiches in the hedge and then gave each of them a sack and lined them across the field. The field was wet, muddy, sticky and heavy. The farmer climbed up into his waiting tractor, drove to one end of the field, lowered his digger and began to turn up the first row of potatoes.

Philip Jonas looked at it in astonishment. "I never knew spuds grew in fields," he said.

"Vool," commented Joe. "Where do ee think they growed then?"

"In gardens I suppose. I just hadn't really thought about it at all."

The digger worked on a spiral, circular system and threw the potatoes anything up to three yards from the row. As it passed, each boy began work, collecting the potatoes and putting them in his sack. Soon all conversation stopped as the boys worked desperately to try to keep up with the tractor.

When Joe's sack was full, with a twirl of his body, he lifted it onto his shoulder and carried it over to the cart. An old man took it from him, emptied it on the cart and gave Joe the sack again. By this time Roger and Jonas both had full sacks.

"I can't lift my sack," admitted Roger.

"Neither can I," said Jonas.

"Gyaw. Bliddy townies," snorted Joe. " 'Tis only about a hunderdweight. You'm soft, the lot of ee. Gi' us your sack Jonas."

With another twirl of his body he lifted it onto his shoulder and set off for the cart. Roger took hold of the top of his sack, twirled his body and lifted – and landed flat on his back. Joe gave up picking up potatoes and took to supervising a group of boys and carrying their sacks to the cart.

They hadn't been working long when Jonas picked up a potato that squelched and collapsed in his hand, squirting a nasty mixture of liquid potato all over his clothes.

Joe shouted, " 'ant you got no sense at all. Can't ee zee when tiddies is bad? My gor." He showed Jonas which potatoes were bad and which were good. Roger watched carefully. The bad ones were obvious when you knew what to look out for, but how were they to know?

They worked on. Bend down, pick up, into the sack, bend

down, pick up, into the sack, on and on all morning. It was murder. But at last it was lunch-time. The boys collapsed into the hedge exhausted. A cart-load of potatoes had gone up to the farm and emptied its load. Now it returned with the farmer's wife and a great urn of tea. The boys drank thankfully and ate their sandwiches but they still felt hungry when they had finished.

" 'Ad enough to eat boys?" asked the farmer's wife, "or do ee think you could manage some of those yer?"

She uncovered plate after plate of pasties. Suddenly the day didn't seem so bad after all. But Joe warned Roger, "Don't ee be a pig mind. Us got to work after an' if you pig yourself you'll be sick as a dog."

So Roger ate but didn't stuff. The farmer's sons ate sensibly but some of the others ate until they were fit to burst. Then they leaned back in the autumn sunshine, laying in the hedge ready to sleep off their exhaustion and their food.

"Come on then boys. Us mustn't waste the day."

So they struggled back into line and began again. On and on: bend down, pick up, into the sack; bend down, pick up, into the sack. Just occasionally the digger got stuck and the boys had a brief respite but it was never long enough. The work went on all afternoon, on and on until daylight began to turn to dusk. The horses with their loaded carts set off back to the farm.

"Well done you boys, and thank ee very much." The farmer was a man of few words.

The boys dragged themselves wearily along the lane behind the horses and carts to the farm. They washed their hands at the pump in the yard and rinsed their sweat begrimed faces. Out came the farmer's wife again.

"I specs you could do with a mug of tea boys, and p'raps some bread and cream."

Great hunks of bread and jam and cream lifted their spirits before they made their way back to the coach and to school for a bath, prep, Assembly and bed.

Three weeks later they were off again but this time they were far less enthusiastic about it. They knew what was in store, or so they thought.

This time they were sent to a government-owned farm. They were carried in the carts out to a huge expanse of field where work had already begun. A long line of men stretched across the field and the boys joined them. Dotted around the hedge a few soldiers were loafing about smoking cigarettes. Each of them had a rifle.

At first the boys worked at one end of the line and the men at the other. Work was much easier than it had been the first time. The government farm had the very latest in equipment. The tractor and digger lifted the potatoes onto a kind of chain grid. The potatoes bumped up and down on the grid and then fell onto the earth in a neat row which was much easier for picking up.

Although it was such hard work, the men never seemed to stop talking. They chattered away nineteen to the dozen.

"They're Italian prisoners of war," whispered Jonas.

Every so often one of the men wandered over to the hedge and had a pee. The boys looked in astonishment. They didn't try to hide what they were doing. They just pissed anywhere and everywhere. It was so embarrassing. And then the men would wander over and chat to one of the guards and have a smoke before drifting back into line.

Slowly the men and the boys mingled and worked side by side. Sometimes the men even broke into song. It was all very strange. They seemed to want to make friends but they were enemies. Roger found himself working beside one of them.

"My name is Luigi Baldasarre. What is your name please?"

"Roger Wallace."

"I prisoner of war."

"Yes."

"I damn glad to be prisoner. No more fighting. No more bloody 'itler."

"Oh!" Roger was surprised.

"I no get killed and after war I go home. Iss better no?"

"Well yes, I suppose so." Roger had never thought of war like that. "Being a prisoner is better than getting killed."

"You student no?"

"Yes, I'm at school."

"You study Athens and Sparta?"

"Yes."

"The Spartans and the Germans and the Japanese, they say iss better to die than to surrender. The Athenians say iss better to live. I say iss better too. So I surrender."

"Where were you fighting?"

"In the desert. Iss hot. Iss dirty. Not nice. I surrender. Iss nice camp with my friends. Iss food. Iss bath every week. And now I meet you. Nice English boy."

Roger was embarrassed.

"You got girlfriend?"

"No."

"Course you 'ave. EVERY boy got girlfriends."

"No I haven't." He pointed at Bradders. "He has."

The Italian turned to Bradders. "You got girlfriend?"

Bradders laughed. "Yes, lots."

"Thass right. What is your name please?"

"Oh call me Bradders. Everyone else does."

"You got 6d Bradders?"

Bradders hesitated. He felt suspicious. "Why do you want to know?"

"You got 6d, I make it into damn fine ring for your girlfriend."

"Oh yeah."

"I do. You ask my friends. They tell, I make all kinds of things. Bertolini," he called to one of the other prisoners, "you tell these guys. Don' I make damn fine rings."

"Iss true," answered Bertolini.

So, with some hesitation, Bradders handed over 6d and some of the other boys followed suit. Roger didn't have a girlfriend and he didn't have a 6d.

When they broke for lunch the two groups separated. The boys ate their sandwiches and an urn of tea supplied their drinks, but there were no pasties here, no extras at all. After lunch they went back to work and Luigi amazed the boys by supplying rings to all those who had given him sixpences.

Roger felt quite jealous. How had Luigi managed it? He couldn't have made all those rings in the lunch hour. Roger reckoned that he made rings in the camp and brought them with him, then he swapped them for the sixpences. Did he make a bit of money for himself, he wondered.

There were other spud-digging days each autumn term. The boys were never sure whether they preferred the perks of pasties and cream teas, or the fun of working with Italians. But there came a day which they didn't like at all. It was also on a Government farm and again they were working alongside prisoners of war. But this time there were more guards and they all stayed alert. There was no singing or chatter from the men and there was no mingling of men and boys.

The prisoners were German. They were arrogant and sullen, not at all pleased to be prisoners. They still believed that they were going to win the war and then they would get their own back on these despised British who made them do such menial tasks. The master race was made for better things than putting potatoes in sacks. Roger felt uncomfortable working alongside them, and even a bit overawed and frightened.

At the end of term each boy received an envelope with his wages. They were paid 3d an hour for the hardest work they were ever likely to do. But to boys like Roger whose pocket money was still negligible, it was a small fortune and just in time for Christmas too. But before that end of term pay-day, Roger had to survive one almighty crisis.

21

Unnatural Practices

At the end of that term each form was to produce a one act play. Dave and Roger both had parts in *The Monkey's Paw*. But Roger was hopeless at learning his lines – not that he had many.

Night after night he got into Dave's bed and they rehearsed together with a torch under the bedclothes. One night they were rehearsing as usual when the bedclothes were suddenly pulled off them. Mr Smart stood there.

"Two boys in one bed. And one of them Wallace of course. The Headmaster will be very interested to hear about this."

He paused for a long time and then just said, "Get back to your own bed you filthy boy."

Roger scuttled back to his own bed, but after Mr Smart had gone he crawled over to Dave's bed again. "I'm sorry," he said. "It looks as though I've got you into trouble." He felt particularly guilty because Dave was never in trouble.

"That's all right," said Dave. "Why did he call you a 'filthy boy'?"

"I don't know. He hates me. That's probably why. He always has hated me ever since I was a bucking new snip. I don't know why. But he picks on me every chance he's got."

"He's a bit of a slimy turd isn't he. I don't think anyone likes him."

"Mrs Elliott does. Joe reckons there's something funny going on between Smarty and Mrs Elliott."

"D'you think he's right? They are always chatting together. But then Joe hates Smarty too, so perhaps he's just trying to think up nasty things about him."

"Joe's probably right. He always seems to have a pretty good idea what's going on. But yes, he's hated Smarty ever since he held up his homework in front of us all and made fun of it."

"You'd better get back to bed. You don't want him to catch you again."

"No. But I'm sorry I've got you in trouble." Roger crawled back to his bed.

After lunch the following day they were both summoned to the Head's study. Dave went in first and came out looking as white as a sheet and ready to burst into tears. He fled down the corridor without a word. Roger wondered what on earth was the matter. He had plenty of time to wonder because several other boys were called into the study before it was his turn. When he went into the study he found the Head looking grim. In fact, he had never seen the Head look so grim.

"Mr Smart tells me that he found you in bed with David Shaw last night."

"Yes sir. We were rehearsing our parts for *The Monkey's Paw* sir."

"Do you normally rehearse in bed?"

"I'm not very good at learning my lines sir, so I asked Dave – I mean Shaw sir – if he would help me. We're both in the play together."

The Head mumbled to himself. He often did. It gave him time to think. Both boys told the same story and they both seemed to be telling the truth. He had never known Shaw to be in trouble before. Yet Mr Smart had seemed so certain.

"Mr Smart believes that you were in bed together indulging in unnatural practices."

"I'm sorry sir. I don't know what you mean."

The Head was embarrassed. Was it possible that the boy didn't know? Shaw seemed just as ignorant. "I mean boy that Mr Smart believes that you and Shaw were doing sexual things together."

Now it was Roger's turn to be embarrassed, and shaken too. "I don't know what Mr Smart means sir. I don't know anything about sex except that boys change when they are old enough."

"And are you old enough, Wallace?"

Roger felt so ashamed. His friends were but he wasn't. Come to that Dave wasn't either. "No sir," he said.

132

"Drop your trousers boy."

Roger looked at him in amazement, but then he undid his fly buttons and let his shorts fall to the ground.

"And your underpants, and hold up your shirt tail."

Roger did as he was told and went crimson as the Head stared at his private parts.

"All right boy. Put your clothes back in order."

After Roger had put his clothes back on the Head said, "So you were rehearsing your play part last night in Shaw's bed."

"Yes sir."

"And you don't know anything about sex."

"No sir."

"You don't know the so-called 'facts of life'?"

"No sir."

"Then I'd better come and give your dorm a talking to." He paused. "Understand young Wallace that I will not tolerate boys being in bed with one another for *any purpose*. You hear me: not for *any purpose*."

"Yes sir."

"Very well. Off you go."

"Thank you sir."

Roger walked out of the study and then fled. He found Dave. "He looked at my pills," he said.

"Yes, he looked at mine too. Half the time I hadn't a clue what he was talking about."

"Nor me. He says he's going to come to our dorm and give us a lecture about something called 'the facts of life'."

And that night after lights out that is precisely what he did. One or two of the boys reckoned he came after dark because he was embarrassed. Farmers' sons mocked.

"I reckon ee ant niver zeed a bull goin' vor it with a cow, or a vitty stallion with his mare," chuckled Parsons. "Gyaw. Their cocks get huge when they'm mating."

"I haven't ever seen animals mating," said Roger, "so perhaps he hasn't, I didn't know that's how people have babies."

Parsons was astonished. "You really didn't know."

"No I didn't know. How would I?"

And that is where the whole thing should have come to an end. But it didn't.

Roger was fast asleep the following night and was woken by

another boy slipping into his bed. Who the hell was it? He didn't know why but he suddenly felt scared out of his wits.

"Are you awake Wallace?"

"Yes," he whispered as he turned to face the intruder. He knew who it was now. It was a senior boy called Thornton. And Roger could feel his cock pressing against him. It felt huge and hard.

"I hear you like getting into other boys' beds."

Roger was terrified. "It's not what you think."

"Oh. And what do I think Wallace?"

"Well it's nothing to do with sex."

"So you say. But you can feel me can't you. I'm nice and hard aren't I. Why don't you hold me?"

"No. I don't want to."

"How would you like to feel me between your legs."

Roger gripped his knees tight. "I wouldn't. I don't want anything to do with you."

"Perhaps you'd like me to push myself into your bum."

Now Roger *was* scared. "Get out. Get out of my bed or I'll yell."

"Oh no you won't Wallace. If we are found together you'll be expelled. But I'm leaving school this end of term anyway, so it won't make any difference to me. Now are you going to wank me off or what? Come on. Get hold of me and give me a stroke."

Roger didn't know what 'wank' meant but he grabbed hold of Thornton's cock and pushed it down as hard as he possibly could. Thornton roared with pain, tumbled out of bed and stumbled out of the dorm. Everyone was woken by the cry but no one knew what had caused it and no one saw who it was who stumbled out of the dorm. Roger kept very quiet. He was trembling all over and soaked in sweat. All round the dorm boys were asking one another what had happened. Roger pretended to be just as baffled as the rest of them. As a result, the mystery remained a mystery. No one ever got to know.

But the experience had sickened Roger. He couldn't wait for the term to end. He wanted to go home and he felt he never wanted to come back again.

But the night of the end of term plays drove the experience out of his mind for a while. The boy who took the main part of the father in *The Monkey's Paw* was the best actor in the school. He had put talcum powder in his fair hair to make himself look grey

134

and old. Late in the play, when tragedy struck, he ran his hands through his hair in the agony of the moment. Clouds of talcum powder filled the air. With any other boy it would have brought the house down in laughter and ruined the moment, but such was the power of the boy's acting that nobody laughed: not until afterwards.

And then the term was over. Roger hadn't come face to face with Thornton and now he never would. He went home for Christmas feeling very much happier. Thank goodness old Smarty hadn't found Thornton in his bed. That really would have been trouble.

22

The War Intrudes

The Christmas holidays passed swiftly enough. There were moments when Roger wondered about telling his mother about Thornton's visit to his bed. He wasn't sure that he wanted to go back to school. But he wasn't sure that he wanted to stay at home either. He didn't really know people at home any more.

If he stayed at home he would have to go to the grammar school. It would mean starting all over again, making new friends. He would never see Joe or Bradders or Dave again. And Thornton wasn't at Perspins any more. He decided to keep quiet and go back. There probably wouldn't be any more trouble.

They hadn't been back at school for long before the Russians drove the Germans back from Leningrad. Now it really looked as though the Germans had had it. It was like the defeat of Napoleon's armies all over again. And down in Italy the British and Americans were slowly grinding their way north.

In February there was the first terrible battle for Monte Casino but the Germans held fast. They were proving to be as dogged and determined in defence as they had been brilliant in attack. British commanders still felt that, man for man and weapon for weapon, the Germans were the best soldiers in the world.

There were minor battles around Perspins too, and increasing signs of the preparations for the invasion of France. When he was still living in Beddingford, Roger had seen the first landing craft around the coast. Now they were everywhere. A twenty mile stretch of the coast had been evacuated. All its inhabitants were gone, leaving the Americans free to practise their invasion skills using live ammunition.

And in the countryside near Perspins there were mock battles. The Americans were the attackers. The Home Guard and the school cadets were the defenders, with scouts acting as messenger boys. This was where Mr Emerson's training in wide games should have come into its own.

At the first of these battles, Joe and Roger were assigned to a Home Guard platoon manning a machine-gun post. The Americans began to appear in numbers behind a hedge not far away. The Home Guard sergeant sent Joe back to headquarters to tell Mr Emerson what was happening and to ask for reinforcements.

But reinforcements didn't come. The machine-gunners did well and held up the American advance 'killing' quite a lot of their troops. But eventually the post was overrun and all the members of the platoon were either killed or captured. As one of the captives, Roger was taken back to an American dug-out. He was surprised to see Joe there, spooning baked beans out of a tin.

"How did they capture you?" asked Roger. "You were nowhere near them."

"Well 'tis only a game init. I made sure they captured me."

"Didn't you take your message then?"

"No I got caught long before that."

"But why?"

"Can't ee zee you vool? There's baked beans, peanut butter, condensed milk, chewing gum, chocolate, fags. They got everything yer, an' us can 'ave as much as us likes."

Roger didn't think he could let himself be caught deliberately, not even for all that, but now he was caught he decided to tuck in with all the rest. And the following day he and a group of other boys made their way back over the battle-field. They explored the American dug-outs and scavenged for all they were worth.

They were particularly glad of these supplements to their school diet because it seemed to be even worse this term than it had ever been before. Throughout the previous year German U boats had been playing havoc with shipping in the Atlantic and food supplies were desperately tight. This was still true, even though the tide had turned and the Allies were beginning to win the war at sea.

Parents sent food supplies from home that boys stored in their tuck lockers. Every afternoon before tea, they raided their lockers to add to their school bread and scrape. There were cakes, eggs, tins of spam or corned beef, even cooked chickens sometimes. Almost all the boys shared what they had with all the others on their dining tables.

But they never seemed to have enough. For a hundred years Perspins boys had grumbled about their food. Now they seemed to have greater cause than ever.

At tea, each of them was given a small pat of butter. One day Roger noticed that the boys at the next table had bigger pats than the boys at his table. It wasn't fair. He grumbled to the others.

"Well, why don' ee go and zee Mrs Elliott then?" asked Joe.

"All right I will," answered Roger without moving.

"Git on with ee then."

"What now?"

"Course."

So Roger took his plate with its pat of butter, walked the length of the dining hall and through the door that led to the kitchen. Mr Wilcox didn't even seem to notice him go. The first person Roger saw was one of the kitchen maids called Gladys.

"Can I see Mrs Elliott please?"

" 'Er's in 'er room. Just go and knock on the door."

So he knocked and Mrs Elliott came to the door. She looked at him and at his plate.

"Well, what is it?"

Roger wished the floor would open and swallow him up.

"Please Mrs Elliott, we think the boys on the next table have got bigger pats of butter than we have."

She flushed angrily. "All of you have pats the same size," she said. "We are very careful to be fair."

"But they are not the same size Mrs Elliott. Really they are not. Theirs are fat and ours are thin."

"Oh you stupid boy. It is just that they have been cut in a different way. Come with me."

She took him to the dairy and took a half pound pack of butter. "Now," she said. "I'm going to cut this into sixteen pieces."

He watched while she cut the butter up.

"Count the pieces," she said.

"Sixteen," he counted.

She took another half pound pack of butter and cut that into sixteen pieces of a different shape.

"Count the pieces," she said.

Roger felt a worm. He didn't like Mrs Elliott much, especially because she was so friendly with Mr Smart, but he had to admit that she was right.

"Sixteen," he said. "I'm sorry," he mumbled looking at his feet. "We were wrong."

"Well just you go and tell the boys at your table that we try very hard to give you the best food we can and to be fair to everyone."

Roger went back and told the others.

"The best food! I like that," said Joe. " 'Tis worse than it's ever been."

And over the next few weeks the evidence began to mount that Joe was right.

The previous summer there had been two nasty incidents. The first was on a day when they had stew for their lunch. Suddenly Joe said, "Ugh. There's a fly in my dinner."

He took his glass, drank his glass of water down, turned the glass upside down and put the fly on it. Soon another boy found a fly and did the same. Then another and another. By the time the meal was over they had built a pyramid of glasses, each with a fly on it. Perhaps when the maids came to clear away they would see what the boys had to put up with.

And then there was the day when one of the senior boys found maggots in his rice. He went to the top table and showed it to the Head. The Headmaster stood and called for silence.

"Elliott has brought his bowl of rice to show me. It contains maggots with the rice. I would remind you that there is a war on and that seamen are dying to bring us our food. I would also remind you that meat is very good for you."

He picked up Elliott's bowl of rice and ate every last mouthful. Then he put the bowl on the table, served Elliott with another bowl from the top table and sent him back to his place.

"Now, eat all of you, and be thankful to God and to our brave merchant seamen."

But very few of the boys followed his example and most of the rice went out for pig-swill.

This term it was meat that caused problems. They sat down to their Sunday roast one week and were faced with a meat none of them recognised. Soon the question was being asked all around the dining hall. Inevitably there were a few boys who knew. There always were.

"Horse meat."

"Horse meat?"

"Horse meat."

"I idn eatin' 'orse meat. Tidn right."

"The French eat it all the time."

"Well there you be then. If they eat it, it can't be right can it. They eat frogs and snails too."

There was a lot of argument. On the whole townies were prepared to give it a go but the farm lads wouldn't touch it. Being a Sunday, the Head was eating at home. But he was called. He came and gave them a lecture while their food went cold and the gravy congealed on their plates. Hunger forced them to eat cold vegetables but most of the meat was sent back.

Farm boys had a relationship with horses on their farms such as they had with no other animals. They weren't sentimental about animals but horses were different. They couldn't stomach the idea of eating them. So after a few attempts horse was withdrawn from the menu and the boys went back to short rations until the day when they were faced with another unknown meat.

It was the colour of rubber. The boys forced their forks into the chunks in their stew and were almost convinced that it *was* rubber. And then they chewed and chewed interminably just to try to get a mouthful down. Once again questions whizzed around the dining hall and once more there were a few boys who knew what it was. There always were a few.

" 'Tis whale meat."

"WHALE meat?"

"Yes."

"No wonder it's so tough." This time it was the townies who flatly refused to eat it while the farm lads were prepared to give it a go. But they soon gave up. It was too tough even for their hungry jaws. They ate the stew and left the meat. Their letters home were full of their grumbles and full of pleas that their parents should send whatever food they could.

But there was one reason that their food was particularly poor that term that was hidden from all of them. It had only the remotest connection with the war and it only came to light because of a moment's folly and greed on the very last Sunday of term.

140

23

The Collection

It was Kick Door Sunday, the last Sunday of term. Mr Smart was the master on duty. He inspected the boys lined up for chapel and each of them was issued with a three-penny bit for the collection. Then they set off, kicking the door before moving in crocodile along the half mile path to the chapel.

There Roger and the other choir boys left the crocodile, walked through the cemetery and into the choir vestry. A door from the back of the choir vestry led to the Minister's vestry. Just before 11.00 the door opened and the preacher for the morning joined them. Their hearts sank. It was the Revd. Bishop. They were in for a long session.

He prayed and they filed into the chapel and into the choir stalls, in front of the central pulpit, facing the congregation. Four hymns, two Bible readings and a long prayer later, after some notices and the collection, the choir boys filed out to the corner pews they would occupy during the sermon. They checked the time by the chapel clock – 11.35.

The Revd. Bishop announced his text and began his sermon. He was an old man, tall and lean with a lined, weather-beaten face. He stomped along the pulpit and glowered down at the choir boys to the right of him, of whom Roger was one. He stomped along the pulpit to the other end and glowered down at the choir boys to the left of him. He knew choir boys too well. There would be no messing about in his sermon.

Because of this habit of his of stomping up and down the pulpit the boys called him 'Shuffling Jesus'. Roger looked at him. He had never seen anybody quite so lined. The whole face seemed to be a mass of lines and creases topped with thin white hair. Huge white eyebrows curved above eyes that had sunk right back into their sockets, from which they sparkled, black and menacing. He wore black clothes too, surmounted by the widest clerical collar of any of the preachers. Boys argued about how wide it was:

"Three inches."

"Never."

"I'll bet it is."

"You couldn't get a three inch collar round your neck."

Roger agreed with that. He hardly had any neck at all. But some people had long necks. Was it three inches? Or a bit less? It didn't matter. People said that Protestant Bible punchers had wide dog collars and churchy Catholics had thin collars. Was that true, or did people just wear the collars that fitted them best? Roger didn't know. 'Shuffling Jesus' had quite a big Adam's apple. That collar must be pretty uncomfortable.

Still the preacher stomped up and down. Roger took little notice. He heard familiar phrases: "the Word of Guard" to which some of the older people in the congregation would breathe "Amen"; "the Bible says . . ." and an echoed "Hallelujah"; "Jee-suss" brought more echoing "Hallelujah's" or "Allelujah's". It was a bit like a liturgy or like a man with marionettes: say the right words in the right tone of voice and the preacher evoked the right response.

By now it was not just Roger's mind that was wandering. His eye was wandering. He recognised some of the adults from the village. And up in the balcony he saw the three village girls who were almost the only female stimulation the boys ever had – and didn't they enjoy it. Except Pat of course. She'd had a baby and Trevose had been expelled. But Pat's shame didn't seem to last all that long. Roger wondered: did it or didn't it? People in villages had long memories. Pat was there anyway. She always seemed happy enough. Roger's eye wandered further round. There was Rowena. He had spoken to her! He gazed at her, worshipping from afar. And still 'Shuffling Jesus' stomped up and down.

But at long last it was over. He announced the last hymn and the boys checked the clock: 12.28. Fifty three minutes. It was about average for him. The choir filed back into their stalls and sang the last hymn. The blessing followed and then they filed out

142

to the choir vestry. Roger found that he was busting to 'do a leg'. He doubted if he could get back to school in time and he couldn't go in the cemetery as the boys often did at night. There would be people visiting graves.

He looked in the minister's vestry. There was no one in there so he risked it. He ran into the minister's toilet, locked the door, opened his flies with fumbling fingers and loosed the stream. 'Ohhh.' The relief. 'Ohhh. Gosh that was better.'

He went to flush the toilet and then thought better of it. He mustn't make a noise. He unlocked the door, opened it a crack and saw to his dismay that Mr Smart was in the vestry. He had come to collect the boys' three-penny pieces. It was all such a farce. Every Sunday the boys were given their three-penny bits for the collection. And every Sunday they were collected up and returned to the school. The school gave the chapel a regular cheque and 'the collection' appeared as an item on the end of term school bill to parents.

Usually one of the stewards was in the vestry counting the collection and putting the school three-pennies in the school black bag but on this occasion there was no one there except Mr Smart.

He looked through the choir vestry into the passageway to the chapel. No one seemed to be coming. He took the collection plates and quickly poured the money into the school bag – not just the boys' three-pennies but the whole collection. He put the bag of money into an inside pocket of his overcoat and then went and found one of the stewards. Roger took the opportunity to escape so he never heard Mr Smart say to the steward: "Mr Ridge . . . I've just been into the vestry to fetch the school money but it doesn't seem to be there. Perhaps you could show me where you have put it."

Mr Ridge didn't like this teacher much – too sly and smarmy by half. He didn't trust him either. They went to the vestry together and found that the collection had gone. They hunted high and low for it. Eventually Mr Smart said, "One of the boys must have stolen it, probably one of the choir boys. What a terrible disgrace for the school. I'll go straight to the Head and we'll sort it out. With all those three-penny pieces the money is bound to come to light."

And off he went back to school. In his rooms there was a black metal trunk which he was packing ready for the end of term – the end of his last term at the school thank goodness. He deserved something out of his time there. It wouldn't be much, but it was a little bit extra. He slipped the collection bag into the corner of the trunk and then went to see the Head.

"The collection has been stolen from the chapel. It looks as though it was probably one of the choir boys."

The Head was furious but there was nothing to be done until he had the whole school together at Assembly on Monday morning. At Assembly he told the school what had happened.

"I intend to sort this disgraceful affair out before any boy is allowed home for the holidays. At the end of Assembly all members of the choir will report to my study."

It was obvious where suspicion lay. Roger had gone white. He knew that Mr Smart had had the money. But he had had no business to be in the minister's toilet. What was he to do? If it came to his word against old Smarty's the Head would never believe him. But he had to do something.

He put his hand up.

"Not now boy."

"But sir."

"No. Control yourself until after Assembly."

'Stupid man,' thought Roger. 'He thinks I want the lavs. I'll just have to tell him when he sees the choir.'

After Assembly the members of the choir, including Roger, went to see the Head.

The Head took the choir into a meeting room and explained that they were the ones most under suspicion because they had the best opportunity of stealing the money. He told them that he was going to interview each of them in turn. If that achieved nothing their property would be searched. Roger stuck his hand up.

"Not now boy. Wait your turn."

Despairingly Roger put his hand down. With his wretched surname he was one of the last to be called. He stood in the Head's study. The Head looked at him with his piercing blue eyes.

"Now boy. Did you steal the Sunday collection? Answer 'yes' or 'no'."

"Sir, I've been . . ."

"Yes or no boy. That's all I want to know."

144

Roger felt desperate and he was also getting angry. Why would nobody listen to him?

"Sir. You must listen to me sir."

"What did you say?"

Poor Roger. He was scared stiff but he had to make the Head take notice of what he wanted to say.

"I'm sorry if I sounded rude sir, but I know who took the money."

"And you didn't?"

"No sir."

"Was it one of the choir boys who took the money?"

"No sir."

"Or one of the other boys from the school?"

"No sir."

"Hrmph." There was a pause. "But you know who stole the money?"

"Yes sir. It was Mr Smart sir."

"Mr Smart? That's a very serious accusation to make against a member of staff. What makes you so sure that Mr Smart took the money?"

"I saw him take it sir."

"You saw him,"

"Yes sir."

"Perhaps you had better tell me how you came to see him and what you were doing in the minister's vestry – I take it that that is where the money was stolen from?"

"Yes sir. Sir, I know I shouldn't have but I wanted to do a leg – sorry sir. I wanted to go to the toilet real bad after chapel. Shuff. . . I mean, Mr Bishop preached for such a long time."

"Just how long?"

"Fifty-three minutes sir."

"Ah. I thought you would know. Very well, go on."

"Sir, when everyone had gone I went into the minister's toilet. I was just coming out when Mr Smart came into the vestry so I hopped back into the toilet and stood watching him until the coast was clear.

"There was no one else there sir. Mr Smart looked around, emptied all the money from the collection into the school bag, put it in an inside pocket of his overcoat and went into the chapel. I thought he had just picked it up to bring it back to school, sir.

145

When he went into the chapel, I slipped out of the side door and back to school."

"So it's just your word against his."

Roger's face fell. "Yes sir."

"And you tell me that you didn't steal the money."

"Yes sir. I mean, no sir. I mean – sir, no. I didn't steal it."

Inwardly the Head smiled. He'd been inclined to believe the boy from the start, but that little mix up helped clinch things for him. "Hrmph." It was his favourite expression. He was quiet for a time. Then he said, "The choir is still in the meeting room isn't it."

"Yes sir."

"While they are there, all your lockers and desks are being searched. I want you to go back and join the other choir boys but you are to say nothing to anybody. Do you understand?"

No Roger didn't understand. Oh he understood that he mustn't say anything, but he didn't understand why. It didn't matter so he answered, "Yes sir."

"I can trust you not to say a word to anybody? Not even your best friends?"

"Yes sir."

"Very well. You may go."

"Thank you sir." Roger turned to go and then he turned back. "Excuse me sir."

"Well, what is it?"

"About the collection sir."

"What about it?" The Head's mind was still on the theft and what he would have to do.

"Isn't it a bit, well sir, a bit sort of wrong?"

"What do you mean boy?"

"Sir, it's supposed to be a freewill collection but it isn't is it? We all give the money the school gives us and then our parents have to pay whether they like it or not. Shouldn't we give the collection from our pocket money sir?"

The Head looked at Roger in astonishment, but damn it he was right. He'd never thought of it like that. The chapel would certainly lose out if boys started putting farthings and halfpennies on the plate. But for all that, the boy was right.

"You're a cheeky beggar Wallace but I'll think about what you say. Oh. And next time Mr Bishop is preaching remember to go

146

to the toilet before you go to chapel. I don't want to have to cane you for using the minister's toilet do I?"

Roger grinned. "No sir. Thank you sir." As he turned and left the study he thought, 'the Head's not a bad old stick when you get to know him.'

24

A Detective Headmaster

Roger joined the other choir boys. They all wanted to know why he had been so long. Was he the crook? He answered them indignantly but he couldn't actually tell them why he had been so long. As a result some of them continued to suspect that he was the guilty one.

The search of the choir boys' lockers and desks revealed nothing, but that was precisely what the Head expected by now. Yet, as he thought about Roger's story he was baffled. Would Mr Smart really bother to steal the Sunday collection? It wouldn't be more than ten to fifteen pounds. Why on earth would he want to steal a sum like that?

At lunch the Head announced that he had been able to narrow down his list of suspects. He had decided to allow the boys to go home at the end of term with the exception of those who were still under suspicion.

There were cheers and a feeling of general relief swept through the dining hall. Roger wondered what the Head was up to.

In fact the Head had been quite busy. If anybody had known what he had been up to, he could have been in real trouble. But he wasn't the man to allow that to worry him.

During the first lesson after break that morning, Mr Smart had been teaching geography. The Head went to his rooms. He used his master key to enter and searched Mr Smart's overcoat.

He found nothing.

He looked through the rooms and opened drawer after drawer. Nothing. Finally he decided to check Mr Smart's black trunk. It was locked but the Head had noticed the keys in Mr Smart's top desk drawer. He unlocked the trunk. There were several layers of clothes neatly packed on the top. Very carefully the Head turned them back at one end and was astonished at what he found. He laid the clothes back down and repeated the operation at the other end of the trunk. Fury swept through him but it didn't stop him searching with care, and there in the corner of the trunk he found the black bag with the collection still in it.

Once again he laid the clothes carefully back in place. He locked the trunk, put the keys back in the desk drawer and returned to his own study. Once there, he rang the police. They had a long conversation.

"No," he said. "It would be better if you did not come to the school. What I would like to suggest is. . ." and at the end of their conversation he and the police had decided what they would do.

The last few days of school passed slowly and were as meaningless as usual to both staff and boys. It was no use trying to teach. The boys were too excited to learn. At last the final school Assembly arrived. All the staff were present with the Head, and Mrs Elliott was there as well. The Head explained that Mrs Elliott and Mr Smart were both leaving that term and that they had plans to get married. As he thanked them for their services to the school and wished them well, he seemed less inspired and enthusiastic than usual. Was he worried about their replacements? Only Mr Emerson knew why the Head was so cool towards them. Mr Smart and Mrs Elliott were so full of their plans that they never even noticed. Though Mr Smart did feel that even in wartime it should have been possible for the school to make some sort of presentation to them both.

The boys fetched their trunks from the tower and packed for the holidays. Everything had to go. Desks were emptied. Rugby kit was fetched from the sports changing rooms. Their buffaloes were emptied. At last it was all done and their trunks were bumped down the stairs to the courtyard to wait for the coaches or for parents with cars. Mr Smart had called in the services of the school caretaker and groundsman to help with his trunk and with that of Mrs Elliott. Both trunks were exceptionally heavy.

The coaches came to take the train boys and staff. Their trunks were all loaded onto an accompanying lorry. Six miles away they arrived at Downland Halt and unloaded. The drivers and the solitary porter-cum-stationmaster carried Mrs Elliott's and Mr Smart's trunks onto the platform.

"Golly. What have you got in there?" one of them asked jokingly, "the Crown Jewels?"

Mr Smart laughed with his mouth but not with his eyes. They were sliding about all over the place and yet they failed to notice the arrival outside the station of the Head and Mr Emerson in the black school car. Nor had anyone noticed the black police Wolseley parked close to the station entrance. They were all far too busy with their trunks and far too excited to be going home.

The Head and Mr Emerson met two policemen (one of them a sergeant) outside the station. They came onto the platform and the Head breezed over to where Mr Smart and Mrs Elliott stood by their two trunks. Mr Smart looked very uneasy.

"Hello again Mr Smart," said the Head in high good humour. "Just thought that we'd come to see you and Mrs Elliott off. Couldn't let you go without a final farewell could we now? Perhaps you'd like to open your trunk for us before you go."

Mrs Elliott flushed and then turned very pale.

"What did you say?" blustered Mr Smart.

"I wondered if you would mind opening your trunk for us."

"Yes I most certainly would mind. It has taken me a lot of time and trouble to pack everything into my trunk and I've no intention of getting things into a mess now. Besides, why should I?"

"Oh I think you know why you should. You did say that you had had trouble getting 'everything' into your trunk. Please open it and show us what you have inside. Oh, and perhaps you would like to do the same for us Mrs Elliott."

"How dare you. I've never been so insulted in my life. I think you are forgetting Mr Headmaster that you have no jurisdiction away from your rather primitive little school."

At that moment the sergeant of police spoke. "You are Mr Smart are you sir?"

"Yes."

"And you are Mrs Elliott?"

"Yes," she answered in a whisper.

"You have both been accused of theft. I'm sure that there has been some ghastly mistake but if you would both be so kind as to open your trunks, we can clear the matter up right away and send you on your way with our apologies."

At that moment the train entered the station and, with a great hissing of steam, drew to a halt. The boys were in a real quandary. They wanted to see the end of this episode but they couldn't afford to miss the train. There was a bit of time while their trunks were being loaded.

When they could hear themselves think for the noise of the engine Mr Smart was speaking to the Sergeant: "As you rightly said Officer, there has been 'a ghastly mistake'. I'm astonished that the Headmaster should have given any credence to it at all. I would have thought he knew me better. And as for casting suspicion upon Mrs Elliott! I'm sure she feels (as I do) deeply hurt and insulted. Now let us load our trunks onto the train and let there be an end to this nonsense."

The boys' trunks were all aboard. Regretfully the boys tore themselves away from the unfolding drama and jumped on the train making straight for the windows and opening those that would.

"We'll be glad to help you load your trunks onto the train if you would just allow us to have a look inside first sir. After all, if you are as innocent as you say, there can be no harm in letting us have a look."

The engine driver was by now engrossed in the scene back along the platform though he couldn't hear a word. The porter began walking down the train, slamming doors. He came to the little group.

"Are you going to be long? I must get this train away as quickly as I can."

"The key to your trunk sir, please," said the sergeant.

"Oh give it to them Leonard," said Mrs Elliott, "and then we can get on the train. There's nothing to be gained by being difficult."

By now the porter had grown weary of waiting. He went back to the train and slammed the last few doors shut. He signalled to the guard.

Meanwhile Mrs Elliott's meaning had not been lost on Mr Smart. He put his hand in his pocket and drew out his keys. As he went to hand them over, he dropped them onto the platform. The constable bent to pick them up. The guard waved his green flag and the engine's whistle sounded. Mr Smart and Mrs Elliott began to run for the train.

151

Up to this point Mr Emerson had taken no part in the proceedings at all. He had simply been standing, leaning on his walking stick, a benign expression on his face. But as Mrs Elliott ran past him he simply stretched out an arm, linked it with hers and said very quietly, "I don't think that would be a very good idea my dear. The police would only take you off at the next station."

Mr Smart got rather further before a crashing rugby tackle from the Head brought him down.

The boys cheered and the engine driver eased the train forward and out of the station. It was so frustrating. What had those two got in their trunks? They were not to get to know until the following term when the Head allowed the facts to leak out. But he and the police had rather less of a wait for information.

Back at the station the sergeant opened Mr Smart's trunk.

Underneath a few layers of clothing, the trunk was jam-packed full of tinned foods from the school stores. The same was true of Mrs Elliott's trunk. But in Mr Smart's trunk there was one thing more. The Head reached in and fished out the school black bag containing the chapel collection.

"If you hadn't stolen this," he said, "you would have got away with all the rest. You were just that little bit too greedy and one honest choir boy saw what you did and had the guts to report you."

It was Mr Emerson who added with a smile, "You might like to know that the boy was one of my scouts. He'll be made up to patrol leader next term. I expect you know the boy Mr Smart. His name is Wallace."

25

New People, New Things

They were no sooner home than Philip Jonas' father was killed in an air-raid in London. Philip and his mother were lucky. If they hadn't been visiting friends they would have been killed too. As it was, their home was completely destroyed.

The Head took it upon himself to go to London for the funeral. Afterwards they went back to an A.B.C. restaurant for a cup of tea and the usual after-death conversations. Philip stayed close to his mother. When the Head came to talk to them Mrs Jonas said, "I'm so grateful to you for coming. I don't know what we are going to do. We've no home and no money. I shall have to take Philip away from Perspins of course. I can't possibly pay the school fees all on my own."

"Yes, I see that," replied the Head.

"At least I've got a job. If we can find somewhere to live we'll manage somehow."

"What is your job, Mrs Jonas?"

"I manage this restaurant."

"Really!" The Head suddenly became interested.

"Yes. That's about the only good thing this war has done for us." And then, at the thought of what the war had just done for them, she burst into tears.

The Head waited until her tears had run their course.

"I'm sorry," she said as she wiped her eyes. "I'm not very well controlled just yet."

"Don't apologise. You are bound to have lots of bad moments for some time to come."

"Yes."

"But I've had an idea that might be of use to you. I may be able to provide the solution to some of your problems Mrs Jonas. Do you feel up to listening to me for a moment or shall I choose another time?"

Mrs Jonas straightened her shoulders and took a deep breath.

"I'm all right," she said. "Please go ahead."

The Head paused. He didn't quite know how to put this. His normal style was blunt and forthright but he needed to be gentle. He wished his wife were with him. She was better at this kind of thing than he was. Oh well, in at the deep end: "The school needs a new housekeeper. The salary is not generous but there is a small flat which goes with the job. It's part of the salary. If you felt able to accept the post I'm sure we could work something out for Philip. For a start, he would be living with you so he would be treated as a day boy. There would be no boarding fees to pay, only his tuition. I'm sure we can work out some way to cover that."

Mrs Jonas didn't know what to say. She was overwhelmed. Tears flowed again. People were so kind. But this time the Head was rather embarrassed.

"I shouldn't have confronted you with this at such a time. I'll write to you from school confirming my offer. That will give you time to think it over."

"Thank you," she said, "I'm sorry to be so silly." She looked at Philip and hugged him to her protectively. "I don't think we need time to think. I'll give in my notice straight away."

"You're quite sure? I don't want to rush you."

"Oh yes, I'm quite sure. It will be such a relief to get away from London and live somewhere quiet."

"School isn't exactly quiet Mrs Jonas, but I think I know what you mean. If you can get to school a few days before the beginning of term, it will help you to meet your staff and to learn the details of your work."

So it was that at the beginning of that summer term the school had a new housekeeper. They also had a new teacher in place of Mr Smart. But Mr Kendall wasn't a straight replacement. He couldn't teach Mr Smart's subjects. In point of fact he couldn't teach anything at all except art and woodwork and sport – and he couldn't really *teach* them. But he was a decent, likeable chap so the boys took to him, even though it was those who were best at sport who soon became his favourites.

Roger had brought a bike back to school. His birthday was in May and his grandfather had given it to him. He wasn't as grateful as he should have been. It was a wartime A.S.P. Hercules.

"Why do they call it A.S.P.?" asked Jonas when Roger took some of his friends out to the bike sheds to have a look at it.

"Don' ee know that," replied Joe. " 'Tis 'All Spare Parts' because of the war."

Dave ran his hands over the handlebars. "It's a pretty solid looking bike."

"Bit old fashioned," said Bradders, "and bloody heavy I expect."

"Yes it is a bit heavy," answered Roger.

"I 'spose you're lucky to have a bike, but I'd rather have something a bit lighter and a bit more sporty," said Bradders.

"So would I," said Roger, "but at least it's a bike. That's something." He took to riding it around the roads near the school in his spare time, but he wasn't really very keen on cycling. You missed so much that you could see if you were on foot. And his bike *was* heavy and didn't have a three speed. Besides, what was the fun of going out on your own.

So the bike was already being neglected when he heard that his mother was coming to Beddingford for his exeat week-end. He could cycle to spend it with her as a birthday treat. On the Friday he made sure that his tyres were well pumped up and on the Saturday he rose early.

He dressed and made his way silently to the cycle sheds. He took his bike out to the road and began to peddle as fast as he could towards Stebble Cross. After about a mile he eased up and began to ride without hurry. It was all up hill and down so that he often had to get off his bike and push it up the hills but from Stebble Cross onwards it was easy, downhill almost all the way.

He didn't have to peddle and the hedges rushed past him. On and on he went down towards the river, and then he cycled the last stretch into Beddingford to the Riverside Hotel. Twelve miles in three quarters of an hour. 'Not bad,' he thought, 'and I've got here in time for breakfast.'

Margaret was at the hotel with his mother, and they had a good week-end together although it was a bit boring visiting so many old acquaintances. Roger was due back at school in time for Sunday evening chapel. He allowed himself three quarters of an hour, said his goodbyes and set off. He rode hard and then began to climb five mile hill. He rode a bit, walked a bit, rode a bit, walked a bit and began to realise that he should have allowed extra time.

And then he realised something else. His mother had brought a tuck parcel with her for him to take back to school and he had left it behind. Agony. He stood in a lather of indecision. He was going to be late anyway. So if he went back for his tuck he would still only be late, and he might be able to think of an excuse. He went back.

His mother phoned the Headmaster. "I'm afraid that Roger is going to be late back to school."

"Never mind Mrs Wallace. I'm sure that there is a good reason."

"Oh yes," she said. "He was half way back to school when he realised that he had forgotten his tuck parcel. So he came back here for it."

Roger was sitting on the stairs listening. As his mother spoke his heart sank.

"Really."

"Yes, and the poor boy is so tired after leaving school so early yesterday that I thought I'd keep him here with me for one more night and send him back in the morning."

"Was he very early leaving school yesterday?"

"Oh yes. He must have been, to manage to get here in time for breakfast."

If Roger's heart had been in his boots before, it went through the floor now. Exeats didn't begin until after school breakfast.

"Yes," said the Head. "He must have started out early. Perhaps you would ask him to come to my study when he gets back to school in the morning, just to let me know that he has arrived safely."

"Yes, of course."

So the following morning Roger set out for school again. Every turn of the peddle seemed hard work. Climbing five mile hill was murder. His bike seemed to get heavier and heavier.

"Blooming bike," thought Roger. "Why couldn't they have got a sports bike for me. I can hardly push this bally thing."

He reached Stebble Cross at last and set out on the last four weary miles up hill and down again. He put his bike away, took his clothes to his dorm and his tuck to the locker room, and then made his way unwillingly to the Head's study.

"Ah Roger, come in."

The Head was in a high good humour but Roger wasn't fooled. Whenever the Head called him by his first name he was in for trouble.

"Did you have a good exeat? Your mother and sister are both well I hope?"

"Yes, thank you, sir."

"Bit of a liability sometimes, mothers, eh?"

"Pardon sir."

"Never mind boy. It was quite a *long* exeat Roger, or so I understand."

"Yes sir."

"I expect you are quite saddle sore after that ride up the hill from Beddington?"

"A bit sir."

"Hm. We must help you to forget that. You know what's coming?"

"Yes sir."

"And you know the drill."

"Yes sir." ('Pretty well thank you sir,' he thought. 'I don't seem to go many weeks without it.') He removed the cushion from the chair as the Head went to the corner to fetch the cane.

"Four today I think Roger: two for leaving early and two for returning late. Tuck is not really a sufficient excuse for being late back to school."

Roger took his punishment, expressed his thanks and was just leaving the study when the Head said, "Oh, by the way Wallace, you'll have noticed that we have made a change to our Sunday collection arrangements."

"Yes sir." The seniors now put their own money on the plate but the juniors still received three-penny bits.

"I'm grateful to you for bringing the matter to my attention. Never be afraid to speak to me of things that concern you. Off you go."

It had been hard to stand there listening with his bum stinging like hell, but when he thought about it Roger was pleased. He used to be scared of the Head but he wasn't any more. He went to his classroom.

26

The Swap

After school that morning one of the prefects surprised him by asking, "Had a good exeat, Wallace?"

Roger was puzzled. He never remembered Briggs speaking to him before. "Yes thank you," he answered.

"Quite hard work riding to Beddingford and back on that bike of yours I expect."

Roger was even more puzzled. "Yes it was. It's a bit too heavy for me really."

"That's what I was thinking. All right for some one my size but a bit big for you."

While they were talking they seemed to have drifted out to the cycle sheds. "What I was wondering was whether you'd like to do a swap. I've got a sports bike that is a bit small for me now. It isn't new of course . . ."

By now he was standing beside a blue sports bike. It was spotlessly clean except for part of the frame which seemed to have been forgotten. That was coated in mud.

"I thought you might like to do a straight swap Wallace. I know mine's worth a bit more than yours but not enough to make a fuss about. Well, what do you say?"

Roger didn't hesitate. "Yes, I'd be glad to swap."

"Shake hands on it?"

They shook hands.

"It's a deal then. Oh, by the way, there's a bit of a crack on the frame down there where it's muddy. Nothing very much. A bit of welding will soon put that right."

Briggs walked away and Roger realised that he had been done. He rubbed some of the mud away and soon found the crack. He wasn't even sure whether he could ride the bike safely. He felt a right twit being diddled so easily – and angry too. How Joe and Bradders would laugh. No they wouldn't. Not if he could help it. He would bluff it out. And if he could get it welded he really would be better off. Briggs was right. In proper condition this bike was worth more than his. He went off and found Dave.

"Any idea where I can get a bit of welding done?"

"Down the village at Dick Petherick, the blacksmith's. Why? What do you want welding?"

"You know Briggs?"

"Yes."

"Well he had a sport's bike with a bit of a crack in the frame. I did a swap with him. If I can get his bike welded, I reckon I'll have done very well out of the swap. His bike's got a three speed an' all."

Roger collected every penny he had and after school he set off for the village telling Dave that he might miss tea. He came to the blacksmith's and watched as a horse was being shod. The heat in the shop was terrific.

"What can I do for you boy?"

"I've got a crack in my cycle frame. I wondered what it would cost me to have it welded."

"Let's have a look." He sucked in through his teeth. "How much money have ee got."

"Two shillings and four-pence half-penny," answered Roger.

The blacksmith had a struggle to keep a straight face. "I expect you'll be reckoning on stopping at the baker's on the way back to school?"

"Well yes, I did think I would," said Roger, baffled by the question.

"Ah. Vitty bread ee makes, with a good crisp crust. Well now look-see. Us'll have to break the frame yer. Then us'll have to bend this yer end out and fit a sleeve over, and bend'n back and draw the sleeve down yer, and then this yer cycle will be stronger'n it's ever bin in its life. How's that boy?"

"That would be wonderful," answered Roger admiringly. He was thrilled to bits.

"I reckon us could do that for two shillings zactly."

"Two shillings?" queried Roger. "I can afford that right away." He fished in his pocket.

"Right boy. You give me they two shillings and then go off to the baker's. By the time you come back us'll have this yer bike nearly ready for riding on."

Roger was so excited. He handed over the two shillings and went to the baker's. He didn't notice the blacksmith's wife, one of the senior kitchen staff. As he walked off up the hill to the baker's she said, "You'm a proper vool Dick Petherick. Us'll niver make a fortune if you goes on like that."

"No maid I reckon," he said and set to work on the bike.

"But I'm glad you'm helping the lad. He's a good boy that one, always cheerful and polite. Some of they up there treats us kitchen staff like dirt."

Roger went to the baker's and bought a large crusty white loaf.

"That'll be fourpence halfpenny," said the baker.

Roger knew that but it was only then as he handed over his last coins that he wondered about the blacksmith's question. He wondered how much it would have cost to have his bike welded anywhere else. Suddenly he suspected that the blacksmith had been very kind.

He walked slowly back through the village, tearing off chunks of the crust and loving every mouthful. He went on eating as he waited. He watched the blacksmith hammering red hot metal on his anvil, sealing it round the break on his bike, bending it, smoothing it, cooling it. He watched the sparks fly and the steam fizz. In the end the blacksmith had done few of the things he said he would. He had cleaned back the frame and burned off the paint and then he had made a sleeve from a flat length of metal and bound the frame together with it, but he hadn't done any bending of the frame.

"There boy," he said at last. "I reckon you'll find that better an' stronger than it was when it was new."

"When will I be able to ride it?" asked Roger.

"As soon as you get to the top of thicky hill out of the village," came the reply.

"Oh gosh. Thank you ever so much Mr Petherick. I can't tell you how grateful I am."

"Ah, well just you give me a hunk of that bread and don't smash your bike up again."

Roger didn't stop to tell him that he hadn't broken the bike. He just let him take a hunk of bread, put what was left into his saddle bag and set off back for school. He had missed tea but he would be in plenty of time for prep. He pushed the bike up the hill. It felt light as a feather after the other one. Then he jumped on and began to ride.

He overtook a girl. It was Rowena. He stopped and waited for her.

"Hello."

"Hello, Roger Wallace."

She remembered his name!

"Are you on your way home?"

"Yes."

"You can ride my bike if you like."

"And what will you do?"

"If you go slow enough I'll run."

" 'Tis a nice bike." She took it from him and swung her leg over the saddle like a boy. He set off after her. At the cross-roads she stopped and waited. "You'd better have it back now."

"No it's all right. You ride on right home and leave it in the hedge."

So she rode on and he ran on. They passed the school and she stopped by the entrance to a footpath. She wheeled the bike into the footpath, leaned it against the hedge and waited for him. He turned into the footpath panting hard.

"I see you in the choir in chapel."

"Yes I see you in chapel too."

"But you don't come with the other boys to see us girls by the saw-mills on Sundays."

"No."

"Why don' ee come? Don' ee like flirtin' and kissin'?"

Roger felt shy. He would love to do a bit of flirting and kissing but not as one among a crowd. He didn't want to be shown up as awkward and silly.

"Kissing's for in private," he said.

"Us be in private now."

He looked at his shoes. "Yes," he whispered.

"Well come on then. You want to don' ee."

"Yes I do." Clumsily he took her in his arms and they kissed. Then he let her go and stepped back.

"Do it again," she commanded and when they had finished she said, "Any time us be private you can kiss me if you want to."

With that she was gone. Roger didn't know whether he was coming or going. He pulled his bike out of the hedge and rode back to school in a dream. It was a long time after prep had started before he was able to do any work. Yet strangely enough, he was never to speak to Rowena again. For no real reason their romance was ended as soon as it was begun, though she was to continue to be the object of his distant worship and to feature in his dreams for a long time to come.

27

The Evangelist

May still had about another week to run. Sunday saw them all on their way to chapel as usual. As they approached the chapel, in a field on the left of the lane they saw a small marquee. At its entrance there was a large placard saying 'The Jesus Tent'.

"Oh my gor," grunted Joe. " 'Mother's got a mangle'."

From further along the line came the response from Parsons: " 'Tis made of wood and lead'." He really was blossoming now that he was free from bullying.

"What are you on about?" asked Roger.

"You'll zee zoon enough," answered Joe. "At least us knows what us be in vor wi' old Sanderson as the praicher."

He might have done, but Roger didn't. He looked at the preacher with curiosity when he came into the choir vestry for their pre-service prayer. Tubby, not very tall, with a cherubic round pink face and twinkling eyes, Roger felt there was nothing special about him and his prayer was nice and short.

Nor was there anything out of the ordinary in the early part of the service. The first Bible reading was announced as 'the Word of the Lord' but quite a lot of preachers used that phrase. But then Mr Sanderson announced that his 'dear wife Dorothy' was going to sing a solo.

It was awful.

Dorothy had a voice with a warble – quite a big warble. It often seemed to clash with the clarity of the note of the organ. But Mr Sanderson was obviously very proud of it.

Before the sermon they sang a hymn Roger liked. It had a good swing to it and he sang enthusiastically as always:

Trust and obey
for there's no other way
to be happy in Jesus
but to trust and obey.

The choir moved to their side pews and Mr Sanderson announced that he was going to talk about being happy. "We all want to be happy don't we boys?" At once Roger's mind began to wander. He thought of a song from a show that his mother loved:

I want to BEEE happy,
But I can't BEEE happy,
'til I make YOU happy TOO.

Mr Sanderson was saying, "we can't be happy without Jesus." That song didn't say anything about Jesus, thought Roger. It was just about flirting and things. He looked up into the balcony at Rowena. It was a pity she liked flirting. He wanted her all to himself. But he wasn't going to let on. Going out with girls was soft.

Mr Sanderson began to talk about a family in the East End of London. The father was a great drunkard. 'So was my great grandfather,' thought Roger. 'That's why my grandpa is so hot against the drink.'

"One day the father was out with his son," said Mr Sanderson, "and they saw an advertisement showing a man and his son. The drunkard's son looked and said, 'That boy's got new shoes.' The father looked at his own son's tattered footwear and felt ashamed. And then they came across a Salvation Army Band playing on the street corner. The preacher cried, 'Give up the drink and come to Jesus and you'll be happy.'

"There and then the drunkard gave his heart to Jesus. He signed the pledge and gave up the drink and before very long he was able to buy his son new shoes with the money he saved.

A few days later his son was walking home from school when he saw some boys throwing mud at a picture of Jesus. He ran in front of the picture crying, 'Don't throw mud at the picture. I've got a new pair of shoes on.'"

Up to that point Roger had been quite impressed, but suddenly the story didn't seem to ring true any more. But Mr Sanderson was already into another story of a "terrible drunkard and gambler, a man who used to beat his wife when he was in the drink." Roger looked around the chapel. Somehow he couldn't imagine any of the men he saw there as drunkards and gamblers and wife-beaters. But this was another story of the East End. Perhaps they were all like that in the slums.

Again the man gave his heart to Jesus and changed his life style completely. He stopped beating his wife and before long he was able to buy her a mangle to make wash days easier. Suddenly Mr Sanderson began to recite a poem:

> *Mother's got a mangle.*
> *It's made of wood and lead . . .*

Roger never heard another word. He caught Joe's eye and began to giggle. He bent down to try to hide it and to stifle his laughter. It all ended up in a mini-explosion of coughing in his handkerchief.

At the end of his sermon Mr Sanderson pleaded with the boys to give their hearts to Jesus. "As we sing our last hymn come forward and stand at the front of the chapel to show us all that you have given your hearts to Jesus."

They sang a couple of verses and no one came forward. Mr Sanderson stopped the organist. "My dear wife Dorothy will come forward so that you have someone to stand with. Now boys don't be shy. Give your hearts to Jesus. Learn how to be happy. Come forward and stand with my dear wife."

They sang the rest of the hymn and Dorothy remained alone at the front of the chapel. "It is still not too late," said Mr Sanderson. "Come to me in the vestry afterwards and tell me that you have given your hearts to Jesus. Or come to the meetings every day this week after school and learn more about how to be happy in Jesus."

At last it was all over. Back they went to school for their lunch. They wrote their letters home and went out for their walk. As Roger was crossing the quad, Joe came from the lavs.

"Mother's got a mangle," said Joe.

"It's made of wood and lead," replied Roger and they both

roared with laughter.

The couplet spread through the junior school like the plague. Wherever two boys met one another you could hear one say, "Mother's got a mangle" and the other would reply, "It's made of wood and lead."

After school on Monday Roger asked Joe if he was going to the meeting in the marquee.

"Got to haven't I," answered Joe.

"How's that?" asked Roger.

"That Sanderson knows my dad. He'll tell if I don't go. An' I shall have to go forward some time to give my heart to Jesus or there'll be trouble. Some of us have been forward a good few times."

To Roger that didn't seem right somehow. Perhaps it was right to give your heart to Jesus, but if you did it once that should be enough. Perhaps he would do it when Joe did. He wondered if it would make him feel different.

Joe skipped Tuesday and Thursday. Scouts and cross country running gave him all the excuse he needed not to go to the meetings. As a result, Roger skipped those two meetings as well. On Friday the two set out together with a few more boys whose fathers knew the evangelist.

"It's the last meeting today," said Joe, "so I shall go forward today."

"Can I come forward too," asked Roger.

"Course you can stupid. That's what he wants you to do."

At all of these meetings Dorothy played on a pedal harmonium and they sang choruses:

> *I'm aitch ay pee pee why,*
> *I'm aitch ay pee pee why;*
> *I think I am,*
> *I know I am,*
> *I'm aitch ay pee pee why.*

Dorothy sang more ghastly solos. She and her husband sang duets that were even worse. His voice also had a warble but it was different from her warble so their voices clashed.

At that final meeting Mr Sanderson said that he was going to talk about "Joy, J-O-Y. The significance of those letters is that the secret of joy is putting Jesus first, Others second, Yourself last. Do you get it?"

Yes they got it but he was going to make sure that they got it: J is the first letter of Joy and of Jesus so it's 'Jesus first'. O is the second letter of jOy so it's 'O for Others second'. Y is the last letter of joY so it's 'Y for Yourself last'. Do you see? The secret of JOY is, say it after me:

> *Jesus first,*
> *Others second,*
> *Yourself last.*

Now, if you want to know the secret of joy come and give your hearts to Jesus."

Poor Joe had been groaning away as this was going on. He had heard it all before when Mr Sanderson conducted his mission at Joe's home chapel. "Oh my gor," grumbled Joe. "Us idn as thick as all that. Us can zee what he's on about first time off. Ee don't have to go on and on so." But during the closing chorus he dutifully went forward and Roger went with him. Roger felt quite excited. So did Mr Sanderson.

"We've got twelve more young converts for Jesus this week Dorothy dear — young boys, ripe for the harvest. Our labours have not been in vain."

He took their names to pass on to the Headmaster and gave each of them a booklet of Bible readings. "Make sure that you read the Bible every day. That way you will stay close to Jesus and be happy in him."

He didn't mean to, but Roger dropped his booklet on the way back to school. 'It doesn't matter,' he thought. 'I don't need a booklet to help me read the Bible. I can read the Bible without that.' And he genuinely tried but he didn't get very far. All those verses when someone 'begat' someone else were so boring. And Genesis was full of the names of people who had lived to unbelievably old ages. He didn't see any point in reading things that were so boring, especially when it was obvious that they weren't true.

But it was events of the war that finally drove Mr Sanderson's mission far from his mind. In mid-May, after a week's bitter fighting, Monte Casino finally fell to the Allies at the fourth attempt. It enabled the next major advances in Italy to take place. On June 4th came the news that the Yanks had driven the Germans out of Rome. And then the advance in Italy stuck again. The Germans held their new defensive line right through almost to the end of the war.

But in England none of that mattered. Nothing mattered except the incredible news that at last the Allies had landed in Normandy. On June 6th D Day had come. An enormous armada had crossed the Channel safely and British, Canadian and American troops had established a firm bridgehead on French soil.

There was immense excitement, dampened only by Mr Emerson's typically quiet announcement in Assembly that two more old boys had been killed during the invasion. Unlike the Head he never indulged in jingoistic rhetoric. Roger had known both boys slightly. They had still been at Perspins during his first year. Their deaths brought back Eric's memory. War was horrible.

But in spite of that, the invasion was a glorious achievement. The boys held their breath as the battle for Caen began.

h

28

Doodlebugs

For quite different reasons Roger and his father faced the summer holidays with a good deal of anxiety and uncertainty.

Roger wasn't at all sure that he wanted to take his bike home with him. He hadn't asked permission to swap the one his grandfather had given him. He wondered what his father would say. He was quite capable of caning him and confiscating the bike. He dithered and dithered right up to the last moment before deciding to take it home. Even then he wasn't sure whether he would tell his parents or just wait until they noticed.

But George Wallace had rather more serious matters on his mind. All through the war he had tried to protect his younger children from the bombing. He had insisted on them staying in evacuation when other children were coming home. He had put them in boarding schools away from danger when evacuated schools came home. He had taken a lot of persuading before he finally let them come home for holidays. And now there was a new threat.

At the end of June the Germans began to send over a new kind of bomb. It looked like an aircraft but it was unmanned. As these flying bombs flew over the south east of England to London, there came a point where their engine cut out. At first, people thought they were experimental aircraft in trouble. They ran towards them to help the non-existent crew. But when the engine cut out, the plane glided silently to land where it exploded causing terrific devastation.

Albert was worried sick. If it hadn't been for D Day he would certainly have sent his wife to Beddingford again, to spend the summer there with Roger and Margaret. But D Day filled him with an unwarranted optimism. The Germans would finally collapse now and war would be over in a few weeks. After his First World War experiences he ought to have known better. But in the end, he decided to allow the children to come home.

So for the first time they had a taste of what it was like to be bombed. Oh they had been through the occasional raid before but this was different. Strangely enough, Roger felt no fear of these raids. He tried to explain the difference to himself.

'With ordinary bombing there were lots of planes and lots of bombs and you never quite knew where they were going to land,' he thought, 'so you always thought that the next explosion could be the one that killed you. But with these things, you saw them coming, you heard them cut out and you had a pretty good idea whether you were safe or not.'

He found them interesting and exciting more than frightening, and he was glad he had his bike. He spent a lot of his holidays riding around looking at places where the doodlebugs had fallen and seeing the damage they caused. He was insulated from the hell of them because he never saw the mangled bodies, the dead or the injured, only the ruined buildings and the craters.

His father listened to the news avidly and read the papers eagerly. Roger had never mentioned the bike swap and his father had never noticed. He was far more concerned that it seemed to be taking an age for the Allies to capture Caen and to break out of their invasion bridgehead.

Then came news that restored all his fears for his children.

He was at work when one of Roger's aunts rang.

"Mother was bombed out last night. A flying bomb landed at the bottom of their garden. No one was hurt but the house is finished. I've taken mother and my sisters home to my place. Can you tell Lilian? I don't want her to panic. And can you see to the house and things for us?"

"Of course," George replied. "I'll bring Lil across this evening to see you all, if that's all right."

"Yes. That's fine."

"And I'll get across to the house right away."

"Thanks."

About half of the house was still standing including the stairs.

The roof had gone. Lilian's mother and one of her sisters had been in the cellar and were fine. But another sister had been in her bedroom. She always refused to go to the cellar. She had slept through it all and woke eventually to find herself gazing at the sky and covered in dust and plaster.

Distressed though she was, Roger's grandmother was typically calm and practical.

"Do you remember?" she said. "We were bombed by a zeppelin in the last war. So we know what to do." She turned to one of her daughters. "Glad. You go and phone your sister Verity and ask if we can go to stay with her." And then, turning to her other daughter she said, "We'll start packing the things we need."

By the time George got there the police had cordoned off the whole area and a constable was on duty. They chatted for a while and George walked around to see what could be done and what needed to be done first. He went back to his office and set things in motion, and then he went home and told his wife. She began to panic but he calmed her down, stressing that her mother and her sisters were all well and that he would take her to see them that evening.

Roger was all agog with the news. His parents seemed so wrapped up in one another that it was almost as if they had forgotten his existence so he went and fetched his bike. He cycled off to see his Gran's ruined house. Full of his own importance he told the policeman on duty it was his grandmother who had been bombed out.

The policeman did his best to appear impressed, but he still wouldn't let Roger go and have a closer look. That had to wait until Roger was able to go with his father, by which time things had been tidied up a bit and the ruins had been made safe. Even that experience was too remote to make Roger afraid nor did he share the gloom and depression that seemed to settle over much of London. It only made him more excited and fascinated.

The weeks slipped by. One evening George was listening to the news on the wireless. "Just listen to this," he shouted. There had been an assassination attempt on the life of Hitler. Count von Stauffenburg's plot had failed but it was tremendously exciting. And then the phone rang. "Get that Roger would you please?" Roger picked up the phone and was delighted to find that it was Bradders phoning from London.

"Some of us are going to Lords on the 29th to see the Army play the RAF. Do you want to come?"

"Yes, of course, if my dad will let me."

"When you get there, go in at the St. John's Wood gates. You'll find us as near the front as we can get."

"OK."

"You aren't half lucky to have a phone in your house. This call has cost me bloody three-pence."

"Blimey. Thanks ever so much for ringing. See you at the match."

They weren't boys to waste time on unnecessary conversation but even if they had been the pips would have cut them short. Roger decided not to mention the cricket to his father. He would ask his mother when his dad was at work.

"What was the phone call?"

"Oh just one of my pals from school."

"Kids these days. Wasting their parents' money on the phone."

"No he was using his own money in a call box. His parents haven't got a phone."

"Well just you be careful how you use ours, that's all."

Poor George hadn't recovered from the shock of Alfie's last leave. He had phoned his girlfriend for three quarters of an hour at a time and the phone bill had been enormous. Roger's mother was knitting a pullover. Roger took a skein of wool from her and held it as she wound it into a ball. He moved his hands up and down fitting into her rhythm. His dad walked out of the room and Roger took his chance: "Can I go up to Lords to watch the cricket the day after tomorrow?"

His mother didn't know where Lords was. But she knew what cricket was, a nice quiet game with people dressed in smart white clothes. Roger couldn't get into any trouble watching cricket. And for the whole day. It would be lovely to have him out of her hair.

"Yes, of course, dear."

"Can I take some sandwiches?"

"Yes dear."

"And can I have some extra pocket money please?"

Whatever next. It was always ask, ask, ask with these boys. The others had been just the same. Margaret wasn't like that. But then, George gave her everything she wanted so she didn't need to ask for money did she.

173

"How much do you need?" she asked.

"You couldn't let me have two shillings could you?"

"TWO SHILLINGS! What do you think we are? We're not made of money you know." She gave him *one* shilling. "Just be grateful," she said. "I don't know what your father would say if he knew."

Roger was grateful and did his best to show it. He not only thanked her but gave her a hug as well. Then he took his bike and went to see his favourite grandmother and his favourite aunt. His grandmother thought he had come because they had been bombed out. She gave him threepence without him having to ask and he managed to scrounge a *tanner from his aunt, so he reckoned he was OK.

On the 29th July he took the train up to London and then walked from Waterloo to Lords. It wasn't all that far. He crossed the river and went up to Trafalgar Square, then Piccadilly Circus and up Regent Street. As he walked he realised that although London was so big, all the places any visitor was likely to want to go to were quite close together. There wasn't any need to use the buses or the tube.

He reached Regent's Park and walked in the park as far as Hanover Gate before cutting across to St. John's Wood Road. It was nearly lunch-time. The man on the turnstile said, "Hello sonny. You're a bit late aren't you?"

"Yes, I've come up from Croydon."

"What – on the train and tube?"

"I came up to Waterloo on the train but then I walked. I haven't got much money so I thought I'd better walk."

The man looked at Roger and thought, 'Kids haven't got very much of anything these days with this bloody war going on and on.' He said, "Have you got three-pence?"

"Yes," said Roger who had been expecting to pay sixpence.

"Go on in then." And then he shoved a score card into Roger's hand. "You'd better have one of these too."

"Cor thanks mister," answered Roger. He couldn't believe his luck. Once inside he found Bradders and three other Perspins Londoners without much difficulty and settled down to enjoy the match. Bradders seemed to know all the cricketers. He came to Lords quite often. Kent's Godfrey Evans was playing but the

*sixpence

174

person Roger would never forget was Middlesex's Jack Robertson.

He was batting when they heard the drone of a doodlebug. Play stopped as everybody listened. It was still out of sight when it cut out. The players threw themselves to the ground and the spectators either ran for cover or followed the example of the cricketers.

There was the most almighty explosion. Slowly people began to look around and get back on their feet.

"Blimey," said Bradders, "that was close."

It had not been as close as all that. It had fallen two hundred yards from the ground, but it certainly sounded close.

The cricketers were back on their feet by this time, dusting themselves down. The bowler went back to his mark and Jack Robertson settled into his normal stance at the crease. As the ball left the bowler's hand he leapt down the pitch and smashed it into the grandstand for six.

Cheers of relief and excitement rang round the pitch. He had lifted everybody's spirits with that one blow. The boys went to see the damage from the V1 but they didn't see much. The fire engines and ambulances were still there and the police had closed the whole area off. So they said goodbye to one another and set off for home full of their day. But it was a sign that Roger was beginning to grow up that he decided not to mention the doodle-bug. He was beginning to learn that there were some things it was better for parents not to know.

Later he was to wonder why doodlebugs affected him so little, especially his gran's bombing. Something like 4000 came over that holiday and over 5000 people were killed, yet it all made little impact on him. Perhaps it was because by this time, far more people were being killed in bombing raids on Germany.

When his dad learned that he had been up in London he was not very pleased. "In future, when you want to go to London you ask me. Do you understand? I'm not having you miles away from home like that with no one knowing where you are."

"But I told Mum I was going to Lords."

"Hm. So you might have done." George knew that his wife had no idea where Lords was. "In future you ask me, not your mother."

"Yes Dad."

"How did you get from Waterloo?"

"I walked."

"Both ways?"

"Yes."

"Hm." In spite of himself George was impressed. "And how much did it cost to go into the ground?"

"They let me in cheap because the match was already on when I got there. I only paid threepence and the man gave me the score card free."

"Did you write the score card up?"

"Yes I did." He showed it to his dad.

Again his dad was pleased, but as he looked at the score card he realised that this was just the moment he had been waiting for all summer.

"In future when you want to go to cricket or to football matches you ask me, not your mother. It's good to have an interest in sport. You know I like to watch the Palace myself. But sport isn't going to earn you a living. Your school report wasn't very good was it."

"No Dad," said Roger as he thought, 'It's taken him long enough. I've been expecting this all summer.'

"You were near the bottom of your class and teacher after teacher said that you could do better."

"Yes Dad."

"Your Headmaster's comment wasn't very good either was it? What was it he said, 'I find the boy straightforward enough, but he is in trouble far too often and constantly needs to be punished'. What do you say about that?"

"Did you read what Mr Emerson wrote about scouts?"

"That was the only decent comment you had."

"But it was pretty good wasn't it Dad."

Yes it had been pretty good, a tiny bit of comfort in a thoroughly bad report: 'Roger is a keen and dedicated scout and our youngest patrol leader. He will make a fine soldier one day.'

"One good comment isn't enough," said George. "When you go back to school I want you to work hard at your lessons. I never had your chance of a good schooling and I know how important it is."

"Yes Dad. I'll try but I'm not very clever you know."

"No I don't know and I don't care. What I want to see on your

176

reports is that you have tried as hard as you can and done your best. Do you understand?"

"Yes Dad."

"Your Mr Emerson was in the last war wasn't he?"

"Yes, he fought on the Somme but he doesn't talk about it."

"I'm not surprised. If our invasion troops aren't careful they'll get bogged down the way we did."

But they didn't. They broke out of their bridgehead and began to advance fast. In August General de Gaulle entered Paris in triumph. Then, as the Allies entered Brussels the Germans unleashed one final weapon onto the long-suffering Londoners. Almost at the end of the holidays the first V2s began to arrive.

They were rockets travelling faster than the speed of sound and causing immense devastation when they exploded. And yet the only fear they instilled was the fear that vast numbers of them would be coming – the fear of the unknown.

And that was not a fear that entered Roger's mind. He lacked the imagination to look at a possible doom-laden future. For him, the V2s weren't scary at all because when you heard the explosion you knew that you were safe. Precisely because the rockets came faster than the speed of sound, it was some seconds after the explosion was all over before survivors heard it.

So to Roger and to many more, the V2s that came right through until the end of the following March were just the last throw of the dice before the Germans were finally defeated. They killed less than 3000 people at a time when, in a few days 260,000 people were killed in ordinary air-raids on Japan.

Roger went back to his third year at Perspins believing that the end of the war was in sight. Yet it still had almost a year to run.

29

Academia

That third year at Perspins when Roger was in form 4 was to be thoroughly disappointing for Roger's parents although he continued to enjoy life. The academic side of school life began to rear its ugly head and Roger was found wanting. Within limits he worked hard and enthusiastically. But the limits he set himself were not designed to bring about an improvement in his position in class or to find favour with the staff who had taken over the teaching.

He was soon in trouble with the Head who was now teaching them French – not that he was the only one. The Head brought their first French homework back and asked Dave to pass the exercise books around the class. Then he began to circulate.

"Look at the work you have done and examine my comments. See where you have gone wrong and make sure that you do not go wrong again. Take particular notice of my asterisks denoting careless mistakes."

Roger looked at his work. There were three asterisks in the margin. The Head came alongside his desk.

"You see that." He pointed to the first asterisk. " 'Le' is masculine. 'Femme' is feminine. The two do not go together. Careless boy," and he thumped the side of Roger's head.

He pointed to the second, explained it, thump. Then to the third and a final thump. The class soon learned when to sway to lessen the impact but the thumping did nothing to drive the lesson home and only led them to dislike studying French.

Then Roger was in trouble again over a particularly bad maths homework. At the end of morning school Mr Barlow sent him to the Head. Roger took his maths work and a covering note and knocked on the familiar study door.

"Come in."

Roger handed over his book and waited while the Head read Mr Barlow's note and examined his homework.

"Mr Barlow doesn't think much of your homework."

"No sir."

"Neither do I. There's very little work here and most of that is wrong. Why didn't you finish the work you were set?"

"I didn't have time sir."

"What do you mean, you didn't have time," the Headmaster rumbled.

"Sir, I did my best sir but I don't really understand it sir, and we only had half an hour to do it in. Mr Barlow set too much sir."

"What do you mean you 'only had half an hour'?"

"Sir we have an hour and a half for prep and three subjects so that's half an hour each."

"You've mastered that much maths I see. How is it that other boys manage to finish their homework and you don't?"

"Sir, they do their homework in their spare time."

The Head was flabbergasted. The boy was utterly serious. He didn't see why he should work in his spare time. No wonder he was always having balls confiscated and being caned for playing football in the classroom.

"What do you want to do when you leave school Wallace?"

"I've no idea sir. That's too far away to worry about."

"Hrmph," the Head growled. "Perhaps, but if you are going to do *anything* worthwhile it will mean hard, dedicated work and it will mean making sacrifices. Whatever you choose to do will be given a good start if you make sacrifices now and achieve good exam results."

"Yes sir."

"Go on then boy. Work hard. Play hard. Always give of your best."

"Yes sir. Thank you sir." Roger was astonished. He hadn't been scatted.

"How did ee get on?" asked Joe.

"He never scatted me. He just told me to work harder. But it's no good, I shall never understand this stuff."

179

"But it's easy. 'Tis just decimals and fractions."

"I don't understand decimals and fractions."

"Gyaw us did they at junior school!"

"I never did. P'raps I missed them between schools when I was an evacuee."

"Us'll 'ave to teach ee then won't us. 'Ave you got your sweet coupons?"

"Yes."

" 'Ave ee got any money?"

"No."

"Same's usual – my money then and your coupons. Let's get a bar of chocolate."

So they went to the tuck shop and bought a bar of chocolate.

"How many squares is there?"

As they walked down the worn stone steps from the tuck shop and along the corridor to their classroom Roger counted the squares: "Twelve," he said.

"You eat one and I'll eat one." They did. "There, us've eaten a fraction of the bar."

"I know that stupid but that doesn't help me understand."

"Break up the other ten pieces. We're going to pretend that those ten pieces make a whole bar."

Roger broke the pieces up with his knife and they nibbled the crumbs that fell away. Nothing must be wasted.

Joe said, "The whole bar is ten pieces, right. So one piece is one tenth of the whole bar."

"Yes," said Roger bemused.

"And two pieces is two tenths and three pieces is three tenths . . ."

Light dawned. "I get it," said Roger excitedly. "Four is four tenths, five is five tenths . . ."

"And so on. That's fractions! That's all there is to it."

"Gosh isn't it easy. Oh wow, I can do fractions! Thanks Joe. But what about decimals?"

"That's just as easy," answered Joe. "Look at those ten pieces again and remember we're pretending we've got a whole chocolate bar there."

"Yes." Roger was eager to learn now and concentrating hard.

"How many chocolate bars have us got then?"

"One, of course."

180

"And how many pieces?"

"Ten."

"Get a piece of paper and put a full stop on it. In Maths that's called a decimal point."

"I know that," said Roger irritably as he put the decimal point on his sheet of paper.

"Take one piece of chocolate and put it on the paper behind the dot."

Roger was baffled but he did as he was told.

"There," said Joe. "That's point one of the chocolate bar. Now do the same again."

Roger hadn't got this sorted but he did as Joe said.

"Zo what have you got?"

"I've got point one of the chocolate bar," said Roger uncertainly.

"Yes, but you've got point one twice haven't you?"

"Yes," answered Roger doubtfully.

"Two point ones is point two, just like ordinary adding up."

"So if I put another one down that's point three?" asked Roger.

"Zacly."

They stopped and there was a moment's silence while Roger tried to work out what he was doing and where he was going.

"Go on then. Don't just stop there."

Roger put another piece of chocolate on the paper. "That's point four." And another, "point five" and at last he got it. "And then when I've put them all down I've got the whole one which is one point nought."

"Easy idn it?"

"So point one is the same as one tenth."

"You got it boy! That's decimals and fractions. That's all there is to it. Now you knows that you can work out every decimal and fraction there is, but you'd better put in some practice from our text book."

So while Joe ate the chocolate Roger looked back in his text book at some of the easy early questions on decimals and fractions and set to work, not even noticing that he was doing it in his spare time. He worked out the answers and Joe marked them. He was astonished. They weren't really difficult at all once you'd got the hang of them. He reached out for a piece of chocolate.

"You beggar. You've eaten all the chocolate."

"Yes," said Joe with a grin. "Every last fraction of it."

The ensuing scrap lasted them until the bell went for lunch That afternoon they settled into their desks and took out their English books. As they did, the classroom door opened a fraction and a pocket knife appeared. It made a few carving movements and was followed by part of an arm. The carving went on and the door opened a fraction more.

Those to the left of the classroom saw Mr Emerson leaning against the door and heaving for all he was worth, still carving with his free arm. At last he was inside.

"God, what a fug," he exclaimed. "Open the windows and let some air into this place."

So with a howling gale whistling round their ears he set about teaching them the rudiments of English grammar. This was his first term teaching them and he worked on the fairly accurate assumption that no one had taught them anything in earlier classes.

He drew a line from top to bottom of the blackboard. On the left he wrote 'subject' and on the right he wrote 'object'.

He explained the two halves of a sentence and then boxes began to appear on either side of the line containing nouns, verbs, adjectives and adverbs. Each box was linked to another as the structure of a sentence was created. Roger was fascinated. He liked Mr Emerson. No it was more than that.

Scouting had given him a real respect and affection for the man. And now he felt that he wanted to learn everything Mr Emerson could teach him even if it meant working in his spare time. He felt that he would do anything for Mr Emerson.

One Tuesday afternoon that feeling was put to the test in a big way.

30

Ditch and Dyke, and Victory

It was inevitable that winter that the war in Europe should finally be on everybody's mind, even the minds of 13 year olds like Roger – perhaps especially 13 year olds like Roger.

They had only been back at school a few days when Airborne troops landed behind enemy lines near Arnhem. It was a heroic mission but one which ultimately failed. School was over and the Christmas holidays had begun before the next major excitement. On the 15th December the Germans launched their final great assault in the Ardennes. It was madness. They lacked the manpower, the fuel and equipment, let alone the reserves for such a push.

But they caught the Americans on the hop and drove forward with apparent ease. For a moment it looked as though they would break right through, and in England there was real anxiety. Even Roger felt it. Memories of 1940 were still too fresh. Was it possible that the Germans could repeat what they had done before?

But then the Americans got their act together and by the end of January the German push was all over. The Allies were now poised for the final invasion of Germany from both the west and the south while the Russians were also hammering on the German door from the east.

Excitement was intense. But as the British and American troops began to push into Germany itself the joy of success and of the approaching end of the war began to be disturbed. Even without television to bring the horrors into their homes, images of concentration camps began to appear in newspapers and on cinema screens.

Advancing troops had to deal with more than images. They were faced with the full awfulness of the truth about Nazism. They were faced by the grotesque heaps of the dead and the dying and by the almost greater horror of the skeletal creatures who had survived to tell the tale. For the first time soldiers knew exactly what they had been fighting for – to rid the world of the foulest philosophy that had ever entered the pages of human history; to put an end to this particularly foul expression of 'man's inhumanity to man'.

Back at school it was cold and wet. Just the right conditions, thought Mr Emerson, to take his scout troop out on a ditch and dyke. There was no better way to keep them fit and prepare them for serving in the infantry or even the commandos.

He told them to come to scouts dressed in rugby kit. To their astonishment he led them at the double all the way to the chapel. In the field to the left, where Mr Sanderson's marquee had been, there was now a lake. Mr Emerson lined his boys up along the top of the hedge.

"Follow me," he cried and waded right through the lake.

The boys leapt off the hedge into the water, sending fountains of water over one another and running through. By this time Mr Emerson was trotting on ahead. Grouped in their patrols they followed across a couple of fields, a short way down a road and into a third field. There the Assistant Scout Master (the prefect Briggs) led the troop in physical jerks while Mr Emerson wriggled through underneath a tiny bridge. There was only room for one at a time and there was a small stream running through as well. Mr Emerson called the first patrol through and led them in physical jerks as soon as they emerged. Gradually the whole troop came through and then they were off again, following Mr Emerson down the middle of the stream for a good half a mile before running across more fields.

A brief and energetic wide game followed in which half the troop rose from their imaginary trenches and made a vigorous frontal assault on the enemy 'trenches'. It was a marvellous opportunity for unarmed combat with a great deal of fun and an occasional serious fight between people who had scores to settle with one another.

Before anything could get out of hand they were off again on the homeward journey across fields, through woods on paths thick with sticky mud until they came to a large drainage pipe. Mr Emerson went straight through.

"It's a bloody sewer," exclaimed Bradders forcefully. "I'm not going through there."

"Tidn' a sewer at all," replied Joe. "Where would it get sewage from? There idn no farms around yer. 'Tis just drainage that's all. Idn nothing to worry about."

By this time they were all busy with more physical jerks to keep them warm until their turn came to go through the pipe. Through they all went, including Bradders and so back across a few more fields to school.

"Straight into the tilehouse with you," called Mr Emerson.

In they went. It was the usual drill. Strip off. Wash at the basins and jump in and out of the three rinse baths. But then there came a change. Between the final bath and their towels Mr Emerson stood with a large bottle and a dessert spoon. Every boy received a spoonful and every boy swallowed the stuff down and said 'thank you' before moving on.

"What the hell was that?" asked Bradders.

"Quinine," Briggs answered. "He swears by it."

"He's bloody mad."

"Have you only just realised that?"

Roger kept his mouth shut. He had enjoyed every minute of the ditch and dyke and would happily have done one every week. It was much more fun than trying to pass the tests for his scout badges. Yet he and Joe were busily doing just that. They both had their second class badges and were to become the first boys in anybody's memory at the school to achieve their first class, though they cheated a little bit for that.

When the time came for them to do their twenty-four hour hike, they hiked from school to one of Joe's uncle's farms. They put up their tent and shortly afterwards Joe's parents arrived with a hamper. Sitting on groundsheets, they had a first class evening meal. Roger wrote up their journal which spoke of the meal they had cooked over an open fire. They slept the sleep of the wicked and the following day hiked back to school after a hearty breakfast with Joe's uncle and aunt.

If scouts were supposed to be able to use their initiative and to be able to live off the land, they reckoned they had done pretty well. In his ignorance, after he had read Roger's journal, Mr Emerson thought so too.

But that hike didn't take place until long after the final dramas of the European war. Vienna fell on April 14. The final battle for Berlin was bloody and cruel but the Russians were unstoppable and on April 30, Hitler followed the example of so many of his generals and committed suicide. After that it was only a matter of days before the final surrender on May 7 – a surrender that took a few days more before it was fully implemented.

The excitement in London on VE Day had to be seen to be believed, but at Perspins it was far more muted. The boys were given the day off but they didn't really know what to do with it. Some went down to the village and rang the church bells until they were stopped by a rather anxious vicar who had visions of losing his bells altogether. Others went into the churchyard and overturned the famous 'Devil's Stone' which should only have been turned once a year.

But most of them felt rather lost. They wandered about the school and the countryside knowing that they ought to be excited and happy, but not knowing how. It was easier to settle back into their normal routine the following day. As they did so it slowly dawned on them that the war was not yet over. They hadn't given a thought to the war against Japan for a very long time. But now their minds began to turn to Burma where Field Marshal Sir William Slim's 11th Army of Indian and British troops was driving the Japanese back at last.

And further east the Americans and Australians were gradually recovering lost territory and the American Navy had won the greatest naval battle of the war at Midway. The Japanese fought almost to the last man and it looked as though that part of the war could still go on for a very long time.

As the Allies advanced, every triumph was hard won. And from time to time prisoners of war were released from Japanese camps. Once again images of skeletal human beings hit the pages of the newspapers and the cinema screens. To an insular people these hurt almost more than the concentration camp images because these were our own men and women, not foreigners, not Jews or gypsies. Stories of their sufferings percolated through. Horror, anguish and anger mingled with the relief of those whose loved ones were safe.

But safe for what? Safe to enter a world which for them would often be dominated by their own permanent nightmares and mental scars. Victory when it came might bring some sort of peace to a ravaged world, but it would never bring peace to men and women who had endured the hell of those camps.

Something of all this reached into Roger's heart and mind, but not very much. As end of term approached once more, another awful set of exam results was of more immediate relevance to him. Only in English had he managed a respectable mark.

The Head came into form 4 just before the end of term.

"I have been studying your examination results. They are poor on the whole. And some of you are worse than poor. For a few of you there is some small excuse. You have come through this year early in terms of your age. But any fourteen year olds with bad results should be ashamed of themselves." (Roger had just had his fourteenth birthday.) The Head continued, "If I allowed you to go up to the 5th form next year, very few of you would achieve your school certificate, let alone your matriculation exemption. As you know, you have to pass in six subjects. Half of you haven't a hope of that even with the high quality of the teaching at this school.

"Those of you who are good enough will go up to form 5. The rest will spend another year in form 4 improving their work in preparation for the examination year in form 5."

He pinned up two lists on the notice board. "You will find which form you will be in on these lists. I congratulate those who have done well. I shall expect better results next year from all of you though."

Roger didn't even bother to look at the lists. He knew which he was on. His father wouldn't be pleased but he had done his best – well, up to a point he had. Joe looked at the lists and came back furious. His exam results hadn't been much better than Roger's but he still felt that he ought to be going up.

" 'Tis just a racket," he said. "Ee knows that as soon as I've done my school cert I shall be leaving school to go and work on the farm. So he's kept me down to make my parents pay an extra year's school fees. Tidn right. 'Tis just a fiddle."

"No," said Roger. "He wouldn't do that. You didn't do very well, and you are younger than me. It's like he said, we're not ready to go up yet."

"I'm just as ready as my cousin. He's going up."

Poor Joe. He reckoned he would never live it down.

They went home and faced their parents. Roger's dad gave him a pretty thorough lecture made worse by the fact that Margaret had had a report commenting on the great strides she was making, and emphasising her good behaviour. Roger was incensed. She had no business behaving so well. She ought to mess about more, enjoy herself and get into trouble sometimes.

His father's lecture was soon forgotten as he went to Lords to watch one of the Victory Tests and again to Lords and the Oval to watch Middlesex and Surrey. He lacked the narrow patriotism which prevented some of his friends from enjoying Australians like Miller. He was captivated by his showmanship as well as by the brilliance of his cricket. But there was one Englishman who was just as brilliant and just as much of a showman. Denis Compton dancing down the pitch was every boy's hero. For Roger there were others too: John Edrich, Alec and Eric Bedser, the Surrey twins, and Alf Gover the Surrey fast bowler who never bent down to pick up a ball.

That summer and in summers to come Roger went whenever he could to Lords and the Oval. And in the winter he went to Crystal Palace where the Dawes brothers and Basset were stalwart in defence and where Fred Kurz and Jack Stamp made a brilliant striking partnership. Less often he went to see Arsenal, and there was Denis Compton again, chatting with the crowd from his place on the wing while his brother Leslie held the fort at centre half. For Roger, those years were the dream years for watching cricket and football.

But in August of that year the war returned to the forefront of everybody's attention. War with Japan came to a sudden, dreadful and devastating end. On August 6 the Americans dropped an atomic bomb on Hiroshima killing 80,000 people outright (and another 60,000 over time). Two days later they dropped another on Nagasaki. Six days later the war was over.

But the shock and horror of those two bombs muted the celebrations. They had killed and mutilated multitudes of people and virtually demolished two cities. Against that, people asked how many soldiers' lives had been saved by the abrupt termination of the war.

Yet everybody knew that the world would never be the same again. If Hitler had had such power at his disposal, no one could have stood against him. Joy that the war was ended was more than matched by anxiety for the future. Was there a future for mankind? And if so what did it hold?

Roger went back to school and to a science text book that still claimed that the atom was indestructible. Yet not everything was doom and gloom. There was a new, idealistic Labour government that was going to do wonders for the education, the health and the welfare of the nation.

Roger was caught up with the excitement the new government brought and became more strongly political than he ever would be again. He began to think about a political career when he left school. He didn't want to be Prime Minister. He would start off as Foreign Secretary he thought.

31

'Macbeth Does Murder Sleep'

If his first year in form 4 had been a disappointment to his parents, Roger's second year was to be a time of bitter disappointment to him.

It didn't worry him that he continued to do badly academically. He and Joe were so bored with the same work all over again that they messed about endlessly and were finally separated in class. But that hardly made any difference to them at all. They were still far too bored to work. Roger went right through the year with only two pages of history notes.

It was sport that worried Roger. Now was the time when he should have been playing for the school Colts, the under fifteens. His pals were chosen but he wasn't. He was so upset that he went to the Colts' master.

"Sir, why haven't I been picked for the Colts? All my friends are in the team – well, most of them. I think I'm as good as they are."

"Do you? You're not as fast as some of them are you? And you can't kick like David Shaw at fly half. And you are too small for the scrum. In fact you are smaller than any of them."

"No, I'm not sir. I'm bigger than Williams and I'm bigger than Cob."

"But both of them are specialists, playing in positions where their small size is actually a help to them."

It was true. Little Andy Williams was a brilliant hooker and Roger knew he could never match John Cob at scrum half either.

Roger played hard against the Colts in practice matches. He

joined in with them in all their informal training sessions. There was no proper training or coaching. Mr Barlow, who had taken over the Colts when Mr Smart left, had never played rugby in his life. He didn't know the first thing about it and didn't want to know.

Poor Roger went right through that year without getting into the team. It was a bitter pill. He never managed to get into the Colts cricket team either but he didn't feel so sore about that. He knew that he wasn't good enough at cricket.

Failing in sport and failing in his academic work, it would have been a complete year of failure but for politics. Although he was so young he was caught up by the excitement and the hopes the Labour Government had raised. He decided that he was a Socialist. At school that marked him out. Hardly anybody was a Socialist. The farmers' sons were all Liberal and most of the rest were Conservatives.

Mr Emerson was amused. He was now taking them once a week for a course in Civics and when they finally moved up into the fifth form he took over their history teaching too. He asked them one day, "Those of you who are Conservatives put up your hands."

There were plenty of takers. There were also plenty who put up their hands as Liberals. "Socialists?" Roger was one of about half a dozen.

"Anybody else?"

Philip Jonas put up his hand: "Communist, sir."

"And why are you Communist Philip?" he asked.

"Because no one else is sir."

Mr Emerson grinned. He was more conservative than most but he made no attempt to push his own point of view. Instead, he tried to persuade the boys to read and to think for themselves. He introduced them to Burke and to Adam Paine and to the poets who had been so enthusiastic about the French Revolution in its early days. He told them about Owen's idealistic experiments in industrial democracy; persuaded them to read Cobbett's *Rural Rides* and John Stuart Mill's book *On Liberty*. He forced them to give reasons for their opinions, challenged their reasons and made them think.

Roger responded. He wasn't really aware of it. He just knew that he enjoyed Mr Emerson's lessons and debates, and enjoyed tackling work he didn't fully understand. He was quite unaware of it, but he was beginning to leave boyhood behind and to grow. He was also, at long last, beginning to grow physically. Curiously enough he didn't really notice.

All through school he had cursed his small size. Now that he was growing there were only two things that he really was aware of. His voice had broken and he had moved through the choir, first from treble to alto and then to tenor. He was to end up amongst the basses. Together with the changes to his voice had come the longed-for changes that signalled his manhood. It was Macbeth that signalled that change in a way that he would never have dreamed possible.

Macbeth was one of the set books for School Certificate so Mr Emerson decided that the fifth form should put on a production. As usual, Roger was just given a bit part as Banquo's servant. As the dress rehearsal drew near boys were told to try to obtain kilts. A few got them from mothers or sisters. The Head's wife provided a few from her Scottish dancing class but they were still one or two short.

"Wallace. Go and see Mrs Petherick in the kitchens. See if any of them can help."

"Gladys has got one," said Mrs Petherick. "I don't know about anybody else. I'll ask around. Gladys," she called and when Gladys came she said, "the boys need kilts for some Scottish play they'm in. Can you lend your kilt to this yer lad?"

Gladys was a few years older than Roger, small, neat, with a cheeky snub-nosed face. "Yes," she said. "Come with me up to my room and I'll give it to ee straight away."

"No," said Mrs Petherick firmly. "The boy will wait yer while you go and get it."

Gladys grinned and went on her own. When she came back, Mrs Petherick was busy elsewhere in the kitchen.

"How long do ee want it for?"

"It's dress rehearsal tomorrow and then the performance the night after. Then I'll have it cleaned and bring it back next week."

"No," said Gladys. "You don't need to bother with having it cleaned. Bring it back here after 'lights out' the night you do your performance. I'll meet ee yer in the kitchens."

It seemed a funny arrangement to Roger but he didn't question it. It was her kilt. If she wanted it back that quickly she must

192

have it.

"OK," he said.

She looked around her quickly and then added, "I expect you'd quite like to have me inside the kilt with you when you wear it."

He blushed crimson and she laughed.

"Git on with ee boy."

Her words played havoc with his attempts at getting to sleep that night . . .

The dress rehearsal began. At last they reached Roger's supreme moment. Banquo took his sword from its scabbard and handed it to Roger. Then he undid his sword belt and said, "Take thee that too."

As Roger took the belt Banquo's kilt fell to the ground. Mr Emerson's quiet voice followed the laughter, "Tomorrow, Wallace, you will make sure that Banquo has two belts and is wearing both of them."

"Yes sir."

As a result, if there were imperfections in the final performance, that was not one of them.

Afterwards Roger changed, folded the kilt neatly and then waited for 'lights out'. He wasn't supposed to be about after lights out. Why hadn't he had the sense to make a different arrangement? He put on his dressing gown and made his way quietly to the kitchens. Gladys was waiting.

"Come on boy," she whispered and led him through the kitchens and up a back staircase to an upstairs corridor with a line of small rooms on each side. She opened her door and took him inside. By now he knew that this was going to be more than a simple handing over of the kilt. He felt a mixture of fear and excitement. What was she going to do with him? It never entered his head that he had any say in the matter.

She took the kilt and put it on a chair. "Take your clothes off," she whispered.

That really shook him. "But . . ."

She put her finger on his lips. "Go on." And then she began to take her own clothes off.

He didn't dare really look at her, but she seemed to have a nice figure. There was a painting he had seen with a girl with a small, shapely figure like that and nice breasts that just asked

193

j

to be held.

She took him into her bed and held him close. They kissed, clumsily at first but then with a genuine meeting of lips and timing. And then he found himself wanting to kiss her all over. He kissed her neck.

"Don't bite me," she said, "but you can kiss me wherever you like."

Oh strewth. This was incredible. He roamed free, held her breasts and kissed them.

"Go on," she said. "See if you can milk 'em."

He sucked and her nipples rose in response.

"Oh my gor," she said. "Yer, let me put this on ee." She fished under her pillow, took his manhood in her hands and clothed it in a *French letter. He felt her hands and thrilled to them without altogether knowing what she was doing. And then, as he lay on top of her, she took him and slipped him inside her.

"Oh. . ." It was the longest sigh of his life. He just lay there inside her.

"Come on then. Push boy. Go for it." And as he began, "Don't be gentle. Go on boy. That's it. Oh that's it. Go on boy. Go on."

It was over far too soon. She took the Frenchie and washed it out in the basin and washed herself. Then she came back to bed, nursed him into life again, dressed him in the Frenchie and took him again. There was no point in helping the boy to grow up unless she had her share of fun too.

When it was over they lay quietly together and then he exclaimed, "The Frenchie's coming off."

"Ooh my gor. Pull it out quick." She took it from him and rushed to the basin again. "I 'ope you haven't gived me a baby."

The blood rushed to his face. In total seriousness he said, "If I have, you know that I wouldn't let you down."

She laughed. "Get on with ee boy. There won't be no baby." She sounded more confident than she felt. "Besides, what could you do for me? How old be ee, sixteen . . . seventeen?"

"Fifteen," he answered ashamed that he was so young.

"FIFTEEN. Oh my gor. I did think as you'd be older than that. Well, never mind that. It just shows that you'm too young to be thinkin' about looking after a maid with a baby. But just you think

*a condom

194

about it. If there was a baby, you wouldn't want to marry me and I wouldn't want to marry you. Us have just been having a bit of fun that's all."

"But I couldn't just leave you could I. Besides, it would be MY baby."

"Bless the boy. Now don't ee worry. There idn gwain to be no baby. So just you relax and don't be so serious."

There was a moment or two of silence and then he said, "That wasn't your first time was it?"

"Gyaw no. I had my first time with they Americans when they was yer. Since then, if I finds someone I likes enough, we 'aves a bit of fun like us have had. Sex idn no big deal boy. Think about the animals. The bull gets on the cow and goes for it and then 'tis done and he goes off to look for another cow."

"But we're not like that are we? We get married and stay together for life."

"Sex and marriage idn the same thing boy. 'Tis true you needs to enjoy sex with your husband or wife, but marriage is about friendship, about getting on with one another and about having kids and bringing them up proper. What you want to understand is that it's all right to have a bit of fun now if you'm careful and then when you'm married you can settle down. Come on now, you'd better get back to your dorm before you're missed. And don't expect to do this with me again. 'Tis too risky. Us could both be thrown out."

"I don't know how to thank you," he said. "You are beautiful you know and you've given me a wonderful time."

"Oh get on with ee," she said – but she was pleased all the same. "Take the kilt with ee and give it to Mrs Petherick tomorrow."

She led him carefully down to the kitchens and they kissed one last time and then Roger saw the Head just about to enter the kitchens on his way back to his house.

"Crikey. It's the Head."

"Quick, out through that door. I'll delay him."

Roger fled, through the door into the kitchen garden and round the outside of the school and up to his dorm. He leapt into bed and lay shaking all over. The Head saw the girl on her way to the fridge but he thought he saw something else as well. He shot across to the garden door and opened it. Nothing!

"Who was that?" he said to the girl.

"Who was what sir?" she asked.

"That boy."

"What boy, sir?"

"That boy who left just as I came in. You know who I mean."

"No sir. I know boys do come sometimes and help themselves to food they shouldn't have, but I didn't see anyone."

"What are you doing down here?"

"I couldn't sleep sir so I came down for a glass of milk."

"Hrmph." Perhaps if he went back round the dorms he might still catch someone. And catch someone he did.

Roger needed the toilet. He got up but didn't bother with his slippers and dressing gown. As he was coming back he met the Head.

"Where have you been?"

"To the toilet sir."

"Didn't I see you in the kitchens just now?"

"No sir," lied Roger with a sinking heart.

The Head's mind suddenly made a host of associations. This was the boy accused of unnatural practices by Mr Smart. And wasn't this the boy who had borrowed a kilt from one of the maids? He'd got him. Trapped.

"Macbeth went well didn't you think."

"Yes sir."

"One of the maids lent you her kilt didn't she Wallace?"

"Yes sir."

"Have you just returned it to her?"

Roger couldn't help it. He blushed even as he said, "No sir. I thought I would give it to Mrs Petherick tomorrow."

Got him!

"Would you like to show me the kilt Wallace."

"Yes sir," he answered. As he went to fetch it his heart skipped a beat. He could have jumped for joy. "Good old Gladys. If she hadn't given it back to him . . ." he thought.

"Here it is, sir."

The Head's feelings were mixed. He still wasn't sure about the boy. He hoped that he had been wrong. In fact he hoped that he hadn't seen anybody at all. But that girl was a flighty lass. He must give the boy the benefit of the doubt.

"Wallace, if ever I have reason to believe that you are

misbehaving either with one of the maids or with another boy you will be expelled forthwith. You understand don't you."

"Yes sir." 'I've understood that for a very long time,' he thought.

"Right. Get to bed and sleep well."

As the Head made his way home he thought, 'if that boy *is* at all oversexed, we'd better make sure that he's kept busy on the sports field.'

Roger went to bed feeling very relieved and then very happy. He felt that something wonderful had happened to him that night and he knew that he would always be grateful to Gladys. No, he didn't want to marry her but he would never forget her, that was for sure.

When he went to put his slippers on in the morning he was very thankful that he hadn't worn them to the toilet during the night. They were covered in mud!

After breakfast Roger took the kilt to Mrs Petherick in the kitchens. Above the noise of the kitchens she shouted, "Gladys, yer's the boy with your kilt."

Roger wasn't sure he could look Gladys in the face but she was completely at ease. He looked at her and said, "Thank you ever so much. I'm very grateful."

He hoped that didn't sound over the top for the loan of a kilt. She smiled and said, "Did the play go well?"

"Yes," he said. "Well I suppose so. Of course I only had a tiny part. I don't know how much the audience enjoyed it but those of us who were in it did."

"That's always how it is," said Mrs Petherick. " 'Tis better to do things than just to watch."

Gladys had a hard job to keep a straight face. "Oh yes," she said, " 'tis better to do things."

Roger grasped his opportunity. "I think so too," he said. "I enjoyed myself last night so much that I shall remember it all my life."

When both Gladys and Mrs Petherick said, "That's good then," he felt that he'd better leave before he gave the game away.

"Thanks again," he said. "I'd better be going."

As he left the kitchens Mrs Petherick said, "Nice boy that. I've always liked un."

"Yes," replied Gladys, "I'll take my kilt upstairs."

On her own and free to giggle, she let herself go. In her room she imitated Mrs Petherick, "Nice boy that," and continued, "Yes Mrs Petherick, but you don't have any idea just how nice he is. I wouldn't mind going with he again if I 'ad the chance. 'Tis a pity 'tis so risky doing it anywhere about the school."

32

The Winter of 1947

They returned to school after the Christmas holidays in time for the coldest winter for a very long time.

The last time Roger had seen snow like it was back in 1940 when he had been an evacuee living with Barbara. But that was in Beddingford. This was quite different.

The first thing about thick snow in the heart of the countryside was its sheer beauty. Boys looked around then in wonder at the unspoiled whiteness of it all. But the wonder didn't last. The quad soon became an ice slide from corner to corner. Sport was replaced by organised snow fights which enabled boys to vent their feelings on some of the staff and on each other.

In the mornings their flannels were frozen rigid and washing in cold water was murder. Classrooms were icy too. Boys clung to the heating pipes whenever the chance came. Teachers interrupted classes for a few minutes of physical jerks in the aisles between the desks, anything to try to keep the circulation going and the boys' minds active.

And then the telephones and the electricity were cut off. Effectively that meant that the school was cut off. Mr Kendall called on a few boys and together they made a huge sledge. Hitched up behind the tractor from the school farm, they towed it ten miles to the nearest town to buy in supplies to keep the school going.

Prep was cancelled and members of staff took turns with prefects to keep the boys entertained in the hall throughout the long, cold evenings. By the light of candles and oil lamps they sang songs endlessly and listened to stories.

Briggs was the one who began by mentioning 'Shuffling Jesus'.

"You know 'Shuffling Jesus'," he said. "He's a school governor. There have always been ministers amongst our school governors. In the early days of the school they used to live here and go out preaching to all the neighbouring towns and villages.

"There was one Governor who had a grey mare that became well known throughout the district. Off the governor would go of a Sunday morning. During the day he would preach in three different chapels and then he would set off for school. But by the evening he was always pretty tired so he just used to put the reins down on the mare's neck and say, 'Take me back to school girl'. And she did. She just plodded quietly along and he would sometimes fall asleep on her back.

"One Sunday he went to Beddingford and preached there all day. In the evening he felt properly done in. He mounted the old grey mare and said, 'Take me back to school girl' and she set off as usual. Only he didn't just go to sleep. He died, sitting there in the saddle. She plodded quietly back to school with him upright in the saddle. She thought it was a bit strange when he never dismounted, but she plodded out to the stables and into her stall. Her food and drink was all there ready for her, so she had a good drink and a bite to eat and then, because he was still on her back, she just went to sleep standing up.

"You know old Bill Battersby, the groundsman? Well his grandfather went out to the stables in the morning and found the grey mare standing there and she was dead. She had died in the night. And sitting on her back was the Governor and he was dead, too.

"Sometimes of a stormy Sunday night, if you're in one of the dorms close to the road you can hear the clop, clop of the old grey mare's hooves and if you look out to the road you'll see her come along the road from Beddingford with the Governor on her back. They clop along the road, pause; and then turn into the stables an' then they disappear."

The following mid-day after school, Roger went out to see if he could find Bill Battersby. He found him sitting with his mate in their den at the foot of the tower.

"Mr Battersby," he said, "last night one of the prefects told us

200

a ghost story about the Governor's Grey Mare. Is it true?"

"Ah," said Bill, " 'tis true enough. Us've seed un 'an' us George?"

"Ah," replied George, "an the one out yer."

"Which one out here?" asked Roger.

"Bill will tell ee," answered George and fell back into his normal silence.

"It were in my father's time," said Bill.

"How many generations of you have worked here?" asked Roger.

"Four, man and boy. My great-grandfather started yer when the school first began."

"Gosh."

"But 'twere my father as found the one out yer."

"What one?"

"Ee were a young minister who were a teacher here as well. Ee got mixed up with one of they girls in the kitchens."

Roger blushed.

"Not to beat about the bush, he gived her a baby. Well ee were a decent enough young man zo ee went to zee her parents to offer to marry the girl. But they wouldn't let un near the place. Her dad drove him off, telling him just what he thought of him.

"He comed back yer to school in a real tizzy. He didn't know what to do. If he told the Headmaster he knew he'd be throwed out, and he'd be out of the ministry too. But worse than that, the girl would be throwed out and disgraced. He just didn' know what to do.

"Well then the Mother and the girl went away. They planned for the girl to have her baby where no one knew them, and then to put it for adoption and they would come back and no one would be any the wiser . . . Except that in a village like this, everybody always does know everybody else's business.

"The young man wadn' no fool. He knew what they was up to as soon as they went away. The thought of his baby bein' given for adoption really got to him. He paced up and down and walked round they fields wondering what to do. Eventually he just wrote a note saying as life had got too much for him. That didn't tell no one nothing about the girl. Then he climbed up this yer tower and hanged himself. My father found him and cut him down.

"Every so often us sees him up there, swinging in the wind."

"Never," said Roger. "I don't believe that. There isn't no such thing as ghosts."

"Us sees un I tell ee. Don' us George?"

"Ah," replied George.

"And the Governor's grey mare too. Don' us George?"

"Ah," came George's answer again.

Roger didn't want to sound too dismissive. "Thanks for telling me the story," he said. "But how do you know the teacher gave the girl the baby?"

"She was friends with my mother. She told her all about it. She felt terrible when the man killed his self."

"Yes I expect she did," Roger replied. He left the men in the tower and walked slowly round the rugby pitch. His own escapade with Gladys was fresh in his memory. He wondered what she would do if she had a baby and how he would feel.

Perhaps she was right and sex was 'just a bit of fun' if you were careful enough. But it was a bit of fun that could become very serious. He thought that it would be best only to have sex with someone he really liked, someone he wouldn't mind marrying if he had to. But if he had the chance to go with Gladys again, would he have the strength to say 'no'?

He didn't think he would. He would just be carried along on the strength of the passion of the moment. It would be better to keep away from girls altogether.

He kicked the snow angrily. Just thinking about it made him want to do it. He could see Gladys' shapely little body. Oh hell. He must think about something else. . .

The school's isolation ended with the restoration of electricity and the telephones after five days, but the snow continued. The tractor and sledge went off a couple of times a week for more supplies for the school, and then at last the thaw set in.

As the term drew to a close it was exam time. For the fifth form that meant mock school certificate. Roger's attitude to work hadn't changed. In class he tried hard to learn all he could. Teachers found him enthusiastic and full of questions – too full sometimes. He was a bit of a nuisance.

And he did his prep as well as he could in the time allotted, but he still wasn't willing to 'waste' his precious spare time. Football, rugby, piano, singing, anything was more important than prep. In spite of that he was in for a shock as were his teachers.

As the marks came out that end of term, in subject after subject he was right up near the top of the class. He couldn't understand it. He had never done as well as this – nowhere near as well. The teachers were baffled too. They checked his papers a second time to make sure that they had got it right. And then when all the marks were out and averaged out to give the boys their places in the class, Roger was top. He couldn't believe it.

Neither could the Head. He said to Mr Emerson, "Have you noticed that Wallace is top of form 5?"

"Yes." Mr Emerson didn't enlarge on his answer but he smiled as if to say, "It's no more than I would have expected."

"But the boy has never been anywhere above the bottom half a dozen in his class. And he doesn't even WORK?"

"He could certainly do with working rather harder than he does," replied Mr Emerson. "But when he works, he works very well. And as for his place in class, perhaps he's just a late developer. He's growing in body as well, as I expect you've noticed Headmaster."

"Yes. Perhaps that's it. Anyway, it's a relief to see it. If he keeps it up he might get a good school certificate."

"He might," said Mr Emerson, "or he might rest on his laurels and fail completely. We shall see."

And Roger was tempted to rest on his laurels. In the event, he just went on as he always had done and was very thankful to get his school cert. with matric exemption – but only just. It was General Science of all things that saw him through.

He had never been any good at science. He was supposed to learn a host of letters that represented things. The only one he ever did learn was H_2O for water. Apparently chalk and lime and marble were all related and had similar letters because of it. Every revision lesson old Herries asked him one or other of them. Every time he got it wrong and every time Herries' metre ruler cropped him on the side of the head.

They came up in the exam too. Whether he got them right or wrong, he hadn't a clue – probably wrong.

But a few days before the exam, Herries had shown them three films, each of them three times over. The first was about the amoeba, the second about the hydra, and the third about a dry cell. Roger quite enjoyed the first two, but how could anybody ever be interested in a film about a dry cell?

When the exam came, they had to write three essays, with diagrams if possible. One of the choices was a question on the amoeba. Another was on the hydra. And, what a surprise, a third was on the dry cell. Had Herries seen the exam paper in advance? Was it cheating to have shown them the films? Roger knew that he would never have passed general science without them.

33
Boxing and Rugby

When Roger returned to school that autumn he found life changed almost beyond recognition. Many of his friends, mostly sons of farmers, had left school to work on the land.

He himself was no longer a small boy to be beaten every week or so for some minor misdemeanour. He was a young man ready for responsibility. He found that he was a sub-prefect, secretary of the choir, a librarian and sub-editor of the school magazine. But there was one change the Headmaster had made which Roger disliked. When he and the Head had first joined Perspins, the Head had made a number of changes. One of them was to put an end to Prefects being allowed to scat boys. If they felt that boys deserved to be scatted, they had to take them to the Headmaster. Now for reasons best known to himself, the Head had decided to restore the power to scat to prefects. Roger determined that he would never be responsible for such a scatting.

The Head had also decided that senior boys must learn to box. It was to be compulsory. Roger didn't like boxing, though whether his objection was on moral grounds or just because he didn't like getting hurt, he was never quite sure. He found that quite a lot of his pals objected to the idea that boxing should be compulsory so off he went to see the Head.

"Well Wallace, what is it?"

"I've come to see you about boxing sir."

The Head sensed what was coming and looked black, "Go on."

"Some of us do not like the idea of boxing being compulsory sir."

" 'Some of us' you say. Do you really mean 'some of us' or do you just mean that you are too cowardly to be willing to put the gloves on?"

Roger flushed. "Call me cowardly if you wish sir, but I've not been too cowardly to come and see you. When I said 'some of us', I meant 'some of us'. If you try to force us, I've no doubt that most boys would box. I wouldn't sir. I'm saying to you now that I am not prepared to take part in the sport."

"You have just been given new responsibilities Roger." (That use of the first name was ominous). "You are a sub-prefect."

"Yes sir."

"You realise that that means that I expect your whole-hearted support at all times."

"If you don't wish me to continue as a sub-prefect, I understand that sir. But it seems to me that a sub-prefect has a responsibility to stand up for other boys as well as a responsibility to school rules sir." He took a deep breath. "Whether I am a sub-prefect or not, I am not prepared to do any boxing sir."

The Head admired his guts. "I'll discuss your objections with the school staff Wallace. For the time being you will continue as a sub-prefect and I shall expect you to fulfil your duties well."

"Yes sir. Thank you sir."

Boxing became a voluntary sport and within a few weeks it had fizzled out completely.

There were two other innovations that term for the fifth and sixth forms. Both concerned dancing and both were compulsory. First of all the Head's wife set about teaching them country dancing.

Once again Roger was rebellious. He thought it was soft, but he didn't feel that he could go to the Head again. Fortunately the Head's wife soon realised that she would get far more out of the boys if she made her classes voluntary and rewarded boys with special refreshments. Thankfully, Roger dropped out as did quite a lot of his friends.

But when ballroom dancing classes began Roger was willing to have a go. He still felt that they should be voluntary, but his parents went to dances sometimes so perhaps this was a skill he ought to learn. And he was even more interested when he saw the visiting teacher. She was young, dark and vivacious.

But almost at once his interest was demolished. She lined the boys up in alphabetical order and said.

"In ballroom dancing we all need a partner. So half of you must be boys and half of you must be girls." She walked down the line. "Boy. Girl. Boy. Girl."

Roger was a 'girl'. It finished him. A few weeks later he was thrown out of the class for misbehaving. But that didn't alter the fact that, when a girls' school from Beddingford was invited to the school for a dance, he was included with the rest of the fifth and sixth forms. But that was still a long way off.

The one really important fact that term was that Roger was now a regular member of the second XV. And then, for no reason that he knew of, he was picked to play open side wing forward for the 1st.

He was never to forget his first match for the 1st XV. It was played on their full-sized pitch at Perspins. The visiting team from the south, Kings College, was unbeaten. As they ran out onto the pitch Mr Kendall heard their captain say, "Let's have a score under the posts early on and then we'll take them apart."

He passed the words on, knowing that they would anger his own side. But when Kings scored under the posts a few minutes into the game, it looked as though he had wasted his breath. The try was converted: 5 – 0 to Kings. (Note: scoring in rugby has changed since the 1940s).

As they waited for the conversion, Cotterell, the Perspins skipper came over to Roger. "I don't care how little you shove in the scrum," he said, "as long as you break quickly and take out that fly half of theirs. He is the key."

For the next twenty minutes, every time Kings had a scrum, Roger waited poised. At the first possible moment he launched himself at the fly half with all his fury. He was no great size, but he thumped into the fly half time and time again just as he received the ball. The fly half's passing became wild and his kicking became hopelessly erratic. As a result all Kings attacks died at their source.

By half time Roger was exhausted, but his work was done. The fly half spent the rest of the match getting rid of the ball as fast as he possibly could, without any thought about what he was doing with it. Meanwhile Perspins had come more and more into the game. Theirs was no brilliant rugby team, but it was very fit and that gave it an advantage on their huge home pitch.

Dave Shaw, the Perspins fly half, had benefited from the demolition of his opposite number. He was now commanding the play with the skill of his angled kicks for touch. And he was bringing Bradders and Nobby in the centre into play more and more. Each of them had the ability to jinx past an opponent.

Fifteen minutes from time Bradders did just that. Then he ran straight at the Kings full back and, at the last moment, passed to Nobby who went over in the corner. Dave's kick failed. 5 – 3 to Kings.

But now the school supporters were yelling their hearts out. Even Mr Emerson, standing by the corner flag in his overcoat and trilby and leaning on his walking stick, deigned to clap.

Kings kicked off and Perspins drove them back. Play was messy and time was running out but then right in front of their posts, Kings gave away a penalty. The silence was breathless. Dave ran up as he did fifty times a week in practice and stroked the ball over. 6 – 5 to Perspins.

Back came Kings on the charge. Their fly half kicked off and their forwards hurled themselves after it. As calm as you like, Cotterell took the ball and broke through the onrushing forwards. As soon as he was free he flung the ball wide to Bradders. Again that jinxing, lightning twenty yard dash and again the ball to Nobby. But Nobby had two to beat. A swerve left, a dummy pass and a swerve right and he was clear. again he was over on the wing; 9 – 5 to Perspins. Again the kick at goal failed but it didn't matter. It was the last kick of the game.

Ecstasy for Perspins. Kings did not delay their departure. It was obviously easier to be sporting in victory than in defeat. Unknown to him, Roger's place in the team was secure. The choir was rehearsing Longfellow's *Hiawatha*. Perhaps it was not surprising that Roger's celebration of victory should sound a little like Longfellow:

> *"They had never yet been beaten," he wrote,*
> *we were just an average side;*
> *they came boastfully to beat us,*
> *we had our fair share of pride.*

They set off in search of conquest
pressed us hard and swiftly scored;
we were struggling just to hold them,
touchline school supporters roared.

Pitch was larger than most school fields,
they were fast and they were bigger;
yet we found that we could match them,
we were fit and full of vigour.

Second half was slipping from us
then we crossed their untouched line:
we had scored and we were fighting,
they were angry, we felt fine.

Back they came and back we drove them,
desperation marked their play,
then they fouled and we were given
penalty to win the day.

Over flew the ball in safety,
we were winning — we would win;
back they rushed to prove their valour
kicked and rushed to save their skin.

But we took the ball right through them,
cut through butter as a knife,
left defenders lying helpless,
scored again to end the strife.

Nine to five we beat those boasters.
Sent them back dejected all;
proud, triumphant, we were heroes:
every move we can recall.

34

The School Dance

The very first school dance took place about half way through the spring term of 1948. A coach load of girls arrived from a boarding school in Beddingford. The Head met the coach and led the teacher and her girls to a classroom to leave their coats. The girls were all chattering excitedly, brushing down their frocks, patting their hair, looking at themselves in tiny mirrors. A few of them had risked the wrath of their teacher and put on some make-up in the coach. Such frivolities were frowned upon.

As they entered the hall they fell quiet apart from a few giggles and nudges as they singled out the ones they fancied. They lined one wall of the hall. The boys were already lined up along the opposite wall. Fifth formers wore grey school uniforms. Sixth formers wore a variety of suits. No uniforms had been required during the war. Now that uniforms were coming back, sixth formers were exempt because they would soon be leaving and coupons were still needed for new clothes. Coupons that were in short supply.

There was almost complete silence as boys and girls eyed one another surreptitiously, but it was the Head who caught John Cob's eye.

"Just look at ee," he whispered to Roger. "Like a blaming turkey cock with all those maids around."

The turkey cock made a brief speech of welcome and the teacher from the girls' school responded. Then the music began and the Head took the girls' school teacher as his partner. For a while they had the floor to themselves. Then the dancing mistress took one of the boys and the Head's wife began to tackle boys she knew, sending them across the room to take their partners. Slowly the floor filled up.

Roger sat tight. He couldn't go and ask a girl to dance. How could you ask one and not another? Which one should you ask? He didn't know any of them. He couldn't ask anyone if he didn't know anyone. At last all the girls were on the floor. There were a few boys surplus to requirements including both Roger and John Cob. The Head's wife came to them, turned to Roger and said.

"Perhaps you would like to have this dance with me."

Roger stood and made a fool of himself at once because he went to hold her as if he were the female partner. She sorted him out gently and then led him through the dance. She was lithe and graceful and a beautiful dancer. In spite of himself, Roger found that he was enjoying himself. But when the dance was over and boys and girls separated to their separate sides of the room again, he knew that he would have to face up to asking one of the girls for a dance. He felt physically sick at the prospect and then John Cob said:

"I've had enough of this. I'm gwain off to see Mrs Petherick in the kitchens, see if I can get a sandwich or two."

"I'll come too," Roger responded and the two of them slipped unnoticed out of the hall.

In the kitchens Mrs Petherick and Gladys were loading a trolley with sandwiches and biscuits. The music from the dance came through loud and clear and Gladys was fooling around trying to get Mrs Petherick to dance with her.

"Well, well, well," she said. "We've got two dancing partners or have you just come to borrow my skirt again Roger Wallace?"

Roger blushed but couldn't think of a suitable reply. John looked at Mrs Petherick and said, "We idn much for dancing so we've come to see if we can have a sandwich or two."

"You can if you give us a dance," answered Gladys. She grabbed John and off they went meandering round the kitchen floor to the sound of a slow fox-trot.

Roger turned to Mrs Petherick. "May I have the pleasure of this dance Mrs Petherick."

"Course you may," she said and they also ambled around the floor in a fairly shapeless shuffle. None of the four could actually dance a slow fox-trot. After a break in the music the Gay Gordons

211

struck up.

"Come on boy," said Gladys grabbing Roger. "I knows this one."

Roger knew it too from youth club dances back at home. The two of them careered up and down the kitchen. It was not a dance that made for conversation but Gladys managed to say, " 'Tis a long time since you came to see me."

"Yes," was the only response from Roger. What could he say? They had agreed that it was too risky They continued to gallop up and down the kitchens.

"Tonight would be a good night," she said. "You'll have to wait until 'tis very late but I don't mind. You will come won't ee?"

"I don't know that I should."

"You old cowardy," she teased and no more was said.

They ate their fill of sandwiches, thanked Mrs Petherick and left. They went and changed and had an hour in the gym playing badminton. Then they bathed and changed in time to slip back into the hall just as the evening was coming to an end. The girls climbed back onto their coach with a good deal of assistance from unusually chivalrous partners and spirits fell as the coach drew away.

The boys made their way straight to their dorms. Once in bed, Roger's mind began to whirl. He was in a lather of desire and confusion. He had never expected Gladys to want to see him again but now she had not only invited him, she had almost dared him to go to her.

On the other hand, he didn't like the way she had teased him. She didn't take him seriously. To her he was just a plaything, a toy to be picked up and put down. Or was that just her way? Strewth, he did want her. He tossed and turned, knowing that he shouldn't go. He mustn't go. There, that was an end to it.

But it wasn't. He put on his dressing gown and slippers, crept downstairs, across the corner of the quad and into the passageway that ran the length of the quad to the kitchens. He crouched to try to get below the level of the corridor glass, opened the kitchen door and closed it silently behind him. He ran across the kitchen and through the doorway to the stairs. Climbing as quietly as he could, he came to the top corridor and then to her doorway. He tapped very gently and went inside.

212

"You've come then," she whispered. "I thought you would. So you'm not a coward after all."

"I shouldn't have come. It's too risky – for you as well as for me."

"No, you shouldn't have come. That's right enough. I don't know how you could do such a thing Roger Wallace," she taunted him.

"Perhaps I'd better go," he said and turned but she grabbed his dressing gown.

"Don't be such a fool. Us won't do it again, but now you'm yer us must make the most of it. Come on. Take your clothes off and get into bed with me."

He was so wound up, a confusion of tension and anxiety and desire. It left his fingers like icicles. He stripped off clumsily and slotted into bed beside her.

"Gyaw, idn your hands cold! Lay still there underneath me. I'll soon warm ee up."

Slowly the tension drained out of him in the warmth and pleasure of her bed. After a while she fished under her pillow for a frenchie and put it on him.

"So you were expecting me," he said.

"Course I was. You men got no defences against the power of a woman." She slipped him inside her and rode him happily. "It was true," she thought. "She could make this lad do whatever she wanted. But he was a decent lad. She wouldn't take advantage of him. There were other fish she could fry if she wanted."

Little did she know how accurate that image of frying was for a lad in the turmoil of anticipation and desire. She removed his frenchie and washed it, lay quietly with him and both of them slept for a little while. When they woke he said, "I wish I could sleep with you every night. You're so warm and soft and comfortable."

"Aren't I beautiful too?" she teased.

"Of course you are," he responded seriously. He was going to go on but she put her finger across his lips.

"You'll be asking me to marry you next," she laughed. "Come on. Make love to me once more and then you must go."

They enjoyed one another as if they had been loving for years, easy and content with one another. Then Roger dressed. Gladys said to him, "I idn serious very often but I'm serious now so listen. You mustn't come again. I want you to come but you mustn't. Your future is too important. You understand me?"

"Yes," said Roger sadly. He felt flattened. "I'm not sure that I ought to say it because it is such a big word, but I think I really do love you Gladys. You're the first love of my life."

"Thank you boy. It's nice of you to say so. But just you remember, I shan't be the last. Now git on with ee."

She took him and kissed him and sent him on his way. He crept back to his dorm safely. But though he never visited her room again, night after night she was with him in his thoughts. Just thinking about her frequently left him in a lather of passion.

35

Further Confrontation

Roger was no great cricketer. That summer he only managed to win a place in the second XI by keeping wicket. He wasn't very good at it, and he didn't want to do it, but no one else wanted to either so it earned him a place in the team.

By now his two best friends were Dave Shaw and John Cob. Together they formed perhaps the finest opening pair of batsmen the school had ever seen. Dave was beautiful to watch, stylish and graceful, a player of real class. John had a brilliant eye, a sound defence and unorthodox attacking strokes. The two were a complete contrast and sometimes seemed to win matches virtually on their own.

But Roger wasn't as envious of them as he might have been. The first XI played other school teams. The seconds played village sides. They never won a match but they had some wonderful cream teas.

So summer passed happily and with no serious exams that year, it passed easily too, as did the summer holidays. Alfie was now married. Jerry was back from the Army and swotting hard to get to university. The holidays passed all too swiftly. Roger's final year at school was about to begin. He returned that autumn of 1948 to find himself a school prefect and also vice captain of rugby. Cob was captain and both of them had been awarded their school colours.

But he also found that the Head had brought in a new rule banning soccer. Right through the school boys were furious.

"It's madness," Roger said to John Cob. "What are people

going to do with their spare time. We've always gone out on to the parade to mess about with a ball. You can't mess about playing rugger on asphalt. It's barmy. I'm going to see the Head."

"I'll come with ee," answered John.

"You will?" Roger was surprised. John had always seemed to him to be a strong, quiet sort. The kind who wouldn't make a fuss about anything. "I thought I'd also tackle the Head about prefects' scatting. I don't believe in it and I'm not going to 'ave anything to do with it."

"There's none of the prefects in our house as'll scat. Greg won't. Bill won't. You won't and I won't," said John.

"Gosh," replied Roger. "That's terrific. So we'll tackle the Head about that too."

"Yes."

The Head sensed trouble as soon as he saw the two boys looking so tense and serious. Their being prefects made no difference to his welcome. He didn't invite them to sit down.

"Well," he barked.

"Sir, there are two matters we would like to discuss with you."

"And they are?"

"First is the matter of prefects' scatting sir. We don't believe in it."

"You too, Cob?"

"Yes sir. None of us in Beta house believe in it."

"What about the prefects of other houses?"

"Some do, some don't sir."

"Then those who do will do the scatting."

"That would not be right sir," said Roger.

"Why not?"

"Sir," said Roger with a grin, "it would be degrading for boys of Beta house to be scatted by someone from Alpha or Gamma."

"Then I'll scat them myself."

"Oh no sir. That wouldn't be fair. You are far too strong sir."

"Hrmph." The Head was amused in spite of himself and not displeased. The boy had spunk, no doubt about that, but how to handle him? That was the question. He turned to John Cob.

"I've never thought of you as a rebel Cob?"

"I'm not a rebel sir but I know what I think is right and wrong. I don't think boys are fit to scat other boys."

"Prefects are hardly to be equated with other boys."

"Sir, when one prefect scats the others watch. They egg him on to hit harder and to give more scats than he should. And if the victim cries they laugh at him, not just then but afterwards as well, mocking him in front of other boys. I've even known a prefect take a run the length of the room to hit a boy sir."

"Oh yes," said the Head sarcastically. "You know all these things because you've been there and seen them I take it."

"Yes sir."

The Head pounced. "How can you have seen these things. You have only just become a prefect. You've never been present when prefects have scatted boys."

Cob's farm-tanned face reddened. He was angry now. "You've no business to speak like that sir," he said firmly. "I've been present because I've been scatted by prefects who were furious because I didn't squeal or cry. They did their utmost to make me but they couldn't."

"I see." The Head felt that the rebuke was just but he didn't apologise. "None of this means that prefects should be stopped from scatting. It just means that we should change the way we do things." He paused. "I'll call a prefects' meeting. In future only house captains will scat and they will be watched by one other house captain who will make sure that things are fair and proper."

"Thank you, sir," said Cob.

"But what about boys in our house sir?" asked Roger. "None of us will scat them nor will we support any alternative scatting programme. We would rather not be prefects," he added though he had no right to do so. He hadn't consulted any of the others.

The Head paused. He wouldn't mind losing Wallace but he had great respect for John Cob. Who were the others he wondered? Two more probably. Four prefects would take some replacing from such a small sixth form.

"What do you suggest?" he asked.

"That you leave it to us to decide how best to handle things sir."

"Really!" he said. "Prefects are not fit to scat but they *are* fit to determine how boys should be punished. Your thinking seems somewhat confused to say the least." He paused again. "Very well. You will report to me every week bringing a list of boys punished and details of their punishments."

"Yes sir."

k

"And the other matter?"

"The banning of soccer, sir."

"We have banned soccer in an attempt to improve the school's rugby standards. As the new captain and vice-captain of rugby I'm sure you will welcome that."

"No sir. The whole school is angry about the ban sir, and we believe that it is wrong."

"Oh you do, do you. I'm growing rather tired of the way you oppose my policy decisions Wallace. You are becoming no better than a trades union agitator. Just remember that you are not indispensable. I will not have you undermining my authority. We can soon find another vice captain of rugby you know."

"And captain," said John Cob quietly.

"You too Cob! I'm astounded. I wouldn't have thought it of you. You push me too far."

Both boys decided to stay quiet. At last the Head said, "I'll speak to the sports' master. I suspect that you have misunderstood the ban anyway. It was never intended as a ban on boys playing about in their spare time. It is a ban on full-blown games of soccer on the rugby pitches. Perhaps we should ease that and allow soccer only when the sports' master has been approached and has given his permission. Will that satisfy you?"

"Yes sir. Thank you sir."

They left the study and walked through the corridor.

"Thank you for sticking your neck out like that," said Roger. "It was only because of you that he gave way."

John was still angry at the Head's sarcasm. "He's a bliddy liar," he said. "That soccer ban was a ban on all kinds of soccer. Now he says 'tis just against full matches. When was there last a full-blown soccer match. Can you ever remember one?"

"No I can't," said Roger. The thought hadn't struck him.

"Well there's going to be now," John said. "You and me are going to go and see old Kendall twice a week to ask permission for matches between sides we've picked and us won't give up until the ban is lifted proper."

A few weeks later the sports master quietly gave a blanket permission. The only result of the ban was an increased interest in playing soccer properly instead of just messing about with a ball.

36

Remembrance Day

Roger was now an editor of the school magazine which meant working with Mr Emerson. He spent more and more of his time with him. They worked together in the library where Roger was now head librarian, and of course, they worked together in the classroom.

Mr Emerson set the work but he really made it feel as if they were studying together, as if the discoveries Roger was making in his reading were shared discoveries, shared ideas and shared thinking. Mr Emerson treated his sixth formers as adults – 'in fact,' thought Roger, 'he has always treated us as adults. Perhaps that's why he has never had to punish us.'

"I want you to lead a debate Roger," Mr Emerson said. "Choose your own second. The subject I suggest is, 'That Labour deserves to get back in at the next election'."

Roger realised at once that he hadn't a hope of winning a debate on that subject. "Could we make that 'That the Conservatives do not deserve to win the next election' sir?"

Mr Emerson smiled. "You're a cunning devil Roger. Very well. Have it your own way."

Roger chose Philip Jonas as his second and each of them made speeches. Roger spoke enthusiastically of the idealism of Labour and of all that the Attlee Government had achieved. With the birth of the National Health Service and a whole raft of new social legislation and change, Roger claimed that these were exciting times to live in. Labour deserved to win the next election. There was no doubt about it in his mind.

In his speech Philip Jonas said that Labour was all very well but there were still gross inequalities in British life and the country was still governed by class. "Look at the new education system," he said. "It might have been a tremendous advance when Butler brought in the 1944 act, but we should get rid of independent and religious schools." He won a cheer for that just as a means of shouting against their own school. "They are socially divisive. We need a system that gives all of our population a fair and equal chance in life, and a system that binds us together instead of splitting us apart. What we really need," he concluded, "is a Communist Government and an end to the monarchy."

Jeers followed. The two pro-Conservative speakers had recognised as Conservatives always do, that there is a price to pay for idealism, a price that most people are not willing to pay. They talked about high taxation and then they pointed out how ungrateful the nation had been to Churchill at the end of the war. He deserved the thanks of the nation and electing him would show our gratitude. "Besides," they said, "under Labour we are still suffering rationing and all sorts of other hardships. It is time we began to enjoy the fruits of victory."

The boys in the debating society cheered and it soon became clear from the speeches from the floor that the Conservatives were winning hands down.

Then came the winding up speeches. First the Conservative who repeated the main arguments he had put before. He received great applause. Then it was Roger's turn to make the final closing speech.

"None of you," he said, "will agree with Jonas that we ought to have a Communist government. Nor will many of you agree with me that Labour should have another term. But all those of you who are Liberals" (it was the first time that evening that the Liberals had been mentioned) "will agree with me that we don't want a Conservative government. I ask all of you to join with me in voting for the motion 'That the Conservatives do not deserve to win the next election'."

There was a stunned silence. Mr Emerson smiled that enigmatic smile if his and the chairman for the evening took the vote. Thanks to the liberals, Roger won by a narrow margin.

"Cleverly done Roger," commented Mr Emerson. "Perhaps

you should consider a career in politics. That is the first time the conservatives have been defeated since the debating society began."

Flushed with success and the delight from Mr Emerson's praise, Roger felt like a sports' captain being carried from a field on the shoulders of his team.

"There's another job I'd like you to do for me," said Mr Emerson. "On Remembrance Day I'd like you to be the boy who reads the list of members of the school who died in the two world wars."

It was an honour and Roger was thrilled by it.

"I have not forgotten that one of your brothers was killed in action Roger. If you feel unequal to the task I shall quite understand."

How long was it since he had last thought of Eric? Roger's cheeks burned with shame. It was so easy to forget, to leave the past behind. He was sure his parents didn't.

"Thank you, sir," Roger replied quietly. "I shall be proud to read the list."

But there was much more to it than just reading the list.

Mr Emerson prepared Roger carefully and thoroughly. In his own mind there was no more important task in the whole year than this one. He was determined that Roger would do it well. Remembrance Day came.

Roger read the first 14 verses of Ecclesiasticus 44: "Let us now praise famous men," he began. Some of it didn't seem all that relevant but then he was reading, "And some there be who have no memorial, who have perished as though they had not lived; they have become as though they had not been born."

The reading ended, "Their bodies were buried in peace" and Roger wanted to cry out that that wasn't true but no one knew better than Mr Emerson that it wasn't true. He had fought on the Somme and at least he was trying to ensure that 'their name liveth to all generations'.

Roger paused for longer than he had been taught to do. He hadn't realised how he would need that pause. And then he began to read the list of names from the First World War and then from the Second – names of boys he had known. He finished and then added silently, "Eric Wallace, my brother."

Tears started to his eyes. Again he paused while he took control

221

of himself. Then he began to recite. Young though he was, the words had been part of his whole life:

> *"They shall not grow old*
> *as we that are left grow old.*
> *Age shall not weary them*
> *nor the years condemn.*
> *At the going down of the sun*
> *and in the morning,*
> *we will remember them."*

No one needed to be told. From oldest to youngest the response came back, "We will remember them."

Roger was so thankful that he had been able to recite the words. His eyes were blinded by tears. He couldn't have read what he had to say. He knew his voice had choked once or twice. Perhaps no one had noticed. It didn't matter anyway.

In history later that day Mr Emerson began his class by saying, "History is not just the study of the past. It is an entrance into our inheritance. In part, we are what we are because of that inheritance.

"There are two inescapable parts of that inheritance that I propose to talk about today. The first is our imperial past and the second, inevitably, is war.

"Yours may well be the last generation to be brought up to be proud of the British Empire. The independence of India is only a beginning. The years ahead will see the steady dismantling of one of the greatest empires the world has ever seen. Whatever its faults and whatever its virtues – and there have been plenty of both – the Empire is an inescapable part of us now. The arrogance and self-confidence of our nation is largely a result of our imperial past.

"We shall probably remain too big for our boots for a long time to come. But if there is to be any national self-confidence in the future, it will have to be built on other foundations. Our nation will also be subject to change. Future immigration will not be from Europe but from Asia, Africa and the West Indies – from the old Empire. We shall have a great deal to learn about mutual respect and tolerance as we seek to build a multi-racial nation living together in harmony and peace.

"Which leads me back to the two world wars. They are ingrained in you whether you like it or not. The life you live, you live because of them and because of their outcome.

"We shall never know how many people have died in this last conflict. But if you were to take the population of England and wipe it out, you would have killed similar numbers. Conservative estimates put the number of deaths at between forty-five and fifty million people.

"The first war was supposed to be a war to end all wars. Given the nature of human beings, I doubt if strife will ever cease but that may be the tired cynicism of an old man. Your generation and the generations that follow have another chance to find the paths of peace. Remembering the past, the shame, the horror and the courage of the past, will always be one way of reminding yourselves of the desperate importance of your task.

"Forgive me if I dismiss the class now. I'm rather tired."

"Roger looked at him. How old was he? In those moments he looked a very old man. He never talked about the Somme. Come to think about it, Roger had never heard Alfie talk about bombing Berlin. Perhaps there were some memories that were so awful that you just blotted them out.

Roger went out and walked around the rugby pitch on his own. He felt that *he* had grown older that day. Protected from the war though he had been, it was a part of him. So was that older war. There was no escaping either of them.

37

The Cross Country Run

If Higher School Certificate year was to be a year of heightened academic endeavour, there was little sign of it that year. Through the winter rugby dominated and then cricket and athletics took over.

Dave and John were now captain and vice captain of the 1st and Roger was captain of the 2nd XI. But Roger was increasingly taken up with the demands of athletics and particularly with preparations for the house cross country. He had the feeling that Beta could sweep the board that year.

So out he went with the eight junior runners and put them through their paces again and again. He did the same with the middles. He would have liked to have done the same with the seniors but half of them were unwilling to train – notably John Cob.

"You idn gettin' me rinnin' around. Us done all the rinnin' us needs in the past on punishment runs, and tidn' no fun."

Roger thought it *was* fun but it was a waste of breath arguing.

The day of the cross country arrived and he called the three teams together. "I believe we can win all three races today," he said. "I don't ever remember that happening before. Those of us in the seniors will be watching you juniors and middles to see how you get on and to cheer you home. If you both manage to win, and I'm sure you will, John Cob and I will make you a promise."

John had not really been paying attention. "Stupid waste of time, this yer pep talk," he thought, but he was prepared to humour his friend.

"If Juniors and Middles win, then Cob and I will come first and second in the seniors and the senior team will win to make it a clean sweep. So off you go and do your best. Give Beta the victory!"

They cheered and left to get ready for their races.

"Blaming fool," said John. "What did ee want to go and say that for. 'Tis all very well telling them that I shall win, but you haven't a hope of coming second."

"I wasn't thinking of coming second," said Roger. "I was thinking of beating you."

John laughed his earthy laugh. "You haven't a hope boy. All that training will have worn you out."

They watched the juniors set off and a quarter of an hour later they watched the middles go. Then they changed into their running kit and went back out to see the younger boys come in. As Roger had hoped, both the juniors and the middles won their team races.

Now it was up to them.

Twenty-four seniors from the three houses lined up across the starting field. With the off they rushed diagonally across the field to the corner gateway, to try to get through in the first bunch. Two more small fields led to a six foot high hedge surmounted by a wooden fence.

They clambered over into a huge ploughed field. Even though it was so early in the race, that ploughed field drained them and the runners began to be pulled apart.

A narrow strip of woodland led them across the road to the saw-mills and onto a long stretch of bridle path. It was the easiest running of the whole race, tending to be downhill all the way. Roger, in the first group of boys, looked around for John. He was nowhere to be seen. The return half of the race would be mostly uphill and Roger knew that he was at his worst on the uphill stretches. He must try to build up a lead now. He stretched his legs and pulled away from all but three or four of the others.

They left the bridle path for a narrow footpath beside a quickly running stream. Roger was in the lead closely followed by the leading pack. He dared not look back. Where the hell was John? He ought to have come out training.

Roger led the way into the water splash and through the

225

stream. He dragged himself up the far bank and across two fields with a gradient that grew steeper as they ran. It was hard work being the front runner. There was no one to pull you on. He felt himself slowing, his legs growing heavy with the upward haul.

Suddenly, there was John beside him. "Come on boy," he said. "What's happened to all that training."

John took up the lead and Roger followed, into a wood following a wet and muddy path. Roger slipped and fell. John turned and that great, earthly laugh rang out through the woods. As Roger pulled himself to his feet, John fell flat on his face. Roger was too weary to laugh, but he now took the front again, slipping and slurping through the mud, down to a small stream and up the other side, across another path and out onto another bridle path where the going was firm.

"Have ee seed who is right behind us?" gasped John.

Roger glanced back. There were only three boys in sight, one of them from Beta house. But hard on their heels was a boy no one had considered. Cockney Pitt had been on just about every punishment run it was possible to go on ever since he had been at the school. Now it was paying off. How the school would laugh if he managed to beat these giants of school sport and win.

Anxious now, John and Roger ran side by side along the bridle path. There was a new urgency in their running and they increased their lead while the going was good. Back across the road and through the narrow wood they ran and then they were faced with that huge ploughed field. They hit it together but then John showed how true he was to his name. With all the stamina of a working pony, he leapt across the furrows. Roger struggled after him but the gap between them increased. He was done for. He glanced behind. Pitt was gaining on him.

At last he made it to the hedge. John had climbed the hedge and the fence almost as if there were no obstacle at all. Roger dragged himself to the top. He really was finished. He straddled the fence and watched Pitt, full of running, cross the last few furrows.

But that brief stop had given Roger the respite he needed. He swung his leg over the fence and let the hedge push him off in pursuit of John. He found that he had a new, last burst of energy. He sprinted after John across those two remaining fields and through the gate. As they climbed the last field towards the tape boys were cheering and shouting them on.

John was only just ahead. He caught him. They ran level pegging. Again Roger found himself struggling, chest heaving, legs dragging, eyes misting over. John increased his pace, seemingly without effort as if he could go on for ever. He left Roger for dead.

Five yards separated them at the tape. The cheers that greeted them went on. If anything they increased in volume. Twenty yards behind them Cockney Pitt ran into third place with a huge grin on his face.

John and Roger stood by the line, arms across one another's shoulders, and watched as more of the runners came in. They didn't have to wait long. It was soon clear that the rest of their team had done what was needed. Beta had won the team race and swept the board.

The runners went on into the tilehouse to wash and rinse off. As prefects, Roger and John were entitled to proper baths. But would there be any hot water? It was always a bit of a toss up. There was never enough hot water for all seven baths.

They had no need to worry. One of their middle school runners had gone ahead of them and run their baths. They soaked contentedly and Roger began to re-run the race in his mind. During prep that evening, he ran it through again. He began to scribble:

> *A massed rush down across the field*
> *to push our way through a narrow gate*
> *and across two more fields to a high hedge*
> *and a huge field that was newly ploughed.*
>
> *We leapt across from ridge to ridge*
> *to the easy firmness of a narrow wood.*
> *We crossed a road and then*
> *the best of all the race was ours to run.*
>
> *Past saw-mills we were stringing out*
> *in a long line of panting boys.*
> *We came to welcoming woodlands*
> *and an easy-running bridle way.*

A steady run and swinging right
a footpath brought us to a stream.
A smallish group now led the field
beside the stream and then right through.

The ice-cold shock and halting power
delayed all but the strongest now,
climbing across the meadow hill
to enter woodland once again.

The path was slimy sticky mud,
we slipped and fell and scrambled on
out onto a stony road –
we tried to spur each other on.

Once more the narrow, gentle wood
and then the field of furrows ploughed
reaching for ever on and on
to sap the last strength from our limbs

and up the hedge to rest awhile
before the final plunging run
across two fields and through a gate
to cheering boys and broken tape.

38

Prize Day

That summer of 1949 was a glorious summer. Higher School Certificate was a bonus. In the exams, Roger found himself sitting next to a shelf of P.G. Wodehouse novels. When he finished his exams early, as he always did, he began to read them and entered into a new, light-hearted world that was to delight him for weeks to come.

But alongside the exams there came plenty of spare time, time for revision. Only for Roger and his closest friends, revision took the form of a stroll out of school and down to the squire's swimming pool. Sometimes their books went with them, sometimes not. They were rarely opened.

And then the final Speech Day and Prize Giving of their school-days drew near. Roger met the Headmaster on the Quad.

"Am I getting a prize for Latin sir?"

"Do you deserve a prize for Latin boy?

"I am the best in the school at Latin sir."

"Hrmph."

That was the end of that conversation.

Speech Day and Prize Giving day arrived. Parents came and the school assembled out in the huge marquee on the lawns. Sixth formers settled at the very back of the marquee. They could slip out for a quiet smoke or an ice cream while the speeches were on. If anybody noticed, who cared. They were leaving that term.

The speeches were completed. A middle-aged lady dressed in mauve with a large hat and hair to match stood up to present the prizes. The Head faffed around her and sixth formers drifted back into the marquee to watch.

Roger was called up for two prizes, one for History and one for English. When the main prizes had been handed out, the Head said:

"You will see on your lists that there is one prize against which there is no name. It is the most coveted prize of all given for 'grit and determination'. No one teacher is responsible for awarding it. We sit down together and choose the boy we feel most deserves it. This year it goes to . . ." He paused for effect . . . "John Cob."

The cheering that filled the marquee showed that it was a thoroughly popular choice and John walked forward, his ruddy complexion three or four shades deeper than usual.

Roger had never seen poor old John look so embarrassed. He wasn't a boy who was at home in the public eye. The school cheered like mad and sixth formers prepared to slip out of the marquee again. But the Head stepped forward and said, "There is one prize which slipped through the net this year. It is not on your published list."

Curious to see what it was, Roger and his pals waited for the announcement.

"The Junior Latin prize goes to Roger Wallace."

There was only the briefest of unbelieving pauses and then the whole school erupted into hoots of laughter. The parents were thoroughly bewildered. Roger went hot and cold and knew that he was crimson. Slowly he made his way forward to the platform accompanied by a slow hand-clap and cheers of derision. It was utterly humiliating.

The mauve lady was as baffled as the parents but she took the prize book from the Head and handed it to Roger, shaking him by the hand and congratulating him. He thanked her, took the book and prepared to scurry back to his place.

"One moment Roger." He hated it when the Head called him 'Roger'. It always meant trouble. If he called him 'Wallace' it was all right but 'Roger' spelt pain. "I think we should explain to parents about your prize don't you?"

Roger squirmed.

"One day recently," said the Head, "this boy stopped me on the Quad to ask if he was to receive a Latin prize."

There were muffled giggles from the school and the parents sat wondering what it was all about.

"He pointed out that he was top of his class."

Laughter erupted again.

"I have to admit to being thoroughly ashamed of myself. It was so remiss of me. I hadn't noticed. But fortunately there was a book in my study that I've been trying to get rid of for years – the ideal prize for such a boy with such success in Latin. So I decided that since this boy was top of his class" (there was still more laughter and still more baffled looks from the parents) "this was the book for him. Wallace, would you mind in your best loud, clear voice, reading to us the title of your book – in full if you please."

Until that moment Roger hadn't looked at his prize. He looked at it now through eyes that were misted over. Then he read the title in full: "A Child's Garden of Verses by Robert Louis Stevenson done into Latin by T.R. Glover."

The boys hooted with laughter until the Head held up his hand once more.

"Perhaps I should explain to the parents," the Head continued, "that Wallace was not only top of his class," he paused once more, "he was also bottom since there was only one boy in the class. He is the only boy in the school who has taken Latin."

Amidst universal laughter, he finally let Roger go.

That evening Roger read the English pages of the book. Then he presented it to the library and, since he was chief librarian, he accepted the book and entered it in. Finally as editor of the school magazine, he inserted a note in the magazine thanking Roger Wallace for his generous gift to the school library. It was the only way he could get his own back.

39

Farewells

Shortly before the end of term Roger took an exeat. He cycled down to Beddingford to see the people who had been good to him when he was an evacuee. First he went to see Miss Holly.

He arrived just in time to go to chapel with her. She felt so proud sitting with 'her boy' now grown to be a young man. They had lunch together in the tiny cottage and he told her that he had come to thank her for her kindness in days gone by and to say 'farewell'.

"Of course, we shall see each other sometimes," he said, "because mother and dad will keep in touch."

"And what be you gwain to do next?"

"I'm going into the Navy."

"Oh my. What a fine sailor you'll look too," she said proudly.

He hadn't the heart to tell her that he wouldn't actually look like a sailor. His uniform would be a suit – and probably an ill-fitting suit at that.

They talked for a while and then he said, "I thought I would go and see Mr and Mrs Guthrie and Barbara while I'm here, to say good-bye to them. I don't suppose I shall ever see them again."

"Don't ee say that," she said. You'll come to Beddingford for sure and then you'll go and see them. But I'm glad you've thought to visit them now."

So he kissed her and left. He cycled round to Barbara's house. Tom was there and the baby was a very lively eight-year-old. They were pleased to see him and Barbara gave him an affectionate hug, but he found that they had little to talk about now. Their lives had taken their separate paths. He didn't stay long.

He was longer with the Guthries who didn't seem to have changed a bit since he was evacuated there. He stayed for tea and found that Mrs Guthrie still made superb rock cakes. They spoke proudly of their grand-daughter and he felt at ease with them.

He cycled back to school feeling that his day had been well spent. But now came the really hard part of moving on.

Those last few days at school were completely unreal. It was as if he was suspended between two lives. His school life was done, his new life not yet begun. He walked the fields endlessly with friends, but none of them really had much to say to one another. Again and again Roger found himself pretty choked. He hadn't realised just how much school had come to mean to him.

On his last evening he sat at his desk and thought carefully about the people he ought to go to see before he left. He knew some boys had been round the different members of staff. He didn't feel inclined to do so, apart from two of them. Soon he had decided exactly what he would do – and he would leave Mr Emerson to the last.

There was one master, a bachelor, who had let the prefects use his room and his collection of records. He had enriched Roger's knowledge of music and broadened his appreciation. Roger went to him first.

And then he went to the kitchens. He wanted to say 'thank you' to Mrs Petherick. He doubted if many boys thought to thank her but she did so much for them all, and she had certainly been good to him.

"Hello boy, what you doin' yer then?" she said when he arrived at the kitchens.

"I've come to thank you for all you've done for us since we came to Perspins," he said, "and to say 'good-bye'."

"Oh my gor," she exclaimed. She dabbed her eyes with her apron. No boy had ever thanked her in all the years she had worked there. " 'Tis good of ee to come."

They both felt awkward. Roger had said his piece and was stuck. Suddenly he grabbed her and gave her a hug and then he fled.

"Oh my. Oh my dear soul," she exclaimed as she dabbed furiously at her eyes again.

"Whatever is it?" asked Gladys who had just come down from

233

her room.

" 'tis that boy, that Roger Wallace."

"Why, whatever has he done?"

"He's comed and said 'good-bye' and 'thank you' and he was so embarrassed, poor boy, and he gived me a hug too."

"Well so he should," said Gladys. "You'm always doing your best for those boys, and for us too. I shall miss ee when I'm gone." And Gladys also took Mrs Petherick in her arms and gave her a hug.

"Oh get on with ee do," answered Mrs Petherick. "But 'tis true. I shall miss you Gladys. You'm a bit of a rascal but I loves ee like my own daughter. Make sure you comes to zee me when you'm home."

"Course I will."

Roger meanwhile had begun a last quiet walk around the rugby field and the cricket field, before calling on Mr Emerson. As he walked the tears ran down his face. It was crazy but they were quite uncontrollable. This must be something of what people felt when they were heartbroken. Thank goodness he was on his own and it was beginning to get dark. He'd have to pull himself together before he went to see Mr Emerson. How many times had old Emerson said to them, "Try to emulate the Stoics. Don't make a fuss about things and don't display your emotions."

It was easier said than done. In fact he had always suspected that Mr Emerson found it easier to say than to do. Certainly he wasn't a man who ever made a fuss, but Roger suspected that he was a man who had very strong emotions and who didn't always find it easy to keep them under control.

He was walking round the cricket pitch now and his tears had eased. Thinking about Mr Emerson had helped. He began to walk past the cricket pavilion.

"Psst. Roger Wallace."

It was Gladys.

"What are you doing here?"

"You never comed to see me did you to say 'good-bye'."

"I came to the kitchens but you weren't there."

"You went to the kitchens to see Mrs Petherick not me."

By this time she had drawn him inside the pavilion. It never entered his head to wonder how she came to have a key.

"Yes," he answered. "I did go to see Mrs Petherick but I hoped

234

you would be there as well."

"And would you have given me a hug too?" she teased but it was too dark to see his blushes.

"No," he said, "but I would have wanted to."

"Only a hug?" she asked. "Wouldn't you have wanted to love me one more time? I'm leaving too you know."

"Are you?"

"Yes. Every summer the school lays us all off except Mrs Petherick and us goes home and waits until next term and then the school gives us our jobs back."

"Why does the school do that?"

"So's they don't have to pay us stupid."

"But that's terrible."

"No 'tisn't. The school can't afford to pay us for doing nothing. Besides that's the way working people is always treated."

"It doesn't seem right or fair to me."

"Well it doesn't matter to me any more. Mrs Jonas and Mrs Petherick have been training me along and now I'm gwain to the Riverside Hotel in Beddingford as their housekeeper. I shall work there for a bit and then see if I can get a job up to London in one of they big, posh hotels."

"I'll bet you'll do it too."

While they had been talking, Gladys had taken some batting pads from the chests around the edge of the pavilion. She had laid them side by side and end to end on the floor.

"Come on then boy. That'll have to do for a mattress. I idn gwain to let you go without you loving me one more time."

He shouldn't have been surprised but he was. He didn't hesitate for long and soon the two of them were letting go of their emotions with joyful abandon. She was ready for him at once. Suddenly it struck him, "But what about . . . I mustn't give you a baby."

"Donee worry boy," she giggled. "I've come prepared."

And so she had. She clothed him and took him. The two of them enjoyed themselves as if there were no tomorrow.

No tomorrow? It was afterwards while they were lying quietly together that the thought struck him. He might never see her again.

"Will you write to me?"

"What makes you think I can write, Roger Wallace. I'm only a poor little ignorant kitchen maid."

"No you're not. And you know you're not. You're . . ."

"Go on then Roger," she interrupted laughing, "what be I?"

"You always laugh and make fun of me," he said, "but you know that you're special. There's no one else in the world like you."

"That's true any road," she said still with laughter in her voice.

"Oh you know what I mean. I think you're wonderful."

And at last she was serious. "You're a bit special to me as well boy. Look if you want to write to me you can and who knows, I might even write back. You know where I'm gwain to."

"But I don't even know your surname."

"You don't even know my surname and here you be making love to me. What a boy 'tis. My name is 'Tremaine'. 'Gladys Tremaine'. There boy don't ee forget."

"I shan't forget," he whispered.

"Love me again then. I must be going soon."

They loved passionately. It was the last time.

"I wish I could give you something Gladys."

"Do ee boy? Well you can too. Give me that there badge off your blazer."

Roger had always intended to keep his school badge. It meant a lot to him. But he had got a badge on his rugger shirt as well, his school colours. He could keep those. He took out his pocket knife and began to cut the stitches. Before long the badge was off. He gave it to Gladys. They held one another in one long, last embrace and then she left.

"Give me a few minutes before you go," she whispered as she locked the pavilion door. "Be happy Roger Wallace." As she ran back towards the buildings she whispered under her breath, "and find someone good to love. It will be a long time before I find anyone I like so much as you."

236

40

The Eiffel Tower

After what seemed an eternity Roger began to walk around the cricket pitch again. He had almost completed his circuit when he became aware of Mr Emerson standing there. As usual he was dressed in his overcoat and trilby hat, and standing leaning on his walking stick.

"Been saying your last good-byes Roger?"

How long had he been standing there?

But Mr Emerson took the sting out of his question, "I wonder how many boys have walked around these fields for one reason or another."

"I don't know sir. I seem to have walked around them a lot ever since I first came to Perspins."

"And now it's the last time."

"Yes sir. I was going to come on to say 'good-bye' to you sir, and to thank you for all you have done for me."

There was an overlong pause before Mr Emerson said, "It's the Navy next isn't it Roger?"

"Yes sir."

"Just National Service or do you think you'll make a career of it?"

"Just National Service sir. I'm not very good at taking orders."

"No!" Mr Emerson paused a long time. "What are your long term ambitions then Roger?"

"I don't have any sir. When I was a youngster I used to have all sorts of ambitions." In the darkness he didn't see Mr Emerson smile. He was certainly unaware of his teacher's thoughts: These serious young men who had left their childhood behind. Mr Emerson thought of those sad words of St. Paul, 'When I was a child I spoke like a child, I thought like a child, I reasoned like a child; when I became a man I gave up childish ways.'

Only a preacher could speak like that. Paul should have listened to his master on the importance of remaining childlike. All these thoughts flashed through Mr Emerson's mind as he said, "What made you give up your ambitions Roger? A man without ambition is dead."

"It was when I went on that school trip to France last Easter sir. I suppose I was already seeing things differently, but I certainly did after that trip."

"Ah yes, Mr Barlow took you to the *Folies Bergère* I believe."

Roger laughed. "Yes sir. I think he enjoyed it more than I did."

"You didn't enjoy it?"

"Not much sir. Some of it was pretty crude. Funnily enough the one thing I shall remember about the *Folies Bergère* is the vividly colourful costumes."

"Interesting. But I'm sorry, I've led you off at a tangent. You were saying that France taught you to see things differently."

"Yes sir. We climbed the Eiffel Tower and it struck me that that was like a school career at Perspins. We started off right at the bottom as bucking new snips and slowly climbed right to the top of school society."

"So how did that affect your ambitions?"

"Well sir, then I started thinking about the country and the prime minister and so on. He's at the top of the tower. But most of the people who matter to me are nowhere near the top.

"The Eiffel Tower may have led you astray Roger. It is unique. So is the position of Prime Minister. But think about this England of ours. Every little town and village has its church tower, a whole multitude of different towers within one society. So it is with us. There are different towers for us to climb.

"Take your father for instance. He has built up his own business. He has climbed to the top of that tower."

"I see what you mean sir. The trouble is, I haven't the faintest idea what tower I should be climbing."

"It doesn't much matter. Many of us make dozens of false starts before we finally discover the right tower for our own lives. As far as I am concerned there are only two rules in life. They will take you to the top of the only tower that matters.

"The first is, 'Be true to yourself'. While you are in the Navy think about the things you do well, the things you enjoy doing. When you leave the Navy concentrate on those things because that is where your individual talents lie. Find some way to pursue them – at work if you can and in your leisure if you can't. By concentrating on your own abilities and talents and making the most of them you will be true to yourself."

"And the other rule sir?"

"Oh I think you know the other rule Roger."

"Sir?" he questioned.

"You went to say good-bye to Mrs Petherick earlier today?"

"Yes sir." (How did he know that).

"Then I've not much doubt that you know the other rule. It is very simple. 'Be decent and generous in your dealings with other people'."

Roger's cheeks burned and a great joy swept through him. It had been such a natural thing to say 'thank you' to Mrs Petherick but it obviously had meant a great deal to her and it mattered to Mr Emerson too. He appreciated that simple gesture.

"Yes sir. Thank you sir."

"So this is a temporary 'good-bye' Roger, keep in touch."

Roger's heart was full. So were his eyes. Thank goodness it was dark.

"Yes sir, I will sir."

They shook hands and went their separate ways.

After a few weeks holiday a new batch of bucking new snips would arrive and Mr Emerson would take up his task again easing their path to the top of the school's Eiffel Tower. And after those self-same few weeks holiday or something rather less, Roger would fall from the tower and come crashing to the ground to those depths where even his name would cease to signify.

Oh what a fall is that, from the apex of a school society to the bottomless pit signified by a mere Naval number: "DMX 884398 SIR".

Another life. Another story?